Staying on Track

C Fleming

ISBN: 9798655039469

1

Christmas Day in England. If this were a scene from a Hollywood movie, Abigail reflected, there would be a foot of crisp, virgin snow on the cobbles of the yard, fat icicles hanging down from the guttering on the stable block and children decked in thick woollen scarves singing carols in the village square. But it wasn't a Hollywood movie, and the sky was slate grey, there was fine mizzle in the air and children were presumably unwrapping the latest games console and squabbling over which sibling would get theirs set up in their bedroom first.

Despite the reality not living up to a Hollywood depiction, nothing could spoil the magic of Christmas for Abigail. She loved the collective calm that descended over the land as families and friends enjoyed each other's company and just focused in on that one special day. For the first time ever, she was surrounded by all the people that mattered to her: Sam, his parents, her Mum and Dad, Mrs Angel and Charly. Molly was also in residence, and despite her ability to test the patience of a saint, Abigail was determined to be charitable and think nothing but kind thoughts about her all day.

They stood on the damp cobbles and Abigail eyed up the horsebox that Mr and Mrs Ashington had driven over that morning from Sloth. It looked like a motorhome from the outside but was – on closer inspection - the two-berth horse carrier that they sometimes used to transport their racehorses to meetings up and down the land. A bow of tinsel twinkled from the cabin. It had to be Grace. Her Christmas present just had to be the ever-patient pony that had taught her so much about riding over the past few months.

Sam disappeared around the far side of the horsebox. The assembled group waited as sounds of unfastening the sides and lowering the ramp drifted across the yard. From inside, there was an equine snort and the

1

unmistakable shuffle of hooves. Excitement bubbled up in Abigail and she heard Sam mutter calmly to the horse. This was followed by the steady clip- clop as man and beast emerged from the interior.

As the pair came into view around the cabin, Abigail instantly realised she was mistaken. This wasn't Grace. Sam gently led round a perky chestnut, its ears pricked forward with enthusiasm and curiosity, tugging keenly on the rein that tethered it to Sam from its head-collar. Its caramel coloured coat shimmered, and every muscle in its lean body rippled. This was clearly a racehorse.

Sam led it to Abigail and they stood face to face, eyeing each other up.

"Ab, meet the Moody Muppet. Merry Christmas."

For a moment, Abigail was speechless. Sam had bought her a racehorse for Christmas. A jumble of questions tumbled into her brain. Was it to ride? Was it just to own? Would they keep it here?

"Is it a racehorse?" Abigail decided to start with establishing the first fact.

"She was," corrected Sam. "She was a talented racehorse too. Unfortunately, she decided it wasn't for her, and she started to refuse to race."

"She was banned from racing by the authorities earlier this year," explained Mr Ashington, stepping forward to run a hand over the Moody Muppet's smooth, taut neck. "So, her racing career has finished, but she's still young and looking for a new start."

"She's very pretty," Abigail offered, not knowing what else to say. A white star blazed in the centre of the mare's forehead, and her thick mane cascaded through her ears to tickle her eyebrow. The horse's large, almond eyes locked back onto Abigail's and she stretched her muzzle forward to grab the end of Abigail's fluffy scarf and nonchalantly began to chew.

"Oi!" Abigail scolded the horse and yanked the scarf back from its mouth. The Moody Muppet's ears went back for the first time during their encounter and she shifted her weight to indicate she wasn't happy.

"She may be pretty, but she's a feisty madam," Molly chipped in. "Come on," she took the rope from Sam and urged the Moody Muppet to follow her. "I'll get her settled in."

Feisty. Little did Abigail know just how highly strung the horse was. Neither did she know that she would soon look back and identify the arrival of the Moody Muppet as the start of the end of the glorious period of happiness she'd enjoyed since meeting Sam back in May. Abigail had no idea as she stood in the overcast yard that Christmas morning that from this moment on, life would not be the same.

2 – SEVEN MONTHS EARLIER

Abigail was careful not to exceed the speed limit as she ate up the motorway miles in her Dad's car. She'd promised not to bump it, scratch it, get any speeding tickets, leave any rubbish in it, nor consume any food nor drink where the smell may penetrate or stain the fabric. Her Dad didn't have to warn her not to allow any smokers anywhere near his precious motor; that went without saying.

So, when her mobile phone bleeped to indicate a text message had arrived, Abigail was mindful of waiting until the next service station appeared, before even glancing at her phone. She checked her mirrors, indicated left and pulled into the car park where she finally tucked herself into a lone parking space away from the crowded front rows and cut the engine.

"How far away?" read the message from Sam. There were three kisses to end the message; a simple act that still caused Abigail to glow inside.

"About half way – with you by midday. Can't wait." She texted in reply, ensuring that her own kisses were added at the end.

The glorious weather was contributing to her upbeat mood. The sky was flawlessly blue without a single wisp of cloud. The sun beat down and the gentlest hint of a breeze stopped the mercury soaring above thirty degrees.

To stretch her legs, Abigail made her way over to the service station to use the ladies, where she found that some travellers were being typically British and moaning about the heat.

"It's just too much, isn't it?" complained a rotund lady in her sixties, splashing cold water on her ruddy complexion. "We probably need a good thunderstorm."

Abigail smiled in reply and moved away to the hand driers. She could just imagine the lady whinging when the thunderstorm came with its accompanying downpours. "Oh, isn't this rain terrible. What a washout this week has been."

Smiling at the thought, Abigail strode back across the car park to the Audi and set off on her way again. It would be the first time that she had been back to Sam's parents' house in Lower Maisey since leaving the Cotswolds village in April, seven weeks earlier. This time she was returning as Sam's girlfriend rather than a mysterious stranger living out of a tent. What a turn of events, she reflected, since running out of Bartlett's Investment Bank, in a blind panic because she had brought down the whole banking system. Or so she thought. She was embarrassed by the whole episode now - the misunderstanding that could have been avoided had she just thought a few more things through.

"Everything happens for a reason, Ab," her friend Nadine pointed out to her as they discussed the week in which Abigail feared she'd never be able to see her friends and family again. "If you hadn't gone on the run, you wouldn't have met some nice friends, or Sam, or had the courage to set up 'April Smith designs'."

This was true. With the generous injection of cash from Mrs Angel, and the extra confidence and new contacts, Abigail had been able to make significant headway with a new range of dresses, aimed at ladies heading for the races. She had got as far as taking on a few commissions, getting a business loan, starting to build the brand and website, and had an overflowing cupboard full of material in her bedroom. She had plenty enough on her plate for now, with orders starting to back up. She could have done without a long weekend in Gloucestershire over the Spring Bank Holiday, but nevertheless, had made the promise to Sam that she would come.

Sam had visited her in Richmond only once since the Ascot meeting where he'd officially asked her out. He'd driven her home that afternoon, met her parents and stayed in the spare room overnight. They'd spent an enjoyable Sunday walking through Richmond Park, spotting deer, before heading off for a Sunday lunch on the terrace of a riverside pub overlooking the Thames. Both she and Sam were gutted that he had to make his way back to Gloucestershire that night.

Since then it had been a strange three weeks, grabbing time with Sam only when his hectic racing schedule would allow. She'd made the short trip from Richmond to Kempton to watch him lose in a couple of races, and they'd also grabbed an hour in a fast food establishment at Cobham services on the M25. "It won a platinum award for its toilets a few years ago," Sam had explained, as if that made up for the lack of finesse in their rendezvous venue.

"It's the summer," he'd say in apology, when another seven-day week had passed without them being able to find time for their paths to cross. "It's the busy season for me as a flat jockey, but I promise it'll get easier in the autumn."

Abigail didn't want to become the sort of clingy girlfriend that nags her man into spending more time with her. Besides, the more money he could earn, the more he could put towards his plan of buying a riding school. Sitting down with Sam to look over internet listings of equestrian facilities for sale was one of the key things Abigail wanted to do this weekend. If they didn't start soon, Abigail feared he'd just carry on doing what he'd always done and their dream would fade quicker than her jeans. She had to keep their future plans on track.

She turned the radio up and enjoyed the scenery as she left the motorway behind and headed deeper into the countryside. The recent good weather had taken effect on the hedgerows, which burst with life. The trees and bushes appeared taller, bulging cow parsley sprang out into the lanes, and the fields were ablaze with golden rape. It was five past twelve when Abigail swung the Audi between the austere pillars announcing the boundary of "Ashington Yard". It was exactly as she remembered leaving it. The neat gravel, the spacious detached house, the sweeping valley beyond the stabling. Sam was leaning on the Land Rover, awaiting her arrival. Dressed in cut-off jeans and a simple white t-shirt, he was still just as perfect as Abigail could have dreamed of.

"I've made us lunch," Sam announced proudly as Abigail emerged from the driver's seat.

"Beans on toast?" She joked in reply, remembering their conversation in the show flat in Cheltenham

"No, I've made us pizza!" he replied with a grin. He joined her at the car, wrapping her in a tight embrace before taking her case from the boot. She felt a tingle of anticipation, looking forward to the passion that having an empty house to themselves would bring later.

"From scratch?"

"Well, I bought the base but added all the toppings myself."

Abigail followed him over the gravel into the Ashington family home. She'd forgotten how much she adored this house, and wondered momentarily if the budget would stretch to something similar when Sam bought the riding school.

"I've also invited a few friends over this afternoon for a pool party," he added. "I hope you don't mind. I thought you'd be pleased to see Kate."

"Absolutely!" Abigail confirmed. She hadn't seen Kate since the race meeting at Ascot where she'd agreed to be Sam's girlfriend, three weeks previously.

"I've also invited Dan," Sam continued, abandoning the case in the hallway and leading her through to the kitchen. "But Mandy's not coming. They've parted ways it would seem. She stayed in Loughborough after their final exams, but he's come home to set up a personal training business in Cheltenham."

"That's a shame," Abigail lied. Mandy had been an enigma as far as Abigail was concerned. She played games with people, and Abigail had never felt comfortable in her presence.

"Ta Dah!" Sam indicated the pizza on the granite counter top. It looked OK. He'd spread chopped tomatoes over the shop-bought base, and arranged some processed chicken, tinned sweetcorn and grated cheese over the top. "I waited for you to arrive before cooking it, because I've got no idea how to turn the oven on."

Abigail knew she had a task ahead of her. She showed him how to operate the oven, and made a mental note to test his learning before she left on Tuesday.

"Did you bring your swimming things?" Sam asked an hour later when all that was left of the pizza was a few crumbs and a short section of crust that had burnt. Yes, of course Abigail had brought her swimming things. The blistering heat and lure of the Ashington's glimmering pool served as a reminder to pack her pretty pink bikini along with the flip flops that rarely saw the light of day.

"The guest room is the one along from mine," Sam called to her as she picked up her suitcase in the hallway and made to head upstairs. "Although you're also welcome to stay in my room, you know, if you prefer." She glanced shyly at him and gave an enigmatic nod, before climbing the stairs and entering his room. It didn't look any different to how she remembered it. She had taken refuge here in April, after the fateful Grand National party that had culminated in her leaving the village. She'd never imagined then that she would be back in the bedroom again, this time as Sam's girlfriend, sharing his bed.

She slipped on her bikini and threw a floaty chiffon dress over the top. She was ready for the pool. Part of her regretted Sam inviting others over to share their afternoon, she reflected as she sat on a lounger under a large umbrella. It would have been nice to enjoy the quiet, just the two of them, sipping champagne and chatting together rather than...

"Hiya!" Kate's cheery greeting cut through the silence. Aidan trotted ahead of her, restrained on his toddler reins. Dan Witt from the campsite followed behind, arms laden with beers. "What a scorcher!" He commented unnecessarily.

Sam went into host mode, organising drinks whilst Kate set about inflating a rubber dingy that Aidan could sit in, whilst bobbing on the pool.

She forced a sun hat on his head, stuffed his chubby torso into a floatation vest and sat him in the boat, casting him adrift.

"Shout if you hear a splash," she joked, turning her attention to the wine glass that had been placed on the wicker table for her.

"Who else is coming?" Dan asked Sam as he reappeared with suntan cream and a hat. On his pale freckled skin he had to be careful on these rare hot days.

"Just Luke Packer, you know the guy who rides a lot for my Dad? He's on a one day ban today so he can come, along with his fiancée Harriet."

Abigail realised that she had met this pair before, albeit briefly, when she and Sam were shopping in the Betty Boo Boutique in Cheltenham. She remembered Harriet as a carbon copy of Abigail's London self; the designer handbag, straightened blonde hair, the manicured nails, the tan. Abigail realised that she had changed herself in such a short time. Since leaving the world of temping, the need to have St Tropez skin and perfect nails waned, and she hadn't bought a new pair of shoes since April. Her scarce finances, attention and new priorities were now directed into the business, and the latest Gucci product had no role to play. What's more, she didn't miss it.

Nevertheless, Abigail was mesmerised by Harriet. Her body was long and lean, and she carried herself like a ballet dancer, with the lightest of step.

"One can get so used to budget champagne like Veuve Clicquot, don't you think?" Harriet asked Abigail, once she had settled into the lounger next to her. She wore a halter neck bikini underneath a floral maxi dress, but Abigail suspected she had no intention of getting in the pool. Girls like Harriet didn't like to get wet. She sipped at the bubbles with a faraway look in her eye. "I was going to have Bollinger at the wedding, but Papa is adamant on having some Louis Roederer that he found in Fortnums. At the end of the day, I don't care what we have because it's his money, but I think the majority of people won't be able to appreciate the difference and would be happy with this." She lifted her glass to inspect the bubbles chasing each other to the surface and then regarded Abigail. "What do you think? Could you put up with this at the wedding?"

Abigail nodded politely. Harriet was right; the average guest couldn't tell how expensive the champagne was. In her experience, if it was free, nobody had any cause to complain anyway.

"When's the wedding?"

"August 13th, so only ten weeks away. You are coming, I take it? Sam's had the invite."

"I'd love to," Abigail replied truthfully. She adored getting dressed up for a wedding. Mentally she began to make an inventory of her latest dress designs that she could wear for the big day.

"Oh, and why don't you come to the hen weekend too?" Harriet put her glass down, gripped with the ingenuity of her idea. "Me and the hens are being flown in Papa's jet down to Monaco to stay on Uncle Henry's yacht. It'll be such a scream."

Abigail opened and closed her mouth. She'd only been properly introduced to Harriet twenty minutes ago; was she serious?

"Well, thanks, er, I'll have to see..." Abigail replied vaguely. Thankfully, Sam appeared with a fresh bottle of champagne and topped up their glasses like an attentive waiter, breaking the train of conversation.

"Are you all up for a game of water polo later?" he asked. "Boys versus girls."

The water glimmered tantalisingly and Abigail was starting to roast, but Harriet predictably refused on the grounds of not wanting to get wet, and Kate excused herself to give Aidan a feed and put him down for a nap soon. "You boys go ahead," Harriet shooed them away, "and we'll relax and talk about you."

They didn't need asking twice and the testosterone took over, with Sam, Dan and Luke stripping off their t-shirts and dive bombing into the pool. There wasn't much relaxing for Kate as she constantly fussed over Aidan, trying to get him to sit and play with some plastic toys she'd brought, but he was getting grizzly.

"Does Callum have him for the weekend sometimes?" Harriet asked Kate.

"Oh, I wish. He's spending most of his time back in Ireland at the moment."

"Yes, I bumped into him at Punchestown last month when I was there for work."

"What do you do?" Abigail asked, curious to discover what profession could support her high maintenance lifestyle.

"I'm an equine photographer."

Abigail processed this information momentarily. "You take pictures of horses."

"Racehorses, yah."

"What...When they are racing?"

Abigail struggled to comprehend that such a niche job existed.

"No, they have to be standing still. I find it more difficult to take pictures when they're moving. I photograph the foals who are up for auction in the sales, for the catalogues, you know?" No, Abigail didn't know, but she nodded anyway.

"You'll have to do a photoshoot for Abigail," Kate chipped in. "Some dreamy shots of models wearing her fabulous dress designs."

"Oh, yah, I heard you were a fashion designer," Harriet replied. She pushed her shades up to her forehead and Abigail was pleased to see an enthusiastic glint in her eye. "I'd be happy to help. It's a shame I've already chosen the bridesmaids outfits otherwise they could all be parading in one of your bespoke designs. The wedding photos will end up all over the media no doubt. When will you be starting on your next collection?"

Abigail tried not to look fazed, even though she knew she was going to have to blag her way through the next few minutes. In reality, the last month had been taken over just getting a few basics off the ground and establishing a couple of commissions. There was no way she'd even thought about collections, let alone for the upcoming seasons, but Harriet was right. She would need to get organised if her business was to be taken seriously.

"I can't believe Harriet has over 45,000 followers on Instagram," Abigail told Sam later, as they finally had some 'together time' in the swimming pool. The sun was sinking down onto the horizon, and the air had cooled as the sky turned darker. The gathering had dissipated late afternoon and Abigail had spent a couple of hours devouring the content of social media sites whilst Sam caught up with some of the afternoon's racing that he'd recorded, and then disappeared to "do evening stables". Abigail didn't ask what that meant, and busied herself with her laptop and stalked the name "Harriet Whittington". It was so easy nowadays to gather intelligence on a person, especially one who lived her life so blatantly through social media channels.

"Last month she put a photo of her wearing a gold Gucci bikini on Twitter and she got likes and comments from so many important people in the industry - she could be very influential," she continued to tell Sam.

"Well, Papa does own half of Gloucestershire and chunks of Chelsea. Harriet can open a lot of doors!"

They bobbed around the pool in amicable silence, Abigail's arms wrapped around his neck, her legs clamped against his skinny waist. "What shall we do tomorrow?" she asked. "The forecast is sunny, so I thought perhaps you could show me some more of the Cotswolds. We could take a picnic?"

"Well, we'll only have a few hours spare, once I've finished riding out and all the other tasks Dad has delegated to me."

"Oh really?" Abigail couldn't keep the disappointment from her voice.

"I seem to remember it was your idea that my Dad took Mum away for a break," he teased, ducking her backwards into the water, a mouthful of chlorinated pool water flooding her mouth as she gasped. She splashed him back playfully, disentangled herself and swam away from him. His words were true. She'd planted the seed in Robin's head that he should take his wife on holiday to help her healing process after the death of her brother. She hadn't realised at the time, however, that there would be implications of that decision for her.

"Anyway," he called after her to placate her, "we can take a picnic down to the woods at the bottom of the gallops. There's a river running through there and the trees will shade the sun."

"That sounds nice," she replied, imagining a few hours of secluded Sam time. She reached the side of the pool and turned back to face him. "And maybe Monday we could go into Cheltenham for a spot of shopping?"

"Ah." He looked embarrassed. "I'm riding at Windsor on Monday."

"There's racing on a Bank Holiday?" Abigail was amazed and disappointed that he was unable to take a full bank holiday weekend off.

"Of course. You can come with me, or stay here, it's up to you. Charly will be home by then so she could take you riding?"

Abigail shrugged. She would see. She could also go home and get on with her Autumn/Winter collection. That was still two days away, and in the meantime, she had a whole night with Sam ahead of her, and the romantic picnic tomorrow. She was rapidly learning to appreciate any time that Sam *could* spend with her.

3

It was a Friday night, but for Abigail one day rolled into another and there was no such structure as "weekdays" and "weekends" anymore. Sam was nearly always tied up on Saturdays and Sundays, as the high-profile race meetings heaving with roaring crowds were always scheduled for weekends, and that meant bigger prize money on offer.

Abigail began to notice a pattern: he called her on days that he'd ridden winners, and the phone was silent when he'd had "a bad day at the office", as he called it. Some days she'd check his social media profile before ringing him. If it were ablaze with insults from the "armchair jockeys" - that is, people who had lost money betting on Sam's losing run and blaming him - she knew she would get a sulky reaction if she called him.

This Friday was one such day. There was no call by 7pm, so she checked his profile and, sure enough, a man called Jimmy63 had launched into a tirade saying his three-year-old daughter could have ridden the horse better than him. Naturally there were a few expletives thrown in for good measure.

Unable to face talking to a monosyllabic Sam, she rang her best friend Nadine instead.

"You just have to come out with us tonight," she demanded. "Blue Steak are playing at the Mermaid. It's a farewell gig for me, as it'll be the last time they play before I head out to Cambodia next week."

Abigail instantly felt guilty. She'd been so wrapped up in her own life that she'd forgotten her friend was heading off for a year of voluntary work abroad. A night out was just what she needed. She decided to wear one of her latest designs - a recreation of the '80s ra-ra skirt. It was a risky creation, but she would be able to gauge people's reaction to the outfit to see whether she was onto a winner. Some retro designs caught the imagination. Others were best consigned to the back of the wardrobe, as the fashion world wasn't quite ready to see them come around again so soon.

"Oh my God, that skirt is amazing!" Nadine gushed, unprompted, as soon as Abigail walked into the Mermaid an hour later. "I love the way you've used crotchet in the layers to tap into that trend."

Abigail glowed. She'd noticed the way a couple of girls were looking at the skirt on the tube too. Nadine's opinion was only partially valid, though, as she too was a fashion graduate, and therefore attracted to weird and wacky clothing. Tonight, she had on baggy pantaloons that looked like they'd been sculpted from flannelette bed sheets. Knowing Nadine, that's exactly what they were.

The Mermaid was buzzing with a mixed Friday night crowd. Students, the after-work crowd, and Blue Steak fans alike crammed into the South London pub. It was an ideal venue for a party, with a long narrow bar area with banquette seating along one edge. To the rear, a door led to the grotty corridor where customers crashed in and out of the toilets, and drifted to and from the smoking shelter. Off the corridor was an archway that led people to an adjacent entertainment space where they spotted the Blue Steak gang setting up their instruments.

"Abigail!" Dougie greeted her as she wandered in to say hello. "What the fuck are you wearing?"

Abigail grinned at him and gave him a friendly hug, trying not to spill her pint of cider over her apple green suede boots. "I've missed your compliments," she laughed in reply, acknowledging band mates Fish and Craig with a wave.

"We're going to give my sister such a good send-off tonight. You ready to party?"

"Absolutely."

The girls headed back to a banquette in the bar to catch up with the last few weeks' gossip. Around them the bar gradually filled, the air became denser and the level of chatter increased to a frenzied buzz.

"And how's the big romance going?" Nadine asked.

"Great," Abigail replied truthfully. "It was never going to be easy with us living so far apart, but we make the most of the time we have together."

Nadine raised a studded eyebrow knowingly. Abigail went on to tell her about the search for Sam's future stables, and having some more riding lessons from Sam's little sister, Charly, and Mrs Angel's birthday, the application to go on the TV programme, and being invited to Luke and Harriet's wedding. She then realised that she hadn't stopped talking about herself. "So. Are you all packed up for your trip?"

Nadine gave a nonchalant shrug. "I don't take an awful lot with me, so I've shoved some casual clothes in a rucksack and I'm sure I can buy anything I've forgotten at the airport."

Abigail thought of the size of case she packed just for a night or two at Sam's, and blushed. Despite her realisation that the bulging wardrobe of designer clothes and racks of near-identical shoes were never going to make her happy, Abigail hadn't been able to bring herself to downsize quite yet. All in good time.

Through the wall, they could hear the muffled bass of Blue Steak's opening number. "Ready to dance?" Nadine yelled. The volume of the pub had risen to a level where they would have to be shouting at each other to hold a conversation; dancing seemed like the sensible option. The pair vacated the banquette and made their way through the toilet corridor to the "live lounge" as the Mermaid proudly advertised the space. In reality, it was a large converted garage with high ceiling, sticky floor and a smattering of wobbly round wooden tables for customers to abandon their drinks on. A few dozen tipsy customers were already in the centre of the dance floor bouncing up and down and shouting along to the lyrics of "I predict a riot".

Three hours later, Abigail's feet throbbed from dancing along to song after song, and whilst neither had drunk much alcohol, they made their farewells to Blue Steak feeling elated. Arm in arm, they tottered out of the Mermaid and turned right to head back to the tube station.

"I'll miss you, Nad," Abigail sighed as they reached the platform. It was a ritual that Abigail would wave Nadine goodbye on the eastbound platform before crossing the bridge to take her westbound service home.

"Ah, I'll not be gone that long, and maybe when I get back, I'll decide what I want to do with my life and settle down."

Abigail doubted it. Nadine shied away from anything that would commit her long term. The girls waited in silence until finally the rails gave off the hiss that indicated a train was on the way, and they hugged goodbye. Abigail watched as Nadine's dreadlocks disappeared behind a group of travellers alighting the train, and still gazed as its lights faded away down the track.

With a sigh, she turned and began to make the short trip to her platform. Her friend had barely gone half a mile but it felt as though she was already on the other side of the world.

4

"What are you doing?" Erik asked, glancing at Nadine, as she chewed on the end of her pen thoughtfully.

"I'm writing a letter to my friend. I feel bad that I haven't rung her for a month, and now I've lost my phone."

"Is that the dressmaker?" Erik had heard plenty of stories about Abigail.

"The fashion designer," Nadine corrected protectively. To a fashion graduate, there was something negative about being dismissed as a dressmaker. "Yes."

It was late afternoon and they were hanging around at the school where they had both been placed for their volunteering. The classes were finished for the day and it was too early for supper.

Erik was clearly bored and, after momentarily watching Nadine scribble away on an A4 sheet that she'd taken from the office photocopier, muttered something about going to kick a ball around. There was never a shortage of kids from the dusty village to partake in a game of football.

Nadine watched his sexy backside disappear out of the classroom and returned to her task in hand. She could have emailed, but somehow a handwritten letter full of gossip seemed more personal. She could imagine Abigail's delight as the envelope plopped onto the doormat of the home she shared with her parents in Richmond. The exotic stamp showing red temples would break up the monotony of gas bills and pizza leaflets.

Abigail ripped open the envelope, having already identified the sender. It wasn't everyday one received mail postmarked from Cambodia with Nadine's loopy carefree writing on the front.

"*Dear Ab*," she read. "*Soo-a s'day, as they say in Khmer (that's the official language of Cambodia in case you were wondering.). Well, I've been here over a month already, and sorry I haven't rung you but I've lost my phone and to be honest, I don't feel*

14

the need to get another one. Telecommunications isn't really high on the list of Cambodian priorities.

So, my guide book described Phnom Penh (that's the capital where we flew into - I feel the need to explain all this because your knowledge of geography is appalling!) as 'a name that can't help but conjure up an image of the exotic. The glimmering spires of the Royal Palace, the fluttering saffron of the monks' robes and the luscious location on the banks of the mighty Mekong – this is the Asia many dreamed of when first imagining their adventures overseas.' What a load of bollocks, is what I say."

Abigail smiled as she heard her friend's voice in her head. Nadine was never one to mince her words. She continued reading. *"The reality is the city is smelly, filthy, noisy, and the traffic is mental. The people themselves are lovely, but we had to spend the first night here and it was like an assault course every time we stepped out of the hotel. The heat was unbearable. You know me, I like a bit of warmth (I'm half Arabian for starters) but the temperatures soar to about 38 degrees every day and in the city centre, it was like a pressure cooker. Combined with the obnoxious traffic fumes made us feel like we're being steamed alive. The traffic is the worst, though; it makes the North Circular on a Monday morning rush hour look like a doddle. Our taxi from the airport took over an hour but it's only 7km away. I asked the taxi driver if this was normal and he said "yes, every day, same". Every vehicle from 4x4s, tuk-tuks, carts and motorbikes (lots and lots of motorbikes) are pushing past. We've even had motorbikes mount the pavements and come straight at us to get through the traffic. Crossing the road is a leap of faith as they have no crossings or any rules for driving – at all!*

Luckily I met Erik, another volunteer (he's from Holland), on the flight and later that night we hid away in a bar selling cold draught beer for the equivalent of 35p. Thankfully the next day we were out of the shitty city and had a six-hour bus ride northwest to the Sangkae district, where we're based in a tiny community school in a village off the National Highway 5. They are so friendly here and know how to party. Blue Steak should come here; I'm sure the guys would run out of steam before the locals.

Last week, Erik and I passed a gathering of about 15 people having a street party and they invited us to join them. The music was pumping, the beer was flowing and we had a very enjoyable night. As is the tradition, they rub your face with talc (I'm still not sure why) and at one point, we all danced round a potted bush placed on a chair. I asked what it signified and they said 'power' and 'joy'.

The traffic is better here in the countryside and we have access to bikes and mopeds as part of the project. I was worried about cycling in the traffic but it's been fine. There are no traffic lights so at the junctions it just flows (in the same way it does when sets of traffic lights are broken back home) and, although the law of the road is that the biggest vehicle has right of way, they're not doing high speeds and are considerate when overtaking westerners on crappy cheap bikes. They drive on the right here but sometimes it is difficult to tell as vehicles are all over the place.

As for the work, well I'm loving every minute of it. We're really working hard with the community to encourage participation at school. I don't know about you, but I used to bunk off to hover around the bus stop smoking fags. These poor kids don't attend school because they're helping Mum and Dad bring in the harvest, so it's a project aimed at finding solutions to these localised circumstances. I'm only a month in, with another eleven months to go yet, so maybe the novelty will wear off. Erik says we should go back and live in Amsterdam when we finish, but it's early days.

Well, better go, it's supper time – probably a dish that involves fish, ginger and soy beans.
Love Nadine."

Abigail read the letter twice. She could appreciate that Nadine was having a faraway adventure, but there was no asking after her. Would it really have taken much effort to slip in a sentence asking how she was, or how her business was going, and how was Sam?

With a sad sigh, she felt her friend slip further away still.

5

The time had come for the bride to throw the bouquet. An act that, despite the progress of girl power and feminism, still caused single girls to unleash their competitive streak and act in utter desperation to catch it. Abigail was no exception, as she lined up with around fifty other ladies, all pretending that it didn't matter to them, whilst praying that it would land in their grasp. Please God, let it be me, chanted the inner goddesses of every single lady at the wedding.

A shriek went up as Harriet tossed the beautiful bouquet of creamy magnolias and blood red roses over her head. Abigail could only watch in despair as its trajectory sailed it to the other end of the crowd. Amid squeals, a dozen pairs of hands shot up, and with unladylike aggression, the bouquet was snatched. The crowd backed off like the sea retreating from the shore, and Abigail saw that it was one of the bridesmaids who had caught it. It was Molly - the irritating one.

"Ha, I don't think we'll see Molly getting hitched any time soon," smiled Sam, as Abigail and Kate rejoined him on the lawn. There was nothing like the romance of a wedding to prompt girls to fantasise about what their perfect day would look like. Abigail decided that when the time came, she would like her setting to be similar to that of Harriet and Luke's grand country house hotel. With its sweeping lawns, a large white marquee in the centre, with a couple of "pop up" champagne bars, and a string quartet playing at appropriate moments in the proceedings, Abigail was in awe. The weather was perfect too, with blue skies and fluffy clouds, a light breeze and a comfortable temperature. The day could have been a disaster if the heavens had opened. There was nothing worse than horizontal rain pelting the guests during the photographs, or beating down hard on the canvas roof during the speeches, drowning out the jokey anecdotes and the romantic interludes from the string quartet. Meteorological intervention

17

had been beyond the remit and talents of the wedding planner, but an August wedding would suggest a higher probability of sun than most months.

"I'm so glad the damn thing didn't come anywhere near me," laughed Kate, who had been reluctant to join the line up in the first place. "Marriage is a long way off for me. I'd need to get divorced first!" She had been invited to the wedding through Callum's connection to Luke. Weighing room buddies, so it seemed. Callum had been spotted a few times in the crowd, but both parties kept a respectful distance from each other. Whilst children had been invited to the wedding, Kate had decided toddler Aidan would be better off being looked after by his grandma for the day, so there was no reason for Callum and Kate (and more importantly, Abigail) to have any interaction with each other. Since Callum had tried to force himself on Abigail a few months earlier, she could barely bring herself to look in his direction. Luckily, he was preoccupied with friends in the racing circle, and seemed to have no intention of causing any trouble.

Kate's "plus one" was Dan Witt, the son from the campsite. He was now giving her personal training sessions, and Abigail wondered whether that was all he was giving her. She was dying to ask her friend, but there had been no opportunity so far for them to be alone.

"What are you thinking about?" Abigail asked Sam, as he gazed out across the lawn. She wondered whether he, too, was imagining what their wedding day would look like.

Sam smiled, a little guiltily. "I was wondering who would be picking up Luke's rides at Southwell tomorrow. I was just glancing through the lads here. My money's on Craigy boy."

Typical, thought Abigail inwardly; he had a one-track mind. She realised with relief that should Sam ever propose to her, at least they wouldn't have to plan a wedding around the relentless racing schedule once he'd redirected his career into the riding stables business. It had been a miracle that he'd agreed to take this one day off. A Saturday of all days, when he could have had four plum rides at Newbury. His sacrifice couldn't even be rewarded with alcohol. He was abstaining so that he was fresh for his journey and rides at Pontefract tomorrow. Abigail made no such concession, and tucked freely into the champagne on offer.

"Oh, I don't miss that at all," Kate replied. "Day after day of rides here, there and everywhere. Phone calls to the agent, buttering up the owners and trainers..."

"Now it's just me nagging you to exercise," joked Dan. His training sessions were having a visible effect. Kate had lost nearly a stone in weight, toned up her "flabby bits" (her words) and she now looked radiant as she showed off her curves in a new dress that she'd treated herself to for the occasion. It was a "look at what you're missing" message to Callum. Not that she'd want him back.

The sun sloped down to the horizon and it was the awkward pause in weddings proceedings where the ceremony, photographs and reception have all been done and dusted, the guests can't eat another morsel, but it's too early for the evening entertainment to get underway. Drink was flowing and guests stood in small groups making small talk.

Sam looked at his watch and wondered whether he'd be the bad guy for suggesting they call it a day.

"Oh, look out," mumbled Kate under her breath. "Here comes Molly." Abigail looked up. She didn't know it yet, but wavering towards them was the woman that would play a key role in Abigail's future. Dressed in her bridesmaid's outfit, she scrubbed up well. Normally, jodhpurs, baggy t-shirts and hoodies were standard dress code for Luke's sister. But today, resplendent in shimmering red taffeta, she even looked feminine. Her long chestnut hair had fallen from its neat "up do" and now sprawled across her shoulders. Molly had removed her dainty magnolia coloured strappy shoes and they now dangled from her free hand as she walked barefoot across the grass. An empty champagne glass and a lit cigarette occupied her other hand, and from afar Abigail would have thought she were too young to drink and smoke, but as she got closer, she realised that Molly was over eighteen. Maybe only just. Her attire matched the bridal bouquet. Of course.

"Hi guys, are you having a good time? I haven't met you properly yet, have I?" Molly stretched her hand out to Abigail without realising the dangling shoes made it tricky to shake, and continued, without taking a breath. "You must be Abigail, Sam's girlfriend? Luke told me all about the great romance, ha! Anyway, I'm Luke's sister, his little sister, not the older one, that's Kelly over there, the slimmer one – the cow - but I'm Molly." She realised the shoes were preventing a hand shake, tucked them in her armpit and pumped Abigail's hand enthusiastically. "Did you see me catch the bouquet? I couldn't believe it, I haven't even got a partner, let alone a fiancé and I don't think I will in the foreseeable future... Oh, hello," she spotted Dan for the first time. "I don't think I know you, do I? Are you in racing like everybody else here? Are you here with Kate? I know Kate vaguely because of Callum, although I think we only met once at Cheltenham, didn't we, do you remember - that time that Callum and Luke were both in the Foxhunters chase."

"I'm Dan," he interrupted her, stretching out a hand. Kate took advantage of the millisecond pause, and excused herself to go to the loo, and nudged Abigail to accompany her. The pair trotted away as Molly was about to launch into another monologue.

19

"Oh, my gawd," Kate breathed as soon as they were safely out of earshot. "Isn't she a nightmare?"

Abigail giggled. "I'm sure her heart's in the right place, she's just a bit ... er....exhausting."

The pair made their way to the courtyard, where they passed through pergolas adorned with bright yellow roses to enter the cool interior of the Cotswold stone building. "So, you and Dan...?" Abigail ventured, as soon as they were in the quiet surroundings of the toilets. "Is it just personal training... Or is it more?"

Kate grinned. "Can you tell?"

It was still early days for the couple, but Kate and Dan had become an item. Kate loved having a toy boy. Fresh from graduation, Dan was five years younger than Kate, but his level-headed maturity was the most attractive thing about him. Well, one of the most attractive things, alongside his toned body, infectious sense of humour and kind twinkling eyes.

By the time they returned from the trip to the ladies, Molly had moved on to talk incessantly at another poor wedding guest.

"What would you ladies say to us ducking out ahead of the evening disco and heading home?" asked Sam. The evening chill was beginning to set into Sam's sober bones and, although he'd never admit it, he was bored. The thought of sipping coffee whilst luxuriating in the cosy, squishy sofas at home was appealing. The quicker he did that, the quicker he could end up in bed with Abigail.

"No problem," Abigail and Kate sang in unison. For Kate, the quicker they got home, the quicker she and Dan could be snuggled up in front of the telly. Together.

Abigail was just keen not to get stuck with Molly again.

6

The nights were drawing in as summer began to surrender, and in Abigail's parents' spare bedroom, the fashion empire was taking shape. Swathes of fabric samples draped over surfaces, Abigail's sketch books bulged with different ideas and designs and her days were taken over by answering emails, updating her social media sites and refining her website.

In his final season as flat jockey, Sam worked as hard as ever, and Abigail gradually adapted to his hectic schedule. Days off during the summer season were as rare as rocking horse poo, and when there was a gap in the racing schedule, Abigail had to grab the opportunity to spend time with him. Sometimes, when Abigail found herself exhausted from admin, sewing and designing, she would allow herself the luxury of a day off and head to whichever racecourse Sam was destined for that day. It felt odd to stand alone amongst groups of drunken punters or retired men in flat caps and tweed, but she would find a quiet spot by the rail and watch him ride down to the starting stalls, cheer for him during the race until he crossed the finish line, and then hook up with him when his last race was run. By then, Sam was usually tired and - depending on the success of the races - despondent or jubilant, but always pleased to see Abigail. They'd find somewhere for supper, then head their separate ways home.

Spending time in Gloucestershire was Abigail's favourite way to spend time off. Regardless of where Sam was due to be racing, Abigail enjoyed pitching up at the Ashington Yard, where she would share his bed, enjoy breakfast together (after he'd been riding out for two hours, during which time Abigail had enjoyed another dream and a cup of coffee), and grab a few precious hours in the evening before bedtime. She used the trips to call in on Mrs Angel, catch up with Kate, and develop her riding skills on the ever patient and lovable Grace. Abigail realised that if their life together was going to be based on horses, she had better master the basics.

Sam's sister Charly was more than happy to step in as teacher. Without letting on to Sam, they took Grace to the schooling ring every time Abigail came to visit. Over the summer months, Abigail grew in confidence and learnt the basic controls and was soon able to ride off the leading rein. Next came the rising trot, and Charly urged horse and rider to trot round and around until Abigail's thighs were burning. Finally by September Abigail had progressed to cantering, but always grasping the saddle like her life depended on it.

It was during her stays at the Ashington Yard that Abigail pressed Sam to keep looking for stables so that he could pursue his new business venture. Using online estate agents, setting the keyword parameters of 'equestrian', they hunted down the opportunities around the country. It soon became evident that Sam's budget wasn't going to give the couple as many options as Abigail hoped. Whilst years of saving hard had given him a powerful amount to go house hunting with, it didn't stretch so far when you needed a country location, with land, space, stables and a property on site.

"You realise that the business comes first, and the property is the thing we're going to need to compromise on?" Sam stressed as Abigail cooed over a five-bedroomed detached cottage in the Cotswolds with just 2 stables attached. They hadn't properly discussed whether Abigail was going to move in, but on their first viewing, Sam made his feelings quite clear. It was a crisp September morning and they made their way to the South Downs to see a "property of Victorian origins", which, on paper, seemed to tick a lot of the boxes they had in their heads. Although there weren't quite enough stables, it did offer sufficient land to construct more, and being under budget would make this possible. It had good access to London, with ample parking and a two-bedroomed property on site.

Abigail concentrated on the appeal of the kitchen, and whether she could see herself having a bath in the mint green tub in the bathroom, which was "in need of renovation". As she wasn't contributing financially to the venture, she didn't feel in a position to complain. She stood contemplating the bright blue surround to the fireplace with distaste, when Sam dropped the bombshell.

"The stables are perfect," he murmured, quietly enough so that the estate agent wouldn't hear from the other end of the lounge. "But I don't think we can cope with just the two bedrooms."

"How many do you need?" she replied in confusion. Two bedrooms had always been an option in their search.

"Well, we'll need another bedroom for Molly."

"For what?" Abigail racked her brain to think whether Sam had a dog called Molly, or whether this name had featured in their conversations before. Nothing came to mind. Sam looked sheepish and she realised that there was a significant part of the plan that he'd omitted to reveal so far.

"I've come to the conclusion that I can't run this place alone," he said simply, perching a skinny buttock on the arm of the chair. For a moment, Abigail thought he was suggesting she help him run a riding school. The idea was laughable, she couldn't even canter without grasping onto the front of the saddle. "So the thing is, you remember Luke's little sister Molly? Well, she's available to come and work for me in return for nothing but bed and board."

Sam looked at Abigail with doleful eyes, like a puppy imploring its owner to forgive it for shredding the cushion. She wasn't cross with him; it was his business, his investment, and his future, so why did he expect her to react negatively?

"So, a bedroom for you and a bedroom for Molly," Abigail clarified, still confused. "That's two bedrooms."

Sam looked relieved and broke into his boyish grin. "I was hoping more along the lines of a bedroom for us, a space for you to use for your business, and another room for Molly."

Abigail's momentary jubilation at having been asked in a roundabout way to move in was suddenly quashed. Things clicked into place as an image of Molly formed in Abigail's memory. Luke and Harriet's wedding. Molly the bridesmaid. Didn't stop talking. Loud, brash, scatty, a smoker, drinking like a fish... And Sam was expecting them to all live together. That would explain his hesitation.

What choice did she have? He'd just asked her to move in with him, and she felt ready to do that in an instant. It seemed Molly was the compromise she'd have to make. The riding school would be his responsibility, and if he felt he needed an assistant to help run it, who was she to stop him? She may live to regret the decision, but it might also provide her with some vital female company too.

"Well, let's get out of here and start another search," Abigail concluded. "And if Molly drives us nuts, it'll be you with the task of sacking her."

"Yes boss," replied Sam with a grin. Taking her hand, he thanked the estate agent and they set off to pour over yet more internet listings.

7

Sam placed the coffee cup down on the bedside cabinet close to Abigail's ear and its clatter broke her out of the thin level of dozing. "Happy five-month anniversary," he smiled. He was dressed in his riding out uniform, the standard issue black jodhpurs and warm merino wool polo neck base layer. He'd left his outer jacket downstairs: it had been thrown lazily over the bannister.

"How do you remember it was five months to the day?" Abigail marvelled. The ability to remember exact dates of trivial matters seemed like a feminine quality for Sam to possess. She wriggled into a sitting position and took the cup, sipping the edge cautiously even though she knew it would be too hot.

"I asked you out on our birthday. 5th May. Five months ago."

Of course, the day at Ascot where he'd asked her to be his girlfriend. She smiled at him fondly; he was as lovable today as he was then. Especially as he brought her coffee in bed whenever she stayed over.

Those five months had flown by for both of them and, if asked about their high points, no doubt Sam would cite his successes in the 1000 Guineas race at Newmarket, riding at Royal Ascot, the thrill of the Epsom Derby and heading to York for the Ebor. There had been occasional five figure prize money sums that Sam had accumulated over the summer months, which he had tenaciously added to the house-hunting fund.

For Abigail, her five months had more modest highlights. She remembered their picnic by the river fondly, and a few profitable commissions on dresses she had launched as part of the late summer collection. That had boosted her confidence. There was also the day the letter arrived from the makers of the TV show '*Where in the World?*'. She had forgotten all about Kate's application, when out of the blue a letter landed on her doormat inviting her and Mrs Angel to audition for the show in Bristol. When the letter arrived, she shrugged it off, not believing for a second that they would be good enough to make the show. Now that the audition day had arrived, she found her stomach tightening every time she thought of day ahead.

"So, have you decided what you're wearing today?" Sam asked, regarding the nine outfit options hanging on the wardrobe door. She had driven Sam and his mum to distraction the previous evening, trying on each outfit for their approval. She had come to Gloucestershire by train this time so had been limited to what she could squeeze into a suitcase. The shoes for the black shift dress weren't quite right, nor were the heels with the trouser suit. Sam wasn't any help, as he had half an eye on the replays of the afternoon's racing, and Sam's mum had little input beyond "Well, it doesn't look too bad to me".

"No, I think I'll try them all again."

"You'll look great whatever you wear," he promised, leaning in to give her a peck on the lips. "You should just go as you are." She blushed and pulled the duvet over her naked body self-consciously.

"Anyway, got to dash, the second string needs to go out. Good luck!"

With that he vanished from the bedroom and Abigail heard his light footsteps fade down the stairs. She placed the half empty coffee cup back on the bedside table and looked at her watch. There was still three hours before Kate was picking her up, but a girl could never have quite enough time to make herself look gorgeous.

"You look amazing!" gushed Kate, as Abigail opened the front door. After managing to reject eight outfits, she had finally opted for a navy top that she had designed as part of her latest collection. It was styled like a vest that hugged and accentuated her shapely breasts, but the material then flowed into a cape at the back. The skirt was full and patterned with images of blue and fuchsia stilettos. She wasn't happy with the white court shoes, but it was the best combination from limited options.

She waved goodbye to Mrs Ashington and followed Kate out to her silver Corsa that she had parked hastily on the gravel. Mrs Angel was installed in the passenger seat, handbag on lap. Abigail clambered over the biscuit- encrusted child seat to settle herself on the backseat.

"We've found our stables!" Abigail blurted out as soon as the necessary greetings were out of the way, and Kate was pulling out into the country lanes. She told them about their recent trip to the New Forest, and described how she immediately fell in love with the town of Fordingbridge. They had stopped there for lunch on their way to see the equestrian centre that was up for sale. From Fordingbridge, they had penetrated a short way into the national park before turning off the main road onto a winding lane.

It was Abigail's first trip to the New Forest and she was amazed at the numbers of ponies and donkeys grazing at the sides of the road, and meandering aimlessly along the tarmac. Following instruction from his bossy sat nav, Sam indicated right and turned into the bumpy driveway leading to the property.

In the late September dappled sunlight, the scenery looked romantic and appealing and Abigail didn't give a second thought to the winter months, when the nights would draw in by four o'clock and she would need torchlight just to navigate to the end of the driveway.

"It's a cosy two bedroomed cottage with a big open plan space downstairs," she told Kate and Mrs Angel. The pair made encouraging noises in the right places. "It's even got an impressive fireplace so we can heat up the house with roaring fires in the winter. Then there's a converted garage on the end, which will be Molly's space. It's not massive, but she says she's happy with a bed to crash on and a toilet. She'll eat with us, as that's part of the deal."

The bonus was that the stables had been empty for over a year and the owners were desperate for a quick sale. Sam put in a ridiculously cheeky offer and, to his amazement, it was accepted on the understanding that contracts were exchanged by November. As first-time buyers with no chain, this seemed realistic.

"So, you'll be in for Christmas," Mrs Angel pointed out. "It sounds like a charming place. I'd love to see it."

"Why don't you come to us for Christmas?" Abigail suggested. "Sam's parents will be coming, so they can give you a lift over. Just for Christmas Day?"

"You know, that would be smashing," Mrs Angel replied thoughtfully. "I usually spend Christmas Day alone, although most years my friend Doreen pops in for a sherry at some point. And Kate has popped around too, haven't you dear?" Mrs Angel placed a gloved hand on Kate's arm momentarily.

Abigail couldn't conceive of spending a Christmas Day alone, and thought how heartless Mrs Angel's family must be not to come and visit. With low cost airlines providing transport as easy as buses, living in Edinburgh was no excuse for Mrs Angel's daughter and granddaughter not to make the effort at Christmas.

Kate took the scenic route through the Cotswolds countryside towards the M5 at Gloucester, and it was obvious that it had been some time since Mrs Angel had travelled out of the village. Like an excited child, she pointed out places along the way that held memories for her.

"We looked around that house in the seventies," she exclaimed. "It was way out of our price range, and we were just being nosy really, but it had a lovely Aga in the kitchen. Oh, and behind this tall hedge was a perfect spot for shooting grouse. Technically it was poaching, but Andrew - that was my husband, God rest his soul - didn't care about that." She made comment about how the leaves were turning. The chestnut trees, having shed their conkers last month were now preparing to carpet the hedgerows with a layer of crispy, golden brown leaves.

By the time Kate pulled on to the M5, Abigail realised that she was starting to get horribly nervous. She had no idea what tasks lay ahead, but Mrs Angel seemed cool and collected.

"Just smile and be yourself," she advised, as Kate dropped them off an hour later. "Let's pretend we're going to a party and want to make a good impression."

"Just don't start on the booze," joked Kate, helping Abigail to climb back out from the cramped confines of the back seat. Dropping the driver's seat back into position, Kate slid back in, fastened her seatbelt and gave a merry toot as she departed. She was going to make the most of a day off, and planned to head to the new shopping centre in Bristol to treat herself to some clothes whilst Mrs Angel and Abigail faced a grilling.

The pair waved her off until the Corsa disappeared from view around the corner. They were delaying the inevitable.

"Well, here goes," Abigail muttered as she held the door open for Mrs Angel to waddle through.

The warmth of the production offices that greeted the pair were a far cry from the sharp autumnal winds that had been battering Sam through the afternoon on the other side of the country. He hadn't had the best of days at the office, with only one ride placed out of three chances.

"Sam!" Molly squealed with delight as he approached, and without inhibition, she ran to him, flung her arms around his neck and squeezed him tight. "I just wanted to say a huge thank you for letting me come and live with you. Luke tells me you've found a place in the New Forest."

Sam peeled her from him, glancing nervously to check that none of the lads had emerged from the weighing room to witness her extravagant greeting. She was the last thing he was expecting. He didn't have any rides remaining on the Leicester card that afternoon, so was keen to get away promptly in the hope he could get home and have a meal waiting for Abigail's return from her audition in Bristol. He would probably have to pick up a takeaway pizza and warm it in the oven rather than attempt anything from scratch, but it was the thought that counted.

"Molly! What are you doing here?"

"I've been watching the racing. You were unlucky on Daisy Dream in the opener, by the way. I had a couple of quid on it, but not to worry, you can't win them all, eh? Luke was going up North today to see friends, and I saw you were riding at Leicester so I bribed him with a McDonalds to give me a lift and drop me off so that I could come and say thank you in person. So here I am. I couldn't see you on the card for the last two races, so was hovering outside the weighing room waiting for you to emerge. Oh, I haven't seen you for ages. It's so lovely to have some Sam time."

She launched herself at Sam for a second time and pulled him into a bear hug that he couldn't escape from. Her mop of wavy, wild hair tickled his nostrils.

"I wasn't planning on hanging around," Sam warned, starting to walk towards the car park as soon as she let go of him. She trotted alongside, undeterred.

"Would you be able to give me a lift back then? Don't go out of your way, you can drop me wherever, but it'll be a good opportunity to have a chat about how it's all going to work when we move into the stables. Come on, tell me about them, is it a massive place? How many horses are you looking to get? Is Abigail moving in too? I like her, she's so pretty, and wears really nice clothes. Unlike me, look at me, what a state! Oh! You've changed your car."

Molly was just about to walk past the plum coloured Jaguar when Sam's approach brought the car to life with a clunk of the central locking and a flash of the headlights.

"Yep," Sam replied proudly, "I wanted something a bit more practical than the Porsche. The number of miles I clock up, the Porsche really wasn't kind on the wallet."

"It's nice," she agreed, sliding into the leather clad passenger seat. "At least we can make our escape before the majority of the punters kick out."

Sam blocked out her subsequent chatter about what she'd placed bets on that day, her analysis of each ride, and the tale of the woman in a hat that looked like a swimming cap from the seventies. There was some drama about a mix up with a Bacardi and Diet Coke, but Sam had truly stopped listening at that point.

As he got settled into the motorway, Sam found a gap in her monologue to describe the stables and the house to her. Molly punctuated the ends of his sentences with "sounds good, sounds good". He decided to stop talking before it drove him mad. He knew it meant she would take the silence as an invitation to start up her chatter again, but it was the lesser of two evils.

"I haven't got much to bring in the way of furniture. It'll just be me and a suitcase of riding gear. What else does a girl need, eh?"'"

Sam thought briefly to the amount of clothing Abigail might want to bring. The main bedroom wasn't large enough to hold more than a wardrobe to share; he'd have to encourage her to think carefully about her clothing allocation.

"Oh, and I'll be bringing Bessie if we haven't traced her owners," Molly continued. "Did I tell you I found a dog?"

"Found a dog? How do you just find a dog?"

"Well, it was more like the dog found me. I was walking along the lane behind Luke's, you know that track that leads up to Kirk's Farm? Anyway, out of nowhere this border collie comes trotting up to me, looking all lost and confused. She's a lovely little thing, looks quite young, and has these adoring green eyes. She was wearing a collar with a tag that says Bessie, and there was a phone number on the tag but every time we've dialled it, it just rings and rings. No answerphone, no nothing. We've put her photo out on social media and all those sites about lost pets, but nothing so far. It's been three weeks now; I can't believe no one knows who she is. She's not chipped either. We took her to Martin – you know, the vet - but she's not chipped."

"One more mouth to feed then," Sam remarked.

"Yep, let's hope the stables bring in as much money as your racing," she replied lightly. "Although judging by days like today, that won't be difficult. When are you officially retiring from racing, it's nearly the end of the flat season, isn't it?"

Sam's heart started beating a little faster. He hadn't admitted to anyone yet that he wasn't hanging up his breeches until the new business settled down. He knew Abigail would disapprove; he would be breaking his promise to her.

"I'm going to keep my licence going for the time being," he confessed. "You know, just until the stables start bringing in enough income. I haven't told Abigail that yet, so best keep that to yourself."

"Oh Sam," Molly replied, placing her hand lightly on his knee. "My lips are sealed. You know me, I can keep my mouth shut."

Sam tightened his grip on the steering wheel. If only that were true, he mused.

Thankfully the traffic was kind as Sam sped homewards and he only had to put up with ninety minutes of Molly's chatter before he was able to drop her off at the Crown pub in Lower Stanway, where she was temporarily bedding down in their stock room in return for a small wage and washing up six nights a week. With no transport to her name, Molly wasn't able to return back to her dad's caravan at night, so she and Bessie were stuck there for the time being.

"I hope you have a nice meal tonight," she said as a parting shot, clambering out the vehicle. She sounded wistful, and Sam wondered whether she was hankering after an invite. Well tough, she had washing up duties to perform. He wouldn't want to be responsible for her getting kicked out of the pub so soon after being expelled from jockey school.

Speeding back to Lower Maisey, he was relieved to find that he had managed to beat Abigail home, and also his mum seemed to have turned into a domestic goddess in the meantime.

"Goodness, what's this?" Abigail stared open-mouthed at the dining table as she wandered in from the hallway an hour later. The formal tablecloth had come out, with five places laid up. Amidst the condiments, a pair of silver candlesticks sporting long crimson candles dominated the centre of the table, flickering romantically, and a salad and platter of bread sat waiting for the diners. The Ashingtons' ground floor was bathed in an aroma of roasting meat.

"We thought it was high time we all sat around together and ate as a family," explained Sam. "I hurried back from Leicester hoping to get a pizza in the oven for you, but Mum beat me to it."

"It smells lovely," she complimented Mrs Ashington, who had scuttled into the room to add mint sauce to the table. "In all the excitement of the day we forgot to have lunch, although Mrs Angel ate enough Werther's toffees to give her a week's sugar intake."

"Well, take a seat both of you – I'll be dishing up now."

She yelled for Robin and Charly to come and sit up at the table, and for the first time, the five of them sat together. Abigail thought ahead to Christmas, when she would be playing host to these four, plus her parents, Molly and Mrs Angel. Part of her shivered with excitement, but a tiny part of her was filled with dread. How could she produce something as professional looking as the leg of lamb that now adorned the table?

"Dig in," Mrs Ashington urged, indicating all the bowls between them.

Ravenously, Abigail piled on the roast potatoes and veg, adding a few slices of meat and drowning the lot in thick gravy. She glanced at Sam and frowned to see that he had only taken a slice of meat and a few spoonfuls of carrot.

She was about to comment, when Charly interjected to ask who would like wine.

"What shall we drink to?" asked Mr Ashington, nodding to indicate Charly had filled his glass enough. "Certainly not to your lack of winners today," he joked to Sam, who pulled a playful face back at his dad.

"We should drink to Abigail getting on *Where in the World*," Sam said proudly, raising his glass of tap water.

"Oh yes, of course! Tell us about the audition," urged Mrs Ashington. "Did you meet that Henry bloke?"

"No, we only saw the show's researchers," Abigail replied, casting her mind back to the middle of the day. It already felt so long ago. "I think it went OK."

She told them about the way the researchers went over the rules of the game, even though she and Mrs Angel were experts. However, she had politely nodded and looked keen, asked a few questions that she hoped sounded intelligent and tried to act as natural as she could.

The wannabe contestants were then split into small groups and led to a room that was set up like a fake studio and there was a pretend round of the quiz. A few of the contestants were useless, but Abigail realised that there were usually a handful of dunces that made it through each week. The game needed a spectrum of abilities within the contestants.

Mrs Angel and Abigail were then taken into a small office for a more intimate chat with a researcher. It felt like the time Abigail had been to an interview for a place at university. She had gabbled her way through the process then, but that was five years ago. She was a different woman now, and relaxed into the chat, not worrying too much whether she passed or failed the audition. It wasn't as if her future depended on it, the way the university interview had.

"The funny thing is, Mrs Angel refused to tell them her Christian name," Abigail recalled. "They tried to coax it out of her, but she was as bullish as ever, insisting that everybody called her Mrs Angel in the village, and the show shouldn't be any different."

"So, do you think she's blown it for you?" Charly asked, concerned.

"I don't think so. They seemed to compromise that if we get onto the show, we could use 'Angel' as her first name."

"What happens now?" asked Sam, who had unsurprisingly finished his meagre meal. "When do you hear?"

"It's a case of 'don't call us, we'll call you'," she replied. "It's out of our hands, so we'll have to wait and see."

"Well, cheers!" said Robin Ashington, realising that they hadn't ever got around to toasting.

"Cheers!" the four joined in, their glasses clinking as if signalling the start of a new chapter.

31

8

Abigail made a mental list of all the things that would be easier once the riding stables were up and running and she would be living with Sam and Molly in the New Forest.

For a start, she wouldn't miss the wasted time driving on the motorway between Gloucestershire and London, or the constant battle to coordinate diaries so that she could spend more than a couple of hours with Sam. She would be able to have the business paraphernalia in one place; that would be a blessing. There had been a number of times she had arrived home to Richmond to find she'd left her laptop in Sam's bedroom in Gloucestershire, or a vital piece of a customer's outfit in the Ashingtons' lounge, when the rest of it was hanging in the study at home.

She tried to think of these positives as she helped Sam to unload his belongings from the Ashington family Land Rover. It was a cold, blustery November morning, and the legal paperwork had all gone through smoothly. The stable block, yard, numerous crumbling out buildings, two-bedroomed cottage, converted double garage and scruffy paddocks now belonged to Sam.

Abigail carried a cardboard box marked "kitchen stuff" into the house and placed it on the countertop. She winced at the filth around her. There would be days of cleaning ahead. Days she didn't feel she could spare with no steady income and orders to deal with.

"We should have thought to bring some cloths and cleaning things..." Abigail told Sam, who was hugging his games console protectively to his chest. He made a non-committal noise, reminding Abigail that he was a man living away from home for the first time. Cleaning was yet to enter his vocabulary, let alone his routine. She'd have to send Molly out to the shops to get some before she could hope to unload anything from the boxes. That was one positive thing about Molly; she was always eager to make herself useful.

Bessie – her adopted dog – was far from collaborative. She bounded with excitement from room to room, sniffing everything, getting under their feet and sending dust flying into the air as she wagged her tail over surfaces.

"That's everything from the car," announced Molly. She paused and looked around the sparse space. The vendors had left the cooker and carpets, and plenty of dust and house spiders, but with the contents of the car unloaded, the trio realised how much they were lacking. Abigail started a list of "essentials" - comprising a fridge, sofa, crockery, cutlery, pots and pans, washing machine and beds. The less essential list included a dining table and wardrobes, but they could make do without those in the meantime.

"Shit, I didn't budget for any of that," Sam mumbled, when Abigail read out the list. "But at least we've got a telly and PlayStation."

"You can get the furniture at the British Heart Foundation shops," Molly suggested. "I know there's one in Salisbury, but there's probably one in Southampton too. We can look it up when the internet's connected."

"Molly, I rode three winners at Royal Ascot this year," Sam spoke to her like a child. "I do not buy worn second hand sofas, or a bed that somebody has died in."

"I was just saying," huffed Molly in response. "You don't want to be spending out loads of unnecessary cash, when you've still got to buy the horses and pay for us to get our qualifications and then there's all the feed, insurance…"

"Yeah, yeah, yeah," Sam interrupted her with a dismissive wave of the hand.

"And don't forget to allow for the marketing budget," added Abigail, partly to wind him up. "If you want me to help, I'm going to need a decent sum for marketing expenses."

There was silence as the three of them stood thoughtfully. The reality of moving into their own place to start their own business was as sobering as it was intimidating.

"Well," Sam spoke to break the silence. "As we have nothing to eat off, we should check out the local pub. My treat."

None of them realised yet, but it turned out to be an expedient suggestion. The Twin Oaks public house was nestled in a thin copse at the end of their driveway. To the front and side of the red bricked property, an expanse of shingle provided a car park, but on this grey Thursday lunchtime, only a couple of cars had been parked up whilst their occupants had lunch.

The trio entered the gloom and Abigail was reminded of the Carpenters Arms in Sloth, with its low ceilings, oak beams and soft hum of the fridges behind the bar, audible in the hushed interior.

At the bar, a man in his thirties sat on a stool, nursing a half pint and reading a newspaper. A liver and white springer spaniel waited reluctantly at his feet, alert to new people entering. Abigail did a quick double take at the man; he looked like a film star with his chiselled good looks. The only other customers were an elderly couple eating ploughman's lunches at the window table.

"So – plan of action." Sam sat opposite the two girls and sipped from his Diet Coke as they awaited their meals. "We need a name for the stables for starters."

"Ashington Stables," Molly was straight in with her suggestion.

"That's a bit similar to Ashington Yard," he replied, screwing his freckled nose up.

"Samolly Stables, you know, a 'what d'you call it' - amalgamation of our two names."

The silent response told Molly that it was a daft idea. "Or Samigail Stables, as technically it should be you two in the name."

"You probably need to work out what you are offering first, as that can have a big influence on the name," Abigail pointed out, her marketing head kicking in. "Are you just teaching kids to ride at the weekends, or offering a riding experience for hen parties, or team building exercises for corporate clients?"

This was a fundamental point, one that should have been worked out months ago and not left to the day they all moved in. Thoughtful silence descended around the table again. In truth, Sam had been too preoccupied with the racing season to give much thought to what the stables would offer. It was all he could manage to keep on top of his races and search for a property. Molly was happy to go with the flow. A free bed and board in return for working with horses, in whatever guise, was enough to satisfy her. As for Abigail, she had left the decisions concerning the stables to Sam. It was his investment, his future. She realised now, as they sat looking perplexed, that she should have encouraged him to think about this sooner.

They were saved by the appearance of their lunch. The lady that had taken their order carried the plates to their table, and placed them in front of the trio.

"There, that'll build you up for the afternoon," she said. Abigail hadn't expected an Essex accent. She was in her early sixties, blond cropped hair doing battle with the grey that tried to push through at the roots. Looking down at her feet, Abigail saw that she was wearing fluffy slippers. "Out walking, are you?"

"No, we're moving in. Next door, the stables," Sam explained.

"Oh, at last!" the lady replied. "That's been empty for such a long time, and it's such a shame to watch the property go to rot. We'll be neighbours then," she beamed. "I'm Anna. Landlady, dogsbody, you know. Just shout if you need anything. Enjoy your lunch."

She toddled off and seconds later, they heard her voice drifting from the backroom, telling somebody else about the youngsters that were moving in next door.

Abigail grinned at Sam. "Sounds like we've got a nosy neighbour. That's good if we need the gossip around here."

"Sounds like we *are* the gossip around here for today," replied Molly, laughing at her own joke.

"I can't believe you've gone for salad on a cold day like today," Abigail observed, as Sam munched on a limp looking salad with a few strips of charcoaled chicken nestled amongst the leaves. "You've got a few days of grafting ahead of you. You should have had something hearty. This hotpot is amazing."

"Ah, he's still watching the weight, aren't you Sam?" Molly replied for him. "Chelmsford on Monday?"

A surge of irritation coursed through Abigail. Not only was Sam continuing to race when he'd promised to give it up to run the stables, but it seemed Molly was fully informed about his schedule when he'd failed to actually tell his girlfriend this.

"Don't forget you've got quite a lot on your plate here now," she pointed out, trying to keep the edge out of her voice.

"I've taken the whole weekend off!" Sam replied defensively. "I'm missing out on some really good rides at Lingfield tomorrow. It's not as if we've got the business up and running yet anyway, so I may as well be earning in the meantime. We have got a lot of furniture to buy," he added, as a final point to score. Abigail's shopping list sat on the pad of paper to her side as a reminder. Over the next hour the list grew as they brainstormed the items that they'd need to get the riding school up and running. From basics like horses, to training, safety equipment, insurance, feed, and tack, the costs soared.

"You can't limit the business to teaching kids at weekends," sighed Abigail. "You've got an expensive asset here with high daily running costs, so you're going to have to operate through the week, which means teaching adults."

"Riding holidays?" suggested Molly, gurgling the dregs of her Coke through the straw like a child. "I went on one when I was twelve. It was in Cornwall. Or Devon maybe, I dunno, somewhere down that end of the country, but it was ace. We stayed in this massive farmhouse in a room full of bunk beds and..."

Abigail had to cut her off. Having finished her hotpot, Molly was back on the chatty side again. "That would be great if we had the accommodation to go with it," Abigail conceded. "Maybe an aspiration for the future. What do we think about corporate away days?"

Abigail explained what she knew about the corporate world to the pair, and outlined what could be done with groups of bankers or marketers from the city and a suite of four legged helpers.

"We could even get them to help muck out!" added Molly, warming to the theme. "And groom them. It'll save us a job, won't it, Sam?"

As Anna's husband, Paul, was sent out to clear the plates - and get a gawp at the trio - they broached the idea with him that the pub could provide the venue for the lunches needed for the corporate away days. It transpired that there was an old skittle alley to the side of the main snug bar that could be used to host up to twenty guests for a buffet lunch.

"It's a bit cold and smelly at the moment," apologised Anna, as she led them into the cold interior of the dejected room, "as we haven't really used it for anything for a while. Don't you worry; we can warm it up, get some fresh flowers in here and make it look pretty. How soon will you be opening?"

"We're aiming for the New Year," replied Sam, to the girls' amazement. This hadn't been discussed, and was seemingly plucked out of Sam's head. But a target date was good. It focused their minds over the next weeks.

9

Abigail would never forget those few weeks settling in to the Twin Oaks Equestrian Centre. Having come to the conclusion that they would offer corporate team building days, the name was chosen as a nod to the two tall oak trees at the end of their driveway. The trees had influenced the name of the pub, which would be a good landmark for visitors coming to the centre. They rejected the term "riding school" for its connotation to teaching youngsters during weekend lessons, and opted for something that sounded professional and business-like. The name plaque was ordered and now swung merrily in the breeze from its sturdy wooden post at the end of the drive.

They had to sleep on the floor for the first few nights, but when the furniture warehouse explained that new beds would take up to six weeks to be delivered, Sam caved in and agreed to buy second hand. The three of them took a trip to Southampton for a shopping spree, and slowly, all the essentials got ticked off the list. The lengthy cleaning sessions made Abigail's arms ache but she adored the feeling of having a place with Sam. Their lives combined, possessions merged and gradually they adapted to the rhythm of each other.

The weather turned colder, but Sam was an early riser all year round. Although he wasn't riding his dad's horses out on the gallops or mucking out, he rose at six o'clock and disappeared. From her semi-conscious slumber, Abigail heard muffled noises that suggested he was taking Bessie for a walk.

She preferred to stay tucked under the duvet until Sam had brought her a coffee an hour or so later. Once the caffeine hit her bloodstream, she felt able to scrape herself out of the warm cocoon, shower and dress before heading into the chilly kitchen to make warm porridge. With her belly satisfied, she'd head to the second bedroom, now transformed into her workspace, and continue to work on the orders that came dribbling in from the website. Alongside her own work, she toiled tirelessly to set up the marketing resources for the Equestrian Centre. A logo, website, social media accounts, branded clothing, business cards and a communications strategy all took time, but since she'd gone through the process that summer with her own business, she took it all in her stride.

Sam's agent would ring up with irritating regularity and offer him rides that were too good to turn down, leaving Abigail to suffer Molly hanging around the house. The TV was on regularly, with sounds of daytime programmes floating up the stairs and distracting Abigail.

"You've got to find her some chores," Abigail begged Sam. There were only so many TV adverts for online bingo games and car insurance that she could tolerate.

To occupy her, Sam subscribed to Horse and Hound magazine, and left her his laptop, urging her to shortlist some horses to buy. To her credit, she pored over listings and made copious notes about potential ponies to buy. When Sam returned from racing, Molly regaled him with every detail. The prospect of horses actually coming to live in the stables seemed to spur Molly on, and to Abigail's relief, the house fell silent for days on end as Molly cleared out the outbuildings and made them suitable as feed stores, demonstration areas and a tack room. With Sam's credit card and the internet at her disposal, she ordered in supplies to be delivered, booked herself onto courses and devised a schedule for the corporate sessions.

"Abigail!" Molly yelled up the stairs one Friday evening in mid-December. "Board meeting!"

It had become a regular weekly activity, with Sam bringing home a giant pizza and dough balls on his way back through Fordingbridge. The three of them would gather on the sofa around the roaring fire and demolish the junk food, updating Sam on the latest progress, raising queries and issues. Bessie watched every mouthful from her dog basket, knowing that if she stayed on her blanket and didn't pester, she would be thrown the crusts as a treat.

"You've done great, girls," Sam smiled. "I think we're on track for our launch on 7th."

Abigail was grateful to be included, otherwise it would simply have become a cosy partnership between Sam and Molly, with the potential for her to feel like a bystander on the sidelines. As well as marketing and promoting the new business venture, Abigail was drafted into the horse purchasing process. Being the most novice rider of the trio - by a long way - she represented the potential clients that would be mounting the horses. Sam and Molly dragged her off to Kent, Devon and Cheshire to see the horses that were for sale. She gave feedback on how the ponies felt to ride.

It was vital to purchase horses that were well-trained, well-mannered and kind, with a quiet, steady temperament. As Abigail nervously asked each horse to walk in large circles around Sam, Molly and the vendor she asked herself whether she could sense its temperament. Did she feel safe? Did it seem volatile? She would signal for the animal to trot, and then gingerly progress to a wobbly canter, cringing with embarrassment at her inadequacy in the face of equine experts.

By Christmas, they had finalised the purchase of all nine shortlisted horses, complete with the green light from a vet's examination. Abigail would struggle to remember which was which. There were two grey mares but whether the one with the dapples on her rump was called Womble, or whether she was Mary, was a mystery.

"Why not get a tenth horse?" she asked Sam. "Nine leaves an empty stable."

"Nine is plenty," he replied dismissively. "Besides, Grace may need a place to retire properly one day."

Abigail glowed at the thought of placid, patient Grace. It would be great if she were to be the tenth resident, and Abigail could continue her riding education. Sadly, things were not to work out quite the way of Abigail's fantasy.

10

Christmas morning arrived. Abigail always woke with an air of excitement on December 25th, even though this year it was only Sam and her waking to see whether Father Christmas had visited. Whilst Sam got up at his usual time and vanished to check on the animals, Abigail felt compelled to get out of bed whilst it was still dark. She padded downstairs, wrapping herself in her dressing gown as she went. She flicked the switch and brought the Christmas tree lights to life. A romantic glow of silver and gold danced amongst the fake green branches.

Under the tree lay a selection of pretty wrapped parcels - some familiar to Abigail, that she had wrapped, complete with bows and ribbons. There were others, unfamiliar wrapping paper, odd-shaped parcels. Abigail couldn't help herself and prodded some of the unfamiliar shapes, but to no avail. She was none the wiser.

No sooner had Abigail filled the kettle, there was a thump as Molly shoved the door with her shoulder and fell into the kitchen, a pile of precarious looking parcels balanced in a stack in her arms. Bessie, having been out in the yard with Sam, was grateful to get back into the cottage and barged past Molly, tail thumping, nose sniffing.

"Morning, morning, Merry Christmas Abigail, I've got some presents here, it's so good of you having me around for Christmas, it's the first time I've not been at home for it, but I guess you're all my family now, although I'll give my dad and Luke a ring later to wish them Merry Christmas."

"Coffee?"

"Yeah, great. Is it your first time away from home at Christmas? It feels strange, doesn't it? I'll put these presents under the tree with the others shall I, Abi? When do you think we should open them?"

Molly finally took a breath and turned from where she was crouching by the tree to face Abigail. She was already dressed, a fleece top over jeans, enhanced by a long cream scarf adorned with a bold pattern of horseshoes. Her baby face broke into a big grin. "Oh, I'm so excited. I know what Sam's got you..." Like a preschool child, she clapped her hands.

"I guess the three of us could open our presents when Sam comes back," Abigail conceded. Although she would never admit it to Molly, she was just as excited about opening presents.

Having made a cafetière of coffee, Abigail checked the instructions on cooking the turkey for the umpteenth time. If her parents and the Ashingtons got to the stables by midday, she would look to serve dinner at two. That meant putting the turkey in the oven at...ten thirty. She suddenly felt very grown up, calculating turkey cooking times and planning a meal for nine people.

"It's a shame it hasn't snowed for Christmas; I love snow," Molly continued. "Although I can't ever remember it snowing at Christmas. It just seems to be mizzley out there at the moment."

"I'm cold," admitted Abigail. "I'll get the fire going."

An hour later, the logs glowed red in the fire basket, a warmth had penetrated through the downstairs and Sam returned from his outside chores, generously gracing the ladies with an hour of his presence. They snuggled together on the two-seater sofa whilst Molly took the single wing backed chair, making small talk whilst all wanting to start opening presents.

"Come on," urged Abigail, rising from the settee and kneeling by the tree. "Let's open ours." She threw a soft package into Molly's lap. "That's a little something from me."

Molly's eyes lit up with delight as she tore off the paper to reveal a handmade patchwork bag. Her current bag had developed a hole that was growing daily and Sam complained that she never ceased moaning about the bag's demise.

"Oh, that's excellent!" She gushed. "Did you make it yourself? My current bag is no good now - I mean look at it. I risk losing my phone every time I take it out anywhere. Thank you so much."

As she busied herself opening up the bag and inspecting the internal pockets, Sam took the opportunity of silence to hand Abigail a large square box. "Merry Christmas, sweetheart."

Abigail had been longing to open his present. It was clear that Molly knew what mysteries lay under the wrapping paper and certainly seemed excited about the gift he'd bought her. The present had clearly been wrapped by Sam, with its clumsily folded paper, and stubby bits of sticky tape holding the ends down. It was devoid of decorative bows or ribbon of course. Inside was a plain rectangular cardboard box, opened by a flap down its longer side. Inside, nestled in tissue paper, a pair of leather boots, shining like tar from their nest.

"Riding boots," explained Sam. "I thought it was about time you looked like a proper horsewoman."

"Oh," was all Abigail could manage in reply. She wasn't sure what she had been expecting, but this wasn't it. She had been raised to be grateful though, so she smiled at Sam and kissed him on the cheek in response.

"I've also got you a riding hat and a pair of jodhpurs, but I left them at Mum and Dad's by mistake so they'll bring them over when they come."

Molly had finished transferring the contents of her broken bag to her new bag, and turned her attention back to the present ceremony. "Sam, this one's for you."

As he pulled the paper off a cardboard box, she threw him a warning. "As I'm not earning any money, I've had to be a bit creative with my presents," she apologised. It turned out the cardboard box was empty, except for a leaf of plain paper, which read in Molly's handwritten scribble "This voucher entitles the bearer to instruct Molly to do additional mucking out on any five days." It was valid for a whole year, and Abigail wondered whether Molly would still be with them in 12 months' time.

"And one for you Ab."

"You needn't have..." began Abigail, but then remembered how many hours she'd put into making the bag for her. It was another empty cardboard box containing a sheet of paper. "This voucher entitles the bearer to five hours of one-to-one equestrian training with Molly."

Equestrian training? What did that mean? "I'll give you lessons in whatever you want," explained Molly, as if reading her mind. "Riding, grooming, tacking up..."

Abigail smiled politely and thanked Molly, reminding herself that Molly was working for free, and this was a sweet gesture. A small part of Abigail bristled with irritation at both her and Sam's insistence of turning her into a better rider.

Once the presents were opened, Abigail went about getting up properly, pulling on her festive red dress with a white cardigan to shield against the damp December cold. Whilst Sam and Molly embarked on a noisy battle of *Champion Jockey* on the games station, Abigail busied herself with preparation for the Christmas lunch.

"Are you getting changed at all?" Abigail enquired, noting that Sam was still in his jodhpurs and scruffy polo neck sweater that he always wore for mucking about with the horses. He'd thrashed Molly five times in a row so far, and despite her protestations that he was cheating, neither seemed to have any desire to stop playing and smarten themselves up.

"No point, we'll be heading out for our Christmas Day ride after lunch," he replied. "Family tradition. Even Mum joins us."

The was no time for Abigail to question Sam any further as the crunch of gravel indicated the arrival of Abigail's parents. In typical fashion of mothers everywhere, Mrs Daycock had come laden with Christmas pudding, a Yule log, a tin of chocolates and a large box of fancy shortbread. The sweet treats contained enough calories to last until next Christmas. More importantly she had followed the instruction to bring along cutlery and crockery so that none of the guests had to eat dinner from plastic plates. It wasn't long after their arrival that the advance party from Sloth arrived. Sam's bubbly sister Charly pulled up in the Land Rover, with Mrs Angel stowed as cargo in the passenger seat.

"Mum and Dad are following behind," Charly explained when Abigail commented that she'd expected them all to come in one car. "You'll find out why in a bit."

It was only five minutes later that Abigail did find out. The arrival of the horse box and one stroppy ex-racehorse called Moody Muppet. For Abigail, the day was thundering by like a snowball rolling uncontrollably down a hill. She was trying to prepare the dinner, and play hostess to a rabble of excitable people. There wasn't time to contemplate the four-legged gift horse that now resided in the tenth stable.

The snug cottage buzzed with warm bodies, chatter and goodwill. Abigail bossed the men around, sending them off to the pub to fetch the extra chairs and tables that Paul and Anna had agreed to loan them. For the ladies, Abigail put Molly to work pouring drinks.

"So, a racehorse, eh?" Mrs Angel smiled at Abigail when there was finally time to take a short break from the sweaty job of cooking. They were sitting in a large circle on an odd assortment of seating, from beanbags to sofa to hard backed dining chairs, sipping at sherry, wine and beer. "How long until you become a lady jockey?"

She was joking of course, but Molly picked up the cue. "Oh, not long, Mrs Angel. I've offered to give Abigail some one-to-one lessons so we'll have her riding in the Grand National in no time. You'll have to come out with us after dinner, Ab, and try out the Muppet. You can wear your new jodhpurs and boots."

Abigail was horrified at the thought. It was quite enough to walk and trot on docile riding school ponies in front of Sam and Molly. Taking out an unfamiliar excitable racehorse in front of Charly, the top eventer, and Robin, the champion racehorse trainer in addition to Sam and Molly was not going to happen.

"It's OK, I'll stay and tidy up here. Somebody will have to keep my folks and Mrs Angel entertained."

"In that case, can I ride her please Abigail. Please?" Molly begged like a small child.

Abigail nodded her consent.

"Just keep an eye out for crisp packets or litter blowing around," Charly warned. "It doesn't take much to spook the silly mare. I got thrown off on Tuesday when I took her down to Morton's fields and a stupid sheep snuffled in the hedge about five metres away. She acted like she'd had a hot poker up her arse."

Abigail blanched. "And Sam thinks this is a suitable gift for his novice riding girlfriend?"

At the sound of his name, Sam looked up from his *Racing Post* annual. "You'll be fine, babe," he replied dismissively.

Abigail bristled. He'd never called her "babe" before and she didn't like the term, let alone the sentiment of her being "fine" on a powerful beast that could kill her at every rustle in the hedge.

Her irritation built over dinner as she watched Sam nibble at a bit of veg and a tiny strip of chicken. The other guests all tucked in with enthusiasm and complimented her on the meal, but Sam refused Christmas pudding and couldn't wait to take his family out for their traditional afternoon ride. He was keen to see what his family thought of their four-legged riding school cast.

Leaving a sea of filthy plates on the table, the Ashingtons and Molly rose and departed, with a cheery farewell, leaving a silence to descend on the cottage in their wake.

"Well," Mrs Angel was first to break the silence. "It's three o'clock. Shall we wash up and then catch the Queen's speech?"

"I've a better idea," Abigail responded. "Let's stack the washing up for Sam and Molly to do when they return, and we'll go to the pub."

11

Anna and Paul had opened the Twin Oaks pub for Christmas afternoon as they considered the villagers to be part of their family. As Abigail pushed open the door for Mrs Angel to shuffle through on her walking stick, a wall of merry chatter hit her. It was warm and inviting, and a middle-aged couple leapt up from the window table to allow Mrs Angel to sit down.

"Merry Christmas, Abigail," Anna called from the far side of the bar. "We've got a free glass of bubbly here for you and your..." Anna wasn't sure who was accompanying her. Abigail approached the bar to save her having to shout back across the crowded room.

"These are my parents, and the lady who's just sat down is a friend, Mrs Angel. The others are all out riding." Abigail's mum and dad hovered at her shoulder, her mum's eyes drawn to the variety of knitted and crocheted Christmas decorations hanging from the beams. Her dad's gaze was fixed admiringly on the barrels of real ale behind the bar. Within seconds, he'd struck up a conversation with landlord Paul over the merits of dark ale.

The ladies took their complimentary glass of sparkling wine - Abigail doubted that it would be champagne - and her first sip confirmed that it was cheap and barely drinkable. The kind sentiment was noted though. Leaving her dad and Paul deep in discussion about darts leagues, they headed back to where Mrs Angel had struck up conversation with a tall dark stranger. Abigail vaguely remembered that he'd been at the bar on their first visit to the pub on moving day. He beamed as they arrived, stirring the recollection in Abigail that she'd pointed him out to Molly that day.

"I hope you don't mind, I thought I'd better entertain this lovely lady in your absence," he began, thrusting out his hand in introduction. "I'm Sol."

Abigail had reached him first and, putting her glass down at the table, shook his hand. It was the confident handshake of the self-assured; the softness of his skin leading Abigail to the conclusion that he was a businessman. His accent had no geography, just the annunciation of the educated.

"Soul?" Her mum questioned, shaking his outstretched hand.

"No, Sol," he repeated with a chuckle. His blue eyes twinkled with flirtation, even though his age sat somewhere between that of Abigail and her mother.

"Is that short for something?" she asked.

Anna, who had begun a circuit collecting empty glasses, sprung up behind them and put a friendly hand on his shoulder. "It stands for 'Sex On Legs'!" She interjected, and then dispersed back into the crowd with a giggle at her own humour.

Sol didn't blush for a second and took the opportunity to skip over the real meaning of his name. "Let me get you ladies a proper drink; this is quite abhorrent." He pulled a face and discarded the full glass on a nearby table. Abigail had finished her wine without realising that she'd been sipping so frequently. It was a bad habit she had developed when nervous or self-conscious.

"I'm not much of a wine drinker to be honest," Mrs Angel agreed conspiratorially, sliding her glass onto the windowsill.

"I bet you're a sherry fan, though," Sol cajoled, and Mrs Angel's blush and giggle confirmed his hypothesis. "And white wine? A nice white wine?" He raised an eyebrow at Mrs Daycock.

"I'll give you a hand," Abigail offered, realising that it would be easier to cross the maze of bodies in one go rather than making two trips.

"You didn't tell me your name," he accused as they made the short trip to the bar.

"Ab," she replied. "Short for Abigail."

They had reached the bar and waited patiently to be spotted by Paul, who was still enjoying the conversation with Mr Daycock. Sol leaned down so that his lips were inches from Abigail's ear and whispered, "or Absolutely Beautiful".

He pulled himself back up to full height and glanced sideways to check her reaction. He didn't know that her stomach had flipped in response, but could tell from her blush that his flattery wasn't unwelcome.

"I've seen you around," he added, returning his voice to a normal volume. "Walking with your dog over by the woodland."

"Ah, Bessie, she's Molly's dog. We're sharing responsibility for taking her out, although I'm not so keen when it's cold and dark every evening."

"I'm looking after my mother's dog at the moment," Sol replied. "She's an unruly spaniel by the name of Daisy. The dog, that is, not my mother."

Over the next hour, Abigail, her parents and Mrs Angel learnt a lot more about Sol's mother, who, as a widower in her sixties had found a new lease of life playing golf in the Canary Islands with increasing regularity. He regaled them at ease with tales of his newly acquired life in the New Forest, having split up from a marriage in London six months ago. Abigail was impressed by his job as a columnist for a broadsheet newspaper, although he shrugged it off as "writing a load of flannel for a pompous rag that nobody reads." In return, Abigail and Mrs Angel explained their relationship to the best of their ability, and Mr Daycock got onto his favourite topic of variable speed restrictions on motorways; a theme that Sol greeted with the same passion.

When Anna clanged the bell for last orders, Abigail was reluctant to drag herself away from the warmth of the bar, and shuffle back to the cottage.

"I'll see you out with Daisy soon then," Abigail called in farewell to Sol, who began to make his way up the lane in the opposite direction.

"Looking forward to it," Sol called back in reply. "Very much," he added under his breath to the crisp night air.

"There you all are!" Mr Ashington greeted as they bustled back through the door. He smiled in welcome, but his tone was accusatory. "We wondered where you could all be at this time of night." It was only half past four, but the winter curtain had descended, and the lack of moonlight meant that the stables were engulfed in a sinister blackness.

As his wife manned the sink, scrubbing hard at grease-ridden roasting tins, Robin was wiping up the stacks of plates already draining on the side.

"We've been to the pub," giggled Mrs Angel, her third sherry still warming her belly. "It's been a long time since I've been to a pub. We met a lovely young man called Sol." She sank back into the armchair with a contented sigh.

"Soul?" Robin questioned; an echo from earlier.

"No, Sol," replied Abigail's mother with a smile. "As in Sex on Legs."

"Where are the others?" Abigail asked, noticing that Molly and Charly were missing. Sam knelt at the fireside, toiling to build up the dwindling fire in the grate that their expedition to the pub had caused to die.

"The girls are out walking Bessie. I hope they took a torch."

Returning to hostess mode, Abigail put the kettle on, knowing that her mum would accept a cup of tea and her dad would be grateful for a black coffee ahead of his drive home.

Having completed the mountain of dishes, the Ashingtons retired to the sofa and reclined with satisfaction. Their cheeks were still flushed from the exertion of riding, combined with the contrasting heat of the cottage.

"Now that I've got a quiet moment," Mrs Angel piped up, "I'd like to talk to you about something." She looked over to Mr Ashington who was sat closest to her. Somberly she placed a wrinkled hand on the sleeve of his burgundy cashmere sweater. "I'm going to be re-doing my will in the New Year, and I wondered whether I could ask you to be executor."

There was an embarrassed silence momentarily; this wasn't appropriate talk for Christmas Day.

"Oh Mrs A, you won't be in need of a will for a long time yet," Robin replied, regarding her fondly. Admittedly, she was going to be 90 next year, and her body creaked and groaned, but she could still climb her stairs slowly and walk a few hundred yards at a time. Mrs Angel still had plenty of spirit left.

"Well, the current one dates back to when my dear Andrew died, and things were very different back then. I just want to make sure that people I care about now are recognised when I'm gone."

"Yes, of course you can put me down as executor," agreed Robin. "It'll be my pleasure."

"Oh, and just to make you aware, there's a suitcase under the bed in the small bedroom upstairs that has quite a bit of cash in it."

Sam exploded with laughter from his spot in front of the fire. He'd got the flames going again and it was now eating into the fresh fuel he'd fed the embers. "What did you do, Mrs Angel, rob a bank?"

"Oh no," she replied with a hearty laugh at the prospect, "I've never got around to putting it in the bank; I was keeping it for a rainy day, but should I die, just make sure one of you takes it and puts it to good use."

Silence fell on the group again. If there were two things that were difficult to talk about, it was death and money.

As if to punctuate the silence, the door opened with a crash and Bessie bounded in, shaking the wet from her coat, followed by Molly and Charly.

"Urgh, it's started to rain quite hard outside now: it's turning really icy," Molly announced to everyone. "Bessie found a stream to play in and she's absolutely filthy." She grabbed one of the dog's blankets from the pile on the dog bed and chased the collie around the downstairs until she caught up with her in the kitchen and began to scrub the worst of the weather from her coat. "We were lucky it stayed dry for our ride, though," she continued. "Oh Abigail, thank you for letting me ride Muppet, she's absolutely brilliant. We galloped over the ridge on the far side of the woods and she's bloody fast. It was really exhilarating. I bet you can't wait to ride her!"

Abigail knew that Molly rarely required an answer to her questions, and she wouldn't have known how to respond to that particular one. The time would come that she would have to get onto her gift horse, and she was dreading it. She felt a pang of guilt; this was obviously a generous gesture from Sam, but she'd have been just as happy with a romantic meal for two. Or a pretty bracelet. Or anything except an over excitable racehorse out to kill her.

12

In Sloth, a twelve-year-old girl's Christmas had been made extra special by an unexpected parcel that had arrived. Penny Fry was ecstatic enough that her mum and dad had got her tickets to see *Lucky Potion*, her favourite girl band, in concert next year. She was delighted to get *Lucky Potion*'s latest CD from her brother, Adam, a pretty stationery set from her school friend, Amy, and twenty pounds from her gran. Then her mum handed her a brown parcel.

"This came for you in the mail yesterday. Who's sending you parcels?"

"You got a secret boyfriend?" teased Adam, glancing up from his supermodel calendar that "Secret Santa" had bought him.

Penny was as baffled as the rest of the family and she ripped the brown paper and pulled out a lump wrapped in bold Christmas paper. Grabbing at the label she grinned as she read "Merry Christmas, Penny. I hope you like these, Lots of love, Abigail (April)".

"Oh, that girl that was in the village earlier this year," confirmed Penny's mum. Subconsciously she glanced out to the poultry housing where ten ex-battery hens pecked happily at the ground. The birds had been purchased with the proceeds of selling Abigail's car boot sale bargain UGG boots, and now provided the family with sufficient eggs, week after week.

"Yes, the one who made me the red devil dress," Penny reminded them. Tearing the paper apart she gasped as more handmade items fell from the package. The first, a crocheted skirt in a blaze of rainbow colours. Penny leapt up to her feet and held the skirt against her.

"Wow, it's amazing. No-one at youth club will have anything like this. It's like a personal designer skirt!" She waggled her hips to sashay the skirt.

"That's called a 'ra ra' skirt," her mother explained. "They were popular in the eighties. Do you remember?" she added to her husband, who was preoccupied with the cartoon film on TV. He grunted a response that suggested he hadn't been listening. "I've never seen one that's half crocheted and half material before. She's certainly creative, isn't she?"

"And this bag matches it!" Penny explained, pulling the second item from the wrapping and posing with the bag on her shoulder.

Abigail hadn't meant to make Penny a bag. It had started out with a clear out at her parents' house back in November, when Abigail tried to decide which essential items to take to the New Forest property. She pulled all her shoes and bags from the wardrobe and laid them on the bed. The surface of the double bed was covered, and a sick feeling rose in Abigail. All this stuff, all hers, mostly never used, hardly needed. She felt ashamed of her previous pointless consumerism.

She began to divide the hoard into different piles. The smallest pile would be essentials to take the New Forest, then a second heap to keep at home in Richmond. Of the remainder, she separated out the most expensive items that she no longer wanted to keep to sell online and raise some much-needed cash. She put some of the mainstream items into a cardboard box to donate to the charity shop, but also kept putting things aside for friends. There was a pair of boots that Nadine had always admired. Abigail couldn't remember the last time she wore them, and since Nadine shared the same shoe size, it would be more useful for her to have them when she returned from her voluntary posting overseas. She put aside some items for Kate, which got her thinking about Sloth. She'd got such a nice feeling donating the UGG boots to Penny's mum in April. It was a simple gesture, knowing that the proceeds from selling them would benefit the family that had been so kind to her. She hunted for something for Penny, but her clothes and shoes would all be too big, and all her accessories seemed too grown up for a twelve-year-old.

When she freed her clothes from the wardrobe to go through the same process, the ra-ra skirt she'd made as an experiment in the summer lay on the top of the pile. Abigail picked it up fondly and smiled. It wouldn't fit Penny, but she could certainly set about making her one. With the leftover material, Abigail whipped up a matching bag, knowing that Penny loved anything bespoke.

She had got it spot on, and Penny couldn't wait to write a thank you letter on her new stationery paper.

Dear Abigail,

Thank you so much for the skirt and bag you made me. I can't believe you've made me them. They are great. The skirt fits really well and I love the bag because it matches it.

I think you are a brilliant clothes designer and I hope a man at Teen Zero wants to buy up your designs, ha ha.

I had a lovely Christmas. Mum and Dad got me tickets to see Lucky Potion next year in Birmingham. I can't wait.

Hope you and Sam had a lovely Christmas. Adam said that Dan said that Kate said (because she saw Charly in the pub) that Sam was getting you a racehorse. Lucky you!

Hope to see you at the Grand National Party in April… Or sooner if you are in Sloth before then.

Lots of love, Penny xxx

Penny put the lid on her fountain pen and read through the letter with pride. She put the letter in its matching pink envelope and wrote Abigail's name on the front. She would have to give the letter to Adam to give to Dan to give to Kate, who would have her address.

She was about to pack away the stationery, when another thought struck her. It was one thing to thank Abigail with a letter, but this idea was even better! With a contented smile she took out a fresh sheet of note paper and began to write.

13

"There's two reasons for phoning you," Mrs Angel said to Abigail a week later. The period between Christmas and New Year had passed with the usual subdued feeling that the world had stopped turning. Few people were back into the routine of work, the shops kept erratic hours and the weather remained grim and uninspiring. Things had been productive at the Twin Oaks Equestrian Centre, though, and Abigail had managed to get on top of the pre-opening marketing, generating a few enquiries that held the possibility of turning into bookings.

"Obviously I wanted to thank you again for such a lovely Christmas Day. I felt truly treated."

"My pleasure," Abigail replied. She had been proud of the day. The cooking had all gone to plan and everyone complimented the meal, the Ashington family had enjoyed their habitual Christmas ride, and her parents and Mrs Angel had a sociable time at the pub.

"I rang to find out if you'd received an envelope this morning."

Abigail wandered over to the kitchen table (a new acquisition from Anna, who decided she no longer needed it at the pub) and flicked through the post. All she could see were boring envelopes to do with insurance, bills, and statements. Being an adult sucked.

"What sort of envelope am I looking for?"

"The one with Whizz Productions logo on the front."

Abigail's heart missed a beat. The decision on their appearance on 'Where in the World'. It had been over two months since their audition and she had forgotten about the process. As the weeks had ticked by, subconsciously Abigail presumed they hadn't been successful and had put it clear out of her mind.

"That will have gone to my parents' address," Abigail replied, her heart pounding at the thought of the TV programme. "What does the letter say?"

Mrs Angel obviously had the piece of paper in front of her and read from it verbatim, "We are inviting you to take part in the programme, on Wednesday 8th March 2017. The recording will take place at the Blueprint Studios in London... blah, blah, and there's the address and lots of terms and conditions and instructions... oh Abigail," Mrs Angel stopped short, breathless.

"Do you still want to do this?" Abigail asked. One word from Mrs Angel and she would happily back out.

"Well, I'm not so keen on going to London, but I'm game if you are."

"Great," replied Abigail with a confidence she didn't feel. "We'd better get swotting up." There was a pause as they both contemplated the task ahead. *Where in the World* wasn't a quiz you could easily revise for. The questions were chosen from a wide and varied pool of subjects, drawing on general knowledge in its broadest sense.

"So, have you got any plans for the rest of today?"

"Yes," replied Abigail, as fresh nerves began to course through her veins. "I'm going out for my first ride on the Moody Muppet."

"Ooh, that'll be nice." Mrs Angel had no idea how off the mark she was, but Abigail didn't correct her.

Sam had spent Boxing Day showing Abigail videos on YouTube of the Moody Muppet in the era when she had been allowed on a racetrack. She had started her career as a hurdler, and Abigail paled when she saw the speed at which the Muppet soared over the brush fences. She took them easily in her stride, with no hesitation, ears pricked and alert, determined and eating up the furlongs with barely a sweat.

"Then this was the day it started to go wrong," Sam explained, calling up a video from the Alder Hey handicap hurdle at Aintree last year. "Luke Packer's on board. That's Moody Muppet there..."

The mare was jiggling on the spot in the pack of excited horses before the race got underway. The dozen horses pranced towards the orange tape that acted as a barrier across the track, all pulling enthusiastically, anticipating that any minute now they would be able to take off and do what they did best. Abigail watched the flag go down, the tape rise and eleven horses surge forwards in a blur of coloured silks. There, at the back, standing stock still, was the Moody Muppet. Luke tried to urge the horse forward, waggling his legs as best as he could in the constraint of the short stirrups. He commanded the mare forward with his reins, but to no avail. Muppet couldn't be bothered that day.

"So, she did that twice in a row, but we could find no reason for her refusal. She would run fine in training, the vets said she was sound, but she obviously took a dislike to the hurdles," Sam explained. "We switched her to the flat. She's obviously got the speed, so I rode her at Newmarket early this summer. Watch this, her odds were 25/1 as she'd never been tested on the flat and everyone remembered the previous refusals."

Sam called up the next video and Abigail watched as Moody Muppet thundered out of the starting stall and took up an uncontrollable gallop ahead of a field of fifteen horses. She led from the start, and increased her lead with every furlong, soaring over the line without Sam having to move an inch on her back in encouragement.

"She broke the track record that day," Sam explained in admiration. "I've ridden some fast horses, but Muppet has an extra gear. It was just a shame that was the only time she emerged from the starting stalls. Next time, the gates flew open and she just leisurely cantered out and pulled herself up within a furlong. It was the same the next time." Sam paused and relived the memory in his mind. "God, I got some grief for it from punters, but I'm fairly helpless up there. I can't make the horse run."

Abigail prayed that Muppet would choose to be the lazy mare rather than the track record breaker as she pulled on her new jodhpurs and boots that afternoon. After a week of reminders and nagging, Abigail had run out of excuses, and couldn't avoid the inaugural ride on Muppet. Sam tacked her up and led her out into the yard, where a new mounting block had been installed ready for the opening of the Equestrian Centre in a week's time. Abigail gingerly swung her leg over and settled into the saddle. Unlike Grace, the only pony Abigail had sat on for more than a quick trial, Muppet was taller, her body lean and slender and her neck seemed to go on forever.

Sam helped Abigail to shorten her stirrups, but Muppet wasn't in the mood to be hanging around. Feeling weight in the saddle, the mare pranced to the side, with the lightness of a ballerina. Abigail grabbed a handful of her mane in panic. She wanted to get straight back off.

"It's OK," Sam soothed, although Abigail wasn't sure whether he was talking to her or Muppet. "First rule, grab your reins when you get on," he spoke sternly, and handed her the reins that had dangled freely on Muppet's neck. "You'll also have to learn to shorten your own stirrups as I won't be around to help you when you go out alone."

Abigail couldn't see herself having the confidence to go out alone anytime this century.

"They feel OK?"

Abigail nodded, not trusting herself to speak.

"Ooh, look at you!" whooped Molly, leading out a dumpy piebald from the far stable. Abigail remembered how docile that pony was when she trotted him around an indoor school a few weeks ago, and would have given anything to swop mounts with Molly right this moment. "The beginning of a great partnership."

Abigail watched enviously as Molly sprang onto the piebald without the need for the mounting block, and adjusted her stirrups whilst the pony stood stock still for her.

"Right, ready?" Sam appeared from nowhere, already mounted on a bay that Muppet seemed to take a dislike to. "Come on Toby."

As Sam clipped past, the Muppet threw her head up, and sharply down, almost pulling Abigail's arms from her sockets.

"Any chance of a leading rein?" Abigail enquired, but Sam dismissed her request with a wave of his hand.

Not wanting to be left behind, with no instruction from Abigail, Muppet broke into a trot to draw level with Toby. Abigail was thrown forward, and just about managed to regain her composure as Sam smiled over at her. "Muppet likes to lead the way," he said simply.

The trio walked down the bridleway at the side of their property without incident. The path led straight out onto the open scrubland of the New Forest. It was a clear, crisp day, and in the distance, they could see the triangle of dense woodland that identified where the deep stream ran through from east to west. Molly had told Abigail in detail about how they had galloped down from the woods on Christmas Day, with Muppet leaping over the stream with ease. If Muppet wanted a repeat of the fun she had on Christmas Day, then she was going to be vastly disappointed.

Abigail wished she had worn gloves. The severity of the cold wind bit against her bare fingers, and she knew they would be numb before long.

"Let's trot," instructed Sam, tapping his heels into Toby's flanks to encourage him to break into a trot. The Muppet needed no encouragement and bounced forward. She had a spring in her step, dainty and eager. Abigail found the rhythm and began to rise in time with her gait, relaxing a little with each step.

Then it came out of nowhere. Before Abigail had time to realise the danger, the firework shot up into the afternoon sky, emitting a high-pitched squeal as it ascended towards the clouds, before bursting into a thousand popping golden shards, followed by an almighty bang.

The Moody Muppet took off in fright, bolting straight into the fastest gallop Abigail had ever experienced. Instinctively she grabbed a handful of her mane and clenched as tight as she could with her thighs. As the wind whistled past her ears, and the cold stung her eyes, it took her several seconds to feel fearful, but as Muppet showed no signs of slowing, the realisation dawned on Abigail that she was in deep shit. The green mossy grass blurred beneath Muppet's hooves, and with her ears back, she maintained a determined gallop towards the stream.

She was going to fall off, Abigail decided in a petrified panic. If she hadn't wobbled off before Muppet reached the stream, then her jumping it would surely mean that they would part company.

Abigail prayed that there would not be another firework shooting up in the sky. Deep down she knew she had to turn Muppet away from the stream, and try and steer her back up the hill towards Sam and Molly. That meant releasing a hand from the mane and tugging on the left rein. She mustn't tug too hard and risk Muppet pulling round too quickly, which would see her exiting over the side. As the stream got closer, Abigail tentatively lifted her left hand from the clump of mane and reached further down the left rein. The adrenaline pumping through her body masked the fact that her thighs were burning with the effort of clinging on, and her hands were shaking with fear. She applied a bit of pressure to the rein, but glancing down Muppet's long neck, she could see that there was no difference in the course she was taking. She pulled a bit harder. Muppet seemed to leave the track she was following and galloped on through the scrubby gorse. Abigail applied a fraction more pressure, and Muppet was soon side on to the stream. With relief, Abigail allowed herself to realise that her plan was working.

There was no time to worry about Muppet stumbling on a rabbit hole, or being spooked by a second firework. Little by little, Abigail concentrated on getting her direction altered so that she was finally heading back up the slope. As Muppet slowed a fraction, Abigail found the courage to release her right hand away from the mane and pull gently to slow Muppet further. By the time she was at the brow of the hill, Muppet juddered back into a trot and seemed to have forgotten the panic of the firework.

Abigail approached Sam and Molly, who were sat motionless on their mounts watching the spectacle.

She pulled Muppet up, and automatically slithered off her back, grateful to have her feet back on firm ground. It was then that she realised she was shaking all over, and fighting back a rage. She stood for a moment at Muppet's head, looking into her wild eyes, before turning accusingly to Sam and Molly.

"Why the hell didn't you come and save me?" she gasped. "I could have been killed."

Sam smiled down at her. There was admiration in his expression.

"If we'd tried to gallop after a racehorse it would have only spurred her on even more. We had to let you sort her out yourself. You coped well."

"I'm so sorry," piped up Molly. "It was my fault for suggesting a ride on New Year's Eve. I didn't think about fireworks or anything."

Abigail felt her lips wobble as the enormity of the feat overcame her. If she had fallen from Muppet's back at that speed she could have been concussed, had broken bones, or even been paralysed or worse. She pulled Muppet's reins over her head and made to walk back.

"Come on, let's go home," she suggested, her voice breaking with emotion at the end. Sam swung himself from Toby and gathered her up in a bear hug.

"You did really well," he whispered into her ear reassuringly. "I'm proud of you."

"I'm bloody frozen," Abigail mumbled in reply. "Come on, let's go."

14

The countdown to the New Year began. In unison, the drunken rabble in the bar chanted in time to the feed from London. "Ten...nine...eight..."

Abigail felt flushed after letting her hair down, dizzy with relief at having survived Moody's bolt. With Sam offering to finish the stable chores, she and Molly were free to head to the pub. Just as on Christmas Day, there was a feeling of a family party going on, with locals welcoming them in and drawing them into conversations and buying them drinks. For those that hadn't heard about the new owners moving in to the stables, they became instant celebrities and had to field a barrage of questions about when they were opening, what they would be doing and what their relationship was with each other.

"So that jockey that won on Port Ferry at Southwell the other day, yeah, he now owns the stables over there?" clarified an elderly gentleman in a flat cap. He pointed his full glass of beer towards the doorway, causing a slosh of ale to tip towards the pair. "And he's your bloke, is he?"

"Yes," Abigail confirmed, amused at his reaction. Not many people recognised the name Sam Ashington outside of Gloucestershire or Newmarket, but when she came across someone who had watched the racing and had enjoyed a successful flutter, it was rewarding to be associated with him.

"Well bugger me! I put a tenner on that because a bloke in Ladbrokes said he'd won by five lengths last time out. I won forty quid from that. I owe him a drink; will he be in later?"

"I don't think so," Abigail replied, without feeling too remorseful. "It's back up to Southwell for him tomorrow, so he'll stay sober and get an early night. No rest for the wicked."

"Got any tips?" It was the most frequently asked question of Abigail once people discovered she was the girlfriend of a jockey.

"I'm afraid not," she apologised. She wouldn't be able to name a single horse he was riding, let alone know whether they were worth risking a tenner on.

"Flightly Al in the opener," interjected Molly. "Don't be put off by his big odds: he's in first time head gear and has been rested for a good performance."

The gentleman looked impressed, and sloshed his pint towards Molly. "Flighty Al," he confirmed. "I'll remember that."

Abigail felt a stab of jealousy that Molly knew more details of Sam's daily life than she did. Then again, she pondered, he wouldn't know which dresses were part of her current collection, who she was working on orders for, nor who her material suppliers were. Couples don't have to have an interest in every intimate detail of each other's business. Do they?

"How are the bookings going?" a voice asked behind them. Abigail smelt Sol before she turned to see him. His aftershave was intoxicating. He smiled down on them with a playful glint in his eye.

"We haven't had any yet," Molly responded, before Abigail had chance to spin a more positive response. "We're trying not to panic, you know, with a yard full of horses, mounting debts and no clients, but hey ho."

"I've got lots of leads out there," clarified Abigail. "It's just not the right time of year to be trying to get anywhere with corporate clients."

"You can be making your fortune at the bookies," chipped in the gentleman in the cap. "All you need is to put money on the horses that this girl tips." He chuckled at the thought and with a gesture of farewell, turned his back to the trio and shuffled off towards the smoking shelter.

In reality, Abigail and Sam could do with an injection of cash. Over the six weeks since moving in, they had developed an unspoken agreement that Sam paid the domestic bills, whilst Abigail met all the costs of keeping them fed. Molly, of course, was exempt from covering any costs, with her free labour available to them. Abigail quickly discovered that Sam had a laid-back attitude to his finances, with unpaid bills littering the kitchen table. When nagged, he deferred the task of writing out the business cheques to Molly, whose response was nearly always "yeah, later." It wasn't hard for Abigail to glimpse bank statements, as they too, were left dismissively on the table, abandoned on top of the envelope that they had been freed from.

The equestrian centre suffered outgoing after outgoing. The list of debits on the bank statement were spread over multiple pages, with a negative balance glaring at the end. It was always going to be that way, with pump priming costs draining the funds before they opened for business, but at the moment, with no bookings on the horizon, Abigail wondered how long they could justify the equestrian centre's existence if it brought in no income.

As for Abigail's fashion empire, she was baulking at the upfront outlay of material in order to fulfil orders. The lag in payments meant that her business account was fleetingly in the black before plunging back into the red. She also needed to find several thousand pounds to display at an upcoming fashion trade event, which would be a great way to showcase her collection. She knew she had to speculate to accumulate, but finding money to fund anything up front was impossible. She tried in vain to keep the fashion business funds separate to her own, and attempted to pay herself a tiny salary, but in reality, both accounts were usually overdrawn.

"Have you met Molly?" Abigail asked Sol, realising that she hadn't been with them on Christmas Day. "Molly's working for us at the equestrian centre."

"Yes, we've met," Sol replied, not taking his gaze from Abigail. "There's not a dog owner within a five-mile radius that I haven't met whilst out walking Daisy. I've seen you and your boyfriend a few times now, haven't I?"

Molly frowned, then blushed. "Oh, you mean Sam." She laughed a forced noise, and flicked her hair. Abigail had noticed the hair flick before, her habit when she felt self-conscious. "That's not my boyfriend, that's my boss!"

"Well he should be here buying you a drink for your hard work. I guess as he's abandoned you both, it falls to me to be a gentleman and get you some bubbly," Sol offered. "It's nearly midnight and you can't have an empty glass for the sounds of Big Ben."

Without waiting for a response, Abigail admired his backside as he pushed his way through the crowd towards the bar. She hadn't known that Sam joined Molly for the dog walks whilst she lay in bed each morning. She presumed he had been up to organise all things equine. It didn't matter, she supposed, but she found that it niggled her all the same.

At the bar, Anna flicked on the TV and cursed the remote control as she tried to work out which channel she needed for coverage of Big Ben. Paul was encouraging the villagers to make sure their glasses were filled for the midnight chimes.

"Here we are." Sol shimmied back to the girls and handed them a flute. "In the nick of time."

The bar erupted into the drunken countdown, then paused in anticipation of the first sombre bong. The sound that denoted a brand new year, a fresh start and the hope and expectation of the unknown.

"Happy New Year!" The shrieks flew around the pub as Big Ben proudly continued to dong twelve times. A flurry of hugs and kisses ensued, and before Abigail had time to think, Sol had pulled her in to a lingering embrace.

"Happy New Year," he said tenderly before placing a kiss on her lips that lasted a second longer than Abigail was comfortable with.

"Happy New Year!" Molly's interruption caused Sol to break away and hug her too.

Blushing, Abigail glanced around her to see whether anyone's prying eyes had noticed Sol's behaviour, but the majority of the crowd was now distracted watching the fireworks explode over the Thames.

Despite the noise in the Twin Oaks pub, Abigail clearly heard the local bursts of pyrotechnics coming from outside.

"Shit," Abigail cursed, grabbing Molly by the arm. "Fireworks! We should check on Moody Muppet. She'll be kicking her way out of her stable."

The girls sprinted out of the pub as fast as their heels would allow, and hammered down the pitch-black driveway towards the stables. Far from acting like the panicked, neurotic horse she had been earlier that day, the pair found the Moody Muppet nonchalantly gazing over the stable door amidst the firecrackers exploding over the sky in a neighbouring village.

"Seems like she couldn't give a monkeys, eh," Molly observed, approaching the stall. "You're a little rascal, aren't you?"

Abigail could think of a list of colourful adjectives to describe Moody, but "rascal" wasn't one of them. She stood and shivered in the bitter midnight air as Molly ruffled the horse's mane. Frost was already painting the ground in white sparkles, and spreading across the tiles of the stable roof. Abigail exhaled and marvelled at how white her breath was against the black night air. An aroma of woodsmoke engulfed the yard; Sam had clearly had the fire burning all night. It was a welcoming country smell, and Abigail yearned for her bed.

"So, a new year," Molly muttered. She reached into her bag for her packet of cigarettes and lit up. It wasn't clear if she was talking to herself, to Muppet or to Abigail. "Are you making any New Year's resolutions?"

She took a drag on her cigarette and turned from Muppet to face Abigail, which invited the mare to chew on the collar of her jacket. Molly pushed her away playfully and fished out a polo mint from her pocket.

"I will ride Muppet without being thrown off?" Abigail didn't attempt to make her reply sound convincing. "What about you?"

Molly had turned back to Muppet to offer her a collection of mints on the palm of her hand. Muppet munched happily, then turned her gaze expectantly to Abigail, as if challenging her to match the sugary treats.

"Oh, that's easy," Molly chirped. She planted a kiss on Muppet's cheek, and with a pat of her neck, started to stroll back towards the cottage. "I'm going to capture the love of my life."

15

The freezing temperatures of that New Year's Eve signalled the start of a harsh January. Sam and Molly appeared to relish the cold, barely flinching as they worked outside together for hours on end. The savage wind would make Molly's blue eyes sparkle even more, and turned her cheeks as rosy as a china doll's.

In the cottage, Abigail layered up her clothes every day, but still found she could not warm up. Her workspace in the spare room had a tiny radiator that creaked and groaned, yet even turned up to the maximum level, only obliged with a lukewarm surface. She was reticent to light a fire downstairs during the day. It seemed a waste to have it burning away to an empty living room, and although the upstairs would gain some benefit, it seemed easier just to tug on another sweater. The days passed slowly; Abigail toiled alone from breakfast to supper time, with only Bessie to talk to when she shuffled downstairs to make yet another cup of coffee. The dependable collie would lift her head from wherever she was snoozing and thump her tail against the furniture in response.

She checked the emails several times a day, willing there to be an enquiry that may lead to a booking for the equestrian centre. The official opening day came and went without being marked in any celebration.

There were a couple of occasions when a car crunched up the drive and a bewildered looking adult climbed out of the driver's seat flanked by a child. Abigail vacated her gloomy workroom, grateful for the temporary distraction, to find the visitor enquiring about child lessons at the weekend. Grateful for any income, Abigail booked them in for weekly slots, which Molly was characteristically eager to embrace.

When a silver Corsa pulled up the driveway, Abigail presumed it would be more of the same. Another back seat of middle-class kids wanting to learn the rising trot and progress onto cantering, jumping, hacking? Pulling her cardigan tighter around her middle, she stepped into her slip-on shoes and opened the kitchen door. She hadn't expected to encounter the sight before her.

"Nadine!" She clamped her hands over her mouth in disbelief, before running up to her friend in delight to embrace her. "This is a surprise!"

She pulled away and then noticed for the first time the tall, tanned man who had exited the driver seat. He hovered awkwardly by the car's bonnet waiting for the formal introduction. He was well dressed, Abigail noted, with a wool jacket more suited to Chelsea than the New Forest, and a cashmere scarf warming his neck.

"Abs, this is Erik," Nadine introduced politely, and he stepped forward to shake her hand formally.

"Shouldn't you still be out in...Cambodia?" She asked, struggling to remember which far flung country Nadine had been stationed in this time.

"Yeah, but we quit early," replied Nadine dismissively. "We missed the gloomy freezing miserable weather so much we were desperate to come home. So, this is the new venture? Show us around."

As Abigail gave them a quick tour of the stables and the paddocks, she learnt that Nadine had decided that she wanted to be a teacher and had come back home to start the process of gaining qualifications.

"The plan is to live in Amsterdam with Erik," she explained, "so I'm just looking at all the options about where to study, so I don't know how long I'll be here in the UK." They paused at the paddock where Moody Muppet was lazily grazing on any sparse grass she could find under the frosty topping. "We only came back a week ago, and we're kipping down with Dougie, which I hope isn't going to be a long-term arrangement. I rang your Mum to get your address."

"I guess you didn't get my Christmas card then," Abigail replied with a hint of bitterness. She hadn't had a card from Nadine. "I put in a letter and included my address."

The Moody Muppet plodded over to the fence and regarded the trio expectantly.

"Oh, the mail was rubbish over there. I hardly received anything," Nadine replied.

Abigail thrust her hands in her cardigan pockets in search of polo mints but found nothing. The Muppet snorted her disapproval and chose to stretch her nostrils forward in the hope of reaching Nadine's headscarf to chew.

"This was my Christmas present from Sam," Abigail explained as Nadine took a step away from the fence in horror.

"You really have become the horsey type; I'd have never had you down as turning into one of those. You'll be shopping in Waitrose next."

It was unlike Nadine to be so judgmental, and Abigail hoped Erik wasn't turning her into a bitchy person.

"Abigail's got a long way to go before anyone can describe her as horsey," came the voice of Molly from behind them. "She's barely been in the saddle, despite having this beautiful beast at her disposal." She paused and regarded Nadine and Erik momentarily. "Have you come to ask about lessons, as we can arrange some adult beginner sessions during the week, or at weekends?" Molly blathered on, joining them at the fence without invitation.

Abigail introduced them to Molly before she made any other ridiculous comments, and seeing Nadine shiver, suggested they all go in the cottage to have a cup of tea.

"Is Sam not here today?" Nadine asked, as they made their way back over the courtyard towards the kitchen door.

"No, he's gone all the way up to Southwell for a few rides. He'll be back for a late supper."

"Southwell? That's Nottinghamshire, isn't it? It's way up north from here!" Nadine raised a studded eyebrow. "That's not exactly twenty minutes down the road. I thought the idea was for him to stop all this jockey nonsense in order to help run this place?"

"Yes, so did I," Abigail sighed. They reached the cottage and Abigail led the way into the kitchen. She suddenly realised how shabby it looked. The lino floor was covered in Bessie's muddy paw prints, toast crumbs littered the countertop from breakfast and Sam had discarded items of clothing and left them strewn over the sofa. Abigail never felt the need to tidy up since visitors were few and far between. Usually.

"He's got a couple of really good rides," chirped Molly, continuing the conversation about Sam's jaunt to Southwell. "He wouldn't normally travel that far but he's riding for Don Knott who's got an amazing set of horses."

"Tea or coffee?" Abigail interrupted, knowing that if she didn't cut Molly off now, Nadine and Erik would be hearing a list of each of Don Knott's stable stars, complete with a potted history of their recent runs. Abigail had learnt quickly the importance of aborting Molly's tales.

They sat around the kitchen table and Nadine began to regale them with tales of life in Cambodia. It was just like their old chats, although every sentence now started with "Erik and I..." or ended in "...didn't we, Erik?"

Erik seemed pleasant enough to Abigail. He was a computer programmer by background, but seemed to be as restless as Nadine when it came to settling down into a job or career. Unlike Nadine's previous lovers, he carried an air of superiority, and Abigail wondered how long their ardour would last.

"Abigail's business is coming on nicely," Molly piped up during a lull in conversation. Abigail regarded her with a hint of admiration. She had been acutely aware that Nadine had neglected to enquire about how things were going with "April Smith Designs", and was impressed that Molly took the initiative to shoehorn it into the discussion. "She made me this bag for Christmas," she continued, holding up her patchwork creation. "And the dresses she's preparing for the next collection are to die for. Not that I'm a dress kind of girl. I don't feel comfortable dressing up in those delicate things. Give me a hoody and jodhpurs any day."

Erik's eyes glazed over as Nadine quizzed Abigail about her collections. Molly made another pot of tea, whilst Abigail showed Nadine her website and the girls collaborated over ideas and bounced suggestions between themselves. It almost felt like the old days at university when they would work on a project together. Nadine's strength was in visualising the impossible, whilst Abigail preferred to play the devil's advocate and counter argue from a variety of perspectives.

This wasn't university, though, and it was gambling Abigail's precious and fragile business. Every decision had to be the right one.

"We'd better think about going, Babe," Erik said, glancing at his watch and trying to stifle a yawn without success.

"You'll have to come and stay with us when we're settled in Amsterdam," Nadine ordered. "Once we get sorted, I'll let you know."

"That would be great," Abigail replied, wondering whether that plan would ever come to fruition. After saying their goodbyes, Abigail, Molly and Bessie stood on the kitchen doorstep to wave them off. Erik gave a short farewell toot of the horn as he drove the hired Corsa down the muddy driveway back towards the lane.

Once again, Abigail watched Nadine leave her life.

16

There was a farm shop in the neighbouring village. It was a timber building that had been purpose built for the business, with a large gravel car park nestled off the main road to Fordingbridge. Abigail discovered its delights when exploring on the muddy track that provided a short cut between the two villages with Bessie.

"Yes, of course I know it," laughed Sol, when she bumped into him and Daisy one chilly January afternoon. The dogs sniffed each other before scampering around after each other in the gorse, whilst Abigail and Sol stood awkwardly watching them in silence. It was too cold to be standing around doing nothing, and both thrust their hands deeper into their pockets and stamped their feet. To break the atmosphere, Abigail asked if he knew of the farm shop. As a nosy journalist, Sol not only knew it was there, but also regaled Abigail with the backstory. It was run by two hard working sisters, who took the plunge when made redundant from jobs in the City ten years earlier. Drawing on their country upbringing and sense of ecological sustainability, the farm shop had now extended into a successful enterprise, employing ten members of staff in its tea shop, local crafts section, deli counter and sophisticated butchery.

"Here's a tip for you," he added conspiratorially. "If you go in between four and five o'clock, the butcher counter reduces all the stock that's going out of date. You can get some good bargains on steak. And it's closed on a Monday so if you head in on Sunday afternoons, there's twice as much reduced."

He winked and made to walk off, touching Abigail lightly on her shoulder as he passed, and calling Daisy to his side. "See you tomorrow," he said in farewell, more as a statement than a question and Abigail sensed he was a man used to getting what he wanted.

Determined not to give Sol the satisfaction of bumping into her the next day, she chose to take Bessie out earlier in the day. She'd not really been in the mood for working all morning. From the time she woke up, a dark cloud hung over her head, a melancholy that made her sigh for no reason and tut as she drew back the curtain to see fat blobs of rain splattering across the windowpane. Sam had already vanished; Abigail couldn't quite remember where he'd gone this time, and Molly had used up all the milk, abandoning the empty bottle on the countertop. There were still no emails requesting to book the services of the Twin Oaks Equestrian Centre, and although she had a couple of dresses she should be working on, she couldn't bear the thought of spending a morning cooped up in that cold room. Instead she pulled on her boots and waterproof coat, and to Bessie's delight, took her lead off the hook in the kitchen. The collie grabbed her tennis ball in anticipation and bounced around in circles.

Determined to avoid Sol, Abigail turned right out of the drive and headed east away from the hamlet. There was little traffic on the back lanes, but it was a nuisance when a car emerged in the distance as Abigail would have to gather Bessie to her legs and huddle tight against the hedgerow. After the third car roared past, Abigail became irritated by this danger and turned down the next public footpath she saw. The rain continued to tap against her hood but the lush countryside around her soothed her mood.

After life in London for so long, she was grateful for the freshness of the air, and the peace and tranquillity of having this stretch of the countryside to herself. She had only passed one other dog walker who nodded in greeting as he ambled past.

Bessie didn't tire of chasing the ball that Abigail threw for her. The footpath spat the pair out on another country lane and Abigail figured that if she turned right and kept heading in a semi-circle then she would end back up in the environs of home. She made her way through a sleepy village then continued alongside a choppy stream that cut through the base of a valley. Another stile to the right took her into a copse, which she trudged through, her legs now starting to complain of the unaccustomed exercise. At the far end of the copse, she followed a trodden path across a meadow and came out on yet another country lane. It looked the same as all the others and she wondered how she could tell where she was. Turning right, she led Bessie onwards figuring that she'd come to a signpost, or someone to ask, soon. The lane slowly rose uphill and as she reached the apex, she stared out over the landscape looking for any familiar landmarks, but all she saw were fields, hedges, and the distant steeple of a church in the distance. Where the hell was she? She cursed, feeling more irritated as the rain persisted, dampening her leggings, and causing a chill to run through her. It was too far to turn around and retrace her footsteps. She couldn't be too far from home, surely?

She continued forward and came to a split in the road. South Gorley was signposted as a mile and a half straight on, Hyde was three quarters of a mile to the right. The names meant nothing to her.

Abigail felt a wave of panic. She'd not thought to bring her phone out with her, trusting her sense of direction, and not planning to walk so far. As the turning right policy hadn't worked for her so far, she carried straight on, hoping for a shop, pub or passer-by with some local knowledge to call upon. Bessie was clearly flagging, and sauntered wearily at Abigail's side. The lane seemed to continue forever, the only sign of life being an occasional horse in a paddock, and birds fluttering between the hedgerows. On a lamppost, a faded poster advertised a drama production in village hall from last August.

"Bollocks," Abigail muttered to herself as she came to the brow of a hill, expecting the village to present itself to her. Nothing but the lane carried on into the distance. A muddy black estate car came towards them, slowing as a wild pony meandered across the lane. The vehicle continued at a crawl as it drew level with Abigail and Bessie, huddling against the hedge. The window lowered and Abigail steeled herself to apologise that she wasn't local and couldn't give directions.

She grinned in relief. "Sol!"

"You're a long way from home." He smiled back, bemused.

"I fancied a good hike. Wear Bessie out, you know. Although I have lost my sense of direction," she admitted.

"Do you want a lift back? I'm heading home."

"That would be great. Sorry we're so damp."

Sol jumped out of the driver's seat to open the back, cursing the rain as he hopped around the car. There was already a scruffy dog blanket lining the boot space, and Bessie jumped in eagerly, sensing the opportunity to rest.

As Sol drove on, Abigail realised that she had been heading completely in the wrong direction. She vowed never to go out without her phone in the future. She'd have ended up in Ringwood if she'd kept going. The warmth of the car was a Godsend. As the car crawled through the picturesque villages and rumbled over cattle grids, Sol explained that he'd been in the area interviewing an economist about the debts of the NHS for an article he was writing for tomorrow's paper.

"Deadlines, eh?" Abigail sympathised. "I have quite a lot on my plate too."

"I'm sure you can spare the time to come in and have a bite to eat?" Sol pulled into his gravelled driveway and cut the engine. Bessie stood up in the rear and stretched in anticipation. Abigail hesitated, but her stomach was growling with hunger.

"Well, if it's no trouble," she replied politely.

"Don't be daft, of course it's no trouble," replied Sol dismissively. "Cheese on toast OK?"

"Perfect."

She and Bessie followed Sol to the back of the house and through the wooden stable door that led into a farmhouse kitchen. Daisy jumped around them in welcome, tail wagging and excited yaps escaping her mouth.

"What a lovely place," Abigail breathed, looking around the space. The aga warmed the kitchen, which had period dark wooden beams over the sink, but modern black granite worktops. Abigail realised how shabby her kitchen was in comparison. Maybe once their finances picked up, they could consider a kitchen renovation.

"I'm just renting at the moment," explained Sol. He placed his laptop and notebook on the solid oak table, and made to prepare lunch, gliding effortlessly around the kitchen, gathering utensils and food as he went. "I'm in the process of selling a property in London so I'll look to buy down here eventually, but this will do in the meantime."

Abigail peeled off her damp coat and hung it on a peg near the back door. She glanced down at her soggy leggings and scruffy sweatshirt and felt self-conscious. She knew that her rain-drenched, windswept hair gave her the appearance of someone dragged through a hedge backwards.

"You've had enough of London life?"

"I can work from home mostly so it makes sense to hide out in the country. It's closer to Mum, when she's at home, and it's so beautiful around here."

Abigail glanced at the photo frames on the wooden dresser. The largest frame contained a picture of a woman and a child of about four. The picture had been taken in a capsule of the London eye; presumably as it reached its highest point, with the vista of London as a backdrop. The woman had wild black hair and piercing dark eyes. She was about thirty and beautiful. The child shared her same mocha skin and pretty smile.

Sol came over to the dresser to fetch the plates and followed Abigail's gaze.

"My soon to be ex-wife," he explained. "And daughter, Beatriz."

"Wow, you have a daughter!" Abigail had not expected him to have any baggage. "Do you see her often?"

"I have access once a month," he replied, emphasising the word "access" with contempt. "Sometimes I bring her here, but otherwise I'll spend time with her in London." He plated up the cheese on toast and indicated for Abigail to sit at the table. "My wife, Rosa, is Mexican," he

71

continued as he settled opposite Abigail.   "She has the Mexican temperament too - fiery cow."

His spiteful words hung in the air as they bit into their lunch.

"So, enough about me. How's the fashion business coming along?"

"Erm… it's kind of challenging," she admitted, choosing her words carefully. "I've got a few online orders to fulfil, as well as trying to prepare the spring / summer public launch on the website." She paused, expecting Sol to jump in and change the subject.   Most blokes didn't have the attention span when it came to fashion topics. Sol, however, was watching her attentively and nodded as he chewed on his toastie.

"There's a trade fair in Birmingham in a few weeks' time," she continued.   "I really feel that I should attend to get my work out there, you know, to try and secure some larger orders."

"But?"

"Well, the hardest thing is the amount of upfront investment I need. It's expensive to have a stand at the fair.   But also, it would be showcasing the Autumn / winter collection so I'd have to work my ass off to get some designs made up in time.   It's not impossible, but it all costs money.   It's such a struggle to work three steps ahead of the season."

Sol swallowed a mouthful and nodded sympathetically.   "I did a piece on the reality of new business set-ups a few weeks ago. Did you know that half of all small businesses fail in the first year and I think it was about 95 percent are gone by the fifth year?   I spoke to some of the failed business owners to get their advice on how people can learn from their mistakes."

"And what were some of their tips?"   Abigail felt as though "April Smith Designs" was teetering on the edge.   Any advice was gratefully received.

Sol regarded her carefully.   "There was a sense that people had rushed into starting their business too soon without sufficient money or resources to survive their mistakes, so they suggested new business owners should take their time.   Your talent and drive will never leave you, so there's no need to put yourself out there to build up debts and make mistakes if you're not ready."

Abigail blushed.   He had just described her last six months.   "But I spent three years temping, and it feels like I've lost that time and am now playing catch up.   I had to start some time."

"Did you save up lots of capital whilst you were temping?"

Abigail felt herself blush even deeper.   In her early twenties she was living virtually rent-free at home with her parents and worked full time. She should have put money away, should have started to build connections and foundations that could be serving her business needs now.   Instead, what did she do?   She bought nice shoes and handbags, blew hundreds of pounds on nights out and splashed the cash on spa days. Should have, could have; hindsight is a wonderful thing.

"Don't look so glum," Sol urged, his face softening. "There was also a conclusion from other people I spoke to that a bit of luck can go a long way. You never know who you're going to bump into, who might be able to do you a favour and what's around the corner."

He gathered up their empty plates and Abigail watched as he took them to the sink. He really did have a lovely body. She shook the thought from her head.

"Listen, how much do you need?" He asked casually as he returned to the table. "This little hamlet isn't the best place to show off your pieces, and the trade show could be the golden opportunity for you. It sounds like the perfect place to meet buyers with their cheque books ready to order from you."

Abigail blushed and no words came.

"Seriously," he insisted. "I can lend you the money."

"Are you sure? You barely know me!"

"But I know where you live," he countered with a cheeky grin.

"I'd pay you back as soon as I could, with interest."

"I have every faith in you. And what about the equestrian centre side of things?"

Abigail sighed, feeling like a bigger failure. "Still no bookings. I was hoping we might have had secured some interest now that the New Year is out of the way. Molly's got a few kids having riding lessons at the weekends, but it's the corporate bookings we want to focus on."

Sol studied his hands as he processed this. They were neat hands. Abigail admired his clean clipped fingernails. "So, what is the offer for corporate businesses?" he asked.

"We offer team building for up to twenty people. They come and learn about horse care and grooming, then have a competition, you know, get into small teams to plait a mane or tail…"

Sol started giggling. "It sounds like 'The Generation Game'! You ought to get them to do it blindfolded."

Abigail had vaguely heard of the Generation Game, but wasn't familiar with the format, and smiled politely. "Then there'll be some riding - like obstacle races on horseback. I don't really know the full details as Molly and Sam have worked it all out between them."

"Have they tested it out?"

Abigail looked blank.

"Had a dummy run to see how the timings work out and what they'll need, and so on."

"Well, er, no. We haven't got access to twenty spare people."

Sol looked thoughtful for a moment, and then stretched back in his chair. Abigail glimpsed skin briefly as his t-shirt rose up, and cursed herself for finding it erotic. "Why don't I ask my editorial team if they'd like to come and try it out? It'll have to be a freebie, but we can buy our own lunch at the pub."

"Would you?" A bubble of excitement rose in Abigail. This could be the start. "That would be great!"

"I can't promise, but I'm going up for the forward planning meeting in a few days' time, so will ask then. And talking of work..."

Abigail leapt out of her chair. "Yes, I know, I really must be getting on with work too. Thank you so much for lunch and for rescuing us." She tugged on her damp, cold coat and called Bessie to her.

"My pleasure. Anytime," he called in reply as she let herself out of the door.

17

Sol was true to his word and rapped on the cottage door a week later with a generous cheque, and to say that he'd managed to persuade a dozen of his colleagues to come to the New Forest for a dummy run of the corporate event. The bad news was that the session would have to be a Sunday so that it didn't disrupt the production schedule, and the soonest they could all get together was the third Sunday in February.

It clashed with the MODA fashion trade fair that she was now able to exhibit at, but Abigail wasn't going to look a gift horse in the mouth. Besides, this was Sam and Molly's thing, and it didn't matter if she wasn't around that day.

"Promise me you won't book in any rides that Sunday," Abigail demanded of Sam soon after he'd walked through the door. He was in a jubilant mood, having won three rides at Kempton that evening. To Abigail's irritation, Molly had stayed up specially to congratulate him, and had been chirping away whilst Abigail tried to finish scheduling social media posts about the equestrian centre and her new season launch.

"You couldn't have timed that better," he confirmed, checking the calendar that hung above the light switch on the pillar in the kitchen. "There's no flat racing that day."

"Cool, it's going to be great," squealed Molly, "Especially having journalists here. They might write up a piece about me. I'll be famous!"

"Don't get ahead of yourself," warned Abigail, "Sol didn't promise anything other than his colleagues coming to help us out."

"Yeah, and you don't want journalists poking around in your past too much," joked Sam. "Just imagine the story they'd write about your time at the racing college."

"Anyway, I'm going to hit the sack," Molly interrupted him, tugging her boots on and heading for the door to return to her side of the building.

"Goodnight!" she called as the door crashed shut behind her. A welcome silence fell on the cottage.

Abigail grinned at Sam as she sank into the sofa. "You seem to have found a way to get rid of her," she marvelled.

Sam threw his coat on the bannisters and flopped onto the cushion next to her. "She doesn't like the racing college to be mentioned."

"Why, what happened?"

"Well, nobody's quite sure of the reason but you know she was expelled. Not even Luke will tell us why."

"Mysterious," conceded Abigail. To be expelled, it must have been something serious. She couldn't imagine Molly dealing drugs or bullying, or thieving; all crimes that would warrant expulsion. She looked across to Sam, who was resting his eyes in sleepy contentment, and decided to drop the subject.

"So, a successful day," she commented. It was the first time they'd had any time together that day, and despite approaching eleven o'clock, she was determined they should have some quality "couple time" before bed.

"Yeah, I'll say." He opened his eyes and looked proudly across at her. "I should have enough for that holiday now."

For a split-second Abigail let herself believe, and a rapid showreel of images flashed through her brain. Sun loungers, beaches, hot sun pounding down on her bare skin, cocktails with pretty coloured umbrellas and the gentle soundtrack of waves caressing the shoreline. But as quickly as the images came, they dissolved as she observed Sam's face and realised she'd misunderstood.

"Holiday?"

"Vegas! The lads were talking about a long weekend in Las Vegas before the flat season gets going again."

"Which lads?"

"Frannyboy, James, Eddie and Smithy."

The regular weighing room gang. Irritation started to ripple through Abigail. She could see bills sat on the kitchen table awaiting payment. Surely, they should take priority over a long weekend boozing, gambling and partying into the early hours? And what did "before the flat season gets going" mean? Sam had promised to retire long before now, but seemed unable to kick his addiction.

"What?" Sam sensed her stiffen.

"Aren't there are more important things to be putting the money towards? Like paying bills. Those stables are not cheap to run and there's no other money coming in at the moment."

"Whose fault is that?" he snapped back. The implication that she was letting the business down stung her, and her irritation turned to anger.

"We're all in this together," she retorted, the volume on her voice rising a notch. "I'm working my socks off trying to get my business into the black, let alone the hours I spend trying to drum up custom for the equestrian centre. It's not my fault if we haven't had any bookings yet, but I'm bloody trying my best."

She knew she sounded petulant, but exhaustion fuelled her vexation.

"I know you are," Sam's voice softened and he reached over to touch her hand. "We all are." Abigail took a deep breath and calmed down. It was impossible to be cross with Sam for long. "I'll make sure the bills get paid," he promised, squeezing her hand.

The clock in the kitchen gave a sombre bong to indicate it was eleven o'clock and Abigail and Sam wordlessly took the cue to rise from the sofa.

"Tell you what," Sam muttered as an afterthought. "If you want to earn a bit of pocket money, stick a few quid on my first ride tomorrow. Horse called Spiral. We think we've cracked the secret to getting him to run better - cheekpieces. A bit of a secret weapon." He put his finger to his lips conspiratorially. "But you didn't hear that from me."

Abigail never betted spontaneously. Deep down, she knew that was no such thing as "a sure thing" as far as racing animals was concerned, but as she lay in bed listening to Sam's breathing descend into the rhythm of the unconscious, she mulled the thought over. It was still in her mind the next day as Sam's Jaguar disappeared off down the lane, and curiosity got the better of her. She reached for the laptop. Opening up a bookies' website, she was overwhelmed by flashing odds, and adverts, but she picked her way through the noise to open an account and transfer her last twenty pounds into the online wallet. She managed to find the race cards and glanced through the runners in the opening race at Southwell.

Sam's horse, Spiral, was priced at forty to one; the least favourite to win apart from some poor nag that was a hundred to one. Twenty pounds at forty to one would bring in eight hundred pounds she calculated, with momentary breathless excitement. That would keep them in food for a couple of months. Surely it couldn't be that simple. Sam had seemed so sure. A secret weapon, he said.

Putting her trust in Sam, she clicked the button and confirmed her bet. Twenty pounds for Spiral to win. A sick feeling lurked in her stomach and stayed there, nagging away at her all morning as she tried to persist with her mundane admin. At quarter to two she flicked on the TV and grappled with the satellite channels until she found the correct one broadcasting Sam's race. She was just in time as the final horses loaded into the starting stalls. They were off and the commentator described the scene in front of her eyes.

"They're racing over five furlongs for this sprint handicap and as they race through the first furlong, Indian River sets the pace in the hood on the far side, far right that is Pearl Harbour, and over on the rail is Ragdoll in the hands of Paul Mullen." Abigail searched the blaze of silks to work out which jockey was Sam, but with the caps and goggles, there was no telling which jockey was which. She just had to listen out for the commentator mentioning Spiral's name. Her prayers were answered quickly. "Down the centre of the course is Spiral, showing speed in the yellow cap, in the hands of Sam Ashington, and next to him in the green and yellow is Jacob's Ladder..."

The line of horses raced virtually shoulder to shoulder and Abigail gripped the arm of the sofa with nerves. Any of the twelve could take the race at this rate. How could Sam be so sure he was going to win it? She leaned forward willing Sam on.

"The favourite, Arches, is racing towards the near side and has just got some work to do in the purple and green colours, and totally outpaced at this stage is Hong Kong Bay. As they head towards the last two furlongs, it's Indian River out in front with Spiral close on his heels and Treaty of Versailles coming up to challenge them..." The three horses picked up the pace and started to draw ahead of the pack. "Come on," muttered Abigail helplessly, like a mad man ranting at the wind in an empty field, "Come on..."

"...but down the centre of the course it's Treaty of Versailles that's come to head Spiral, and in the closing stages he shows he's not disadvantaged by the extra two pounds, to take the sprint handicap. Treaty of Versailles clinches the race. In second place it's Spiral half a length in front of Indian River...."

"No!" wailed Abigail, slamming her fist in fury on the arm of the sofa.

"Oh, is that the 1.45?" Molly's voice behind her made her jump. "How did Sam do?"

"Second," Abigail spat. "He was just about in the lead when that Treaty of something snook over the line."

"Second, that's great!" Molly came closer to the sofa to get a better look at the TV screen. "The cheek pieces seemed to do the trick." She saw Abigail's face and frowned.

"What's up?"

"Sam told me to put some money on, so I've just lost our supper fund."

Molly looked confused. "But he came second... Oh, shit, you bet on him to win, didn't you?"

Abigail blushed and willed herself not to cry. It was only money. Her only money. Wasted. Down the drain.

"You daft thing," laughed Molly. "At forty to one you should always go each way."

Abigail sighed deeply. Trust her to fuck it up - she was useless at everything. "I have no idea what I'm doing with betting," she admitted, ashamed of herself. She rose and made her way to the kitchen where she peered in the fridge. As she suspected, she'd now have to rustle up a meal for three people and a dog from a bag of potatoes, a handful of mushrooms and some frozen peas.

"Do you want to come out for a ride with me?" Molly asked. "It's about time you had another trip out on Muppet."

"Oh, not today, Molly."

Abigail couldn't think of anything she'd like to do less. She felt a twinge of guilt that poor Muppet received no attention from her, and she relied on Molly to keep her exercised and cared for. Fortunately, Molly enjoyed the challenge of taking the frisky madam out, and Abigail had more urgent financial matters to attend to.

"I really need to go and chase up some unpaid invoices," she explained with a grimace, and vanished up the stairs before Molly could ask what was for supper.

18

Abigail glanced over to Sol in the driver's seat, then looked back ahead at the stream of taillights glowing red as they approached yet another bottleneck on the M3. It felt as though they had been driving for hours already, but in reality, they only left the village forty minutes ago. Could this day get any worse, she pondered as the car came to a standstill and Sol yanked on the handbrake. She'd had no idea that this particular Saturday was going to present so many challenges when she'd woken up eight hours ago. It was raining again, but that was nothing new. It seemed as though most of February had been continually raining, and the mud was unavoidable around most parts of the yard. Sam brought her a cup of coffee and disappeared with Bessie at his side before she could even say thank you. She hadn't lingered in bed, as her active mind was already listing all the outstanding jobs she needed to get ahead of today. Pieces that needed finishing for customers, items that needed to be packed for MODA tomorrow, paperwork that was outstanding. The workroom was a blaze of material by ten o'clock when she heard Sam re-enter the kitchen downstairs, Molly's irritating laugh following close behind. She tried to block out the sound and concentrate on her deadlines.

"Have you seen my thermals?" Sam asked, trotting upstairs. "I thought they were in my kit bag but they're not there. Did you wash them?"

Abigail sighed, her concentration broken. "No, I don't think I've seen them."

"It's arctic out there. I'm definitely going to need them."

"Why, where are you off to?" Abigail couldn't remember him having any racing today.

"Lingfield." He vanished into the bedroom momentarily and Abigail heard the thud of Bessie's paws come trotting up the stairs behind him.

Normally she wasn't allowed upstairs, but Sam had a forgetful way of reminding her. The collie was still splattered with fresh muck from her walk, and excitedly spotted Abigail.

With lightning speed, Abigail put down the package she was labelling and tried to intercept Bessie at the door before those muddy feet came anywhere near her finished dresses. She wasn't quick enough and the front paws stamped all over the pale pink satin dress, and her tail knocked numerous reels of cotton from their stack on the shelf.

"Bessie, oh shit! You bad girl!" Abigail yelled at Bessie, who had no idea what she had done wrong but cowered in dread, placing her wet, muddy belly over one of the skirts for display at MODA. Sam came rushing to see what the panic was about.

"Oh, oops," he contributed, trying to stifle a giggle. "Come on Bessie, out you come." He grabbed her collar and pulled her away from the bedroom, revealing the brown disaster she left behind.

"It's not funny," Abigail wailed, holding the skirt up to the light. She might have time to wash, dry and iron it for display tomorrow, but it was an added pressure she could do without. As for the pink satin dress, there was no way that could be sent to the customer. She'd have to try and rectify that next week. "I haven't got time for shit like this."

Having returned Bessie to the lounge and ordering her in his stern voice to stay on her bed, Sam came back upstairs, albeit a little sheepishly. "Bessie doesn't know what she's done wrong. You shouldn't shout at her like that."

"She shouldn't have been following you up here in the first place," Abigail snapped back. How dare he try and make her feel guilty.

"All right, my bad, I'm sorry." He didn't sound very sorry.

"Well, 'sorry's' not going to be any help getting this clean for tomorrow, is it?"

"Calm down. Flipping' heck, it's not really the end of the world."

Abigail could feel her blood starting to boil. "Sam, just piss off to Lingfield and leave me alone," she grumbled.

Sam huffed and went into their bedroom to pick up his kit bag. "Right, I'm pissing off then, and I'll leave Mrs Premenstrual to her strop."

Without waiting for a reply, he stomped off down the stairs and after a brief muffled exchange with Molly, left the house. Abigail presumed he'd not tracked down his thermals, and with a minuscule sense of satisfaction, felt that he would get punished with the cold at least. She wished she'd had time to pull him up on his sexist presumption that she was premenstrual. She wasn't premenstrual: she was just mad as hell that hours of work had been ruined.

It was three o'clock when the call came. Abigail had made some progress through her list of urgent tasks, but felt as though she would be up all evening getting sorted, when her mobile rang. She almost ignored it, as the number was unfamiliar, but then she figured it could be something important concerning the trade fair or the dummy run tomorrow, or just a potential customer.

It was neither. It was the call that Kate said she always dreaded the most when her husband Callum was racing. The call to say there had been an accident.

"Sam's been taken to East Surrey Hospital," explained the clerk of the racecourse. "It's just precautionary, to get checked over as he did lose consciousness for a short while." Abigail barely heard the words, just felt an urgent desire to get to Sam as quickly as possible. The argument this morning was forgotten, the trade fair lost its importance, and the dummy run didn't matter. She just needed to be at his side.

"He won't be able to drive himself home of course, so would you be able to come for him?"

"Oh yes, yes, I'm on my way."

The caller promised to be back in touch with any update in the meantime, and Abigail hung up, her head spinning, wondering how she was going to get to Lingfield. Molly would know. Abigail frantically searched for her around the yard, but it seemed as though she had taken one of the ponies out. The pub was the next best thing, and Abigail crashed through the doors to find it calm now that the lunchtime rush had subsided.

"Oh, 'ello stranger," Anna called from the bar. "Haven't seen you in a while." Her face fell when she saw the anxiety on Abigail's features. "Is everything OK?"

"I need to get to Lingfield," Abigail gabbled in response, "but I've got no transport and I've no idea even where it is!"

"Lingfield, you say?" The interruption came from the flat capped gentleman that she'd spoken to on New Year's Eve. "You can get the train from Salisbury straight up to Clapham Junction, then change onto the line that goes down to … oh, where is it now? East Grinstead I think, but Lingfield is a few stops along that line. You can walk from the station; it'll take about 15 minutes or you can splash out on a taxi."

"You need to go now?" Anna asked, clearly confused by the conversation. Abigail explained with rising frustration, that Sam had been taken to hospital after a fall and she needed to get there.

"Oh, you won't want to go by train then, that'll take hours. I'd get Paul to drive you but he's gone down to Southampton this afternoon." An awkward silence fell over the trio, as Anna realised that she wasn't being any help.

"Oh, Sol might be able to drive you," she blurted. "He was in here half an hour ago, but only had a half. Go and tap on his door. I'm sure he won't mind."

Abigail hesitated for a moment. It was a big favour to ask of someone that she didn't know that well, but she was desperate. She could just ask for a lift to Salisbury and do the train option, she figured.

"Don't be silly," laughed Sol, when she explained her predicament to him. "You don't want to get the train. It's expensive and will take forever. I'll drive you."

"But are you sure? It's quite far… I think. Actually, I have no idea."

She wondered whether the train would have been quicker, as they crawled through yet another set of roadworks.

"He'll be all right," Sol interrupted her thoughts with an encouraging smile.

"He could have picked a better weekend, though, couldn't he?"

"If you need to rearrange the dummy run tomorrow, I can ring round everyone," Sol offered. "It's no problem."

The dummy run. She could barely think that far ahead. Why did it have to be today that he'd fallen, of all days?

"I'm sure Molly can manage on her own. There's nothing like being thrown in at the deep end." She glanced across at Sol who was staring ahead into the traffic queue. "I'll let you know if that's not the case."

"And you'll be there of course," he added.

"No, if all goes to plan, I'll be in Birmingham, exhibiting at the trade fair. We'll see…". She left it hanging in the air. She couldn't presume anything about the next 24 hours until she saw for herself what state Sam was in.

"That would be a shame to miss the event. All that hard work you've put in and money you've spent. I guess you're all ready?"

"Not really." Abigail shuddered as she remembered the pile of pieces still abandoned on the floor back at the cottage. Pieces with and without dirty paw prints. "I thought I had the rest of the today to get it all sorted."

"Well, if you go, you'll be fine," Sol reassured her. "You only really need yourself to promote your company. You're the best asset."

The conversation was interrupted by another update from the hospital. Sam's scans had come back clear, so it seemed he'd had a lucky escape. Subject to some further observation, he should be able to go home in a few hours' time. One of the other jockeys had driven his car and belongings over to the hospital from the racecourse; a logistical detail that hadn't even crossed Abigail's mind. No sooner had she come off that call, her mobile rang again. It was Kate.

"I've just heard about Sam," she said. "Is he OK?"

Abigail relayed all the information she had. If there was one person that would understand what she was going through, it was Kate. She had spent a couple of years as Callum's wife, dreading calls about falls. As a jump jockey, Callum parted company with his mounts with regularity and had endured a broken ankle, fractured wrist, snapped collar bone, broken ribs and a punctured lung in the last few years alone.

"Oh, thank God, that doesn't sound too bad. Call me later to let me know if we're still on for MODA. If not, I'm happy to come to the New Forest for a few days and help out. I've got a week off and no child; it feels great!"

Kate's relaxed attitude put Abigail at ease a little. As someone who could interpret hospital lingo, she trusted her friend when she said it didn't sound too bad. She was grateful that Kate was there for her in whatever capacity. Callum had charge of baby Aidan for the week as he wanted to take him to Ireland to spend time with his grandparents. Kate had agreed instantly and promptly booked the week off work to take advantage of having no ties.

"Thanks Kate. Hopefully I can leave Molly in charge of Sam and we can go to Birmingham as planned, but I'll call you later."

As she hung up on her friend, she noticed Sol had raised an eyebrow. "What?"

"Is it wise to leave Sam and Molly together?"

Abigail regarded Sol incredulously. "Why not? They run the place together."

Sol waved his hand dismissively. "Forget I said anything. It's none of my business...".

"But?" Abigail sensed he was leaving something hanging in the air.

"Nah, forget it. It's just that whenever I see them with the dog, they seem a bit too friendly, you know, for work colleagues."

Molly and Sam did spend a lot of time together. They had to. They got on well, but how much was too well? The other day she'd observed them fooling around in the mud. Molly had the wrong shoes on, some trainers that she didn't want to get mucky, but there was a barrier of ankle deep, sticky mud across the path to the barn where she'd left the grooming kit. Sam offered her a piggyback through the mire, and then threatened to drop her in it as he carried her through. She was screaming and giggling, clinging onto his shoulders, with her legs clasped around his waist, pleading for mercy.

Abigail mulled this over in silence as Sol steered the car to merge with the M25. She was achingly close to her parental home and would like nothing more than to have her mum with her right now.

"Forget I said anything," Sol urged again. "It's none of my business."

Abigail wasn't sure what to think, and right now, she was more concerned about what condition she would find Sam in.

When she did finally navigate through the vast maze of corridors at the East Surrey Hospital and got her first glimpse of Sam, she burst into tears. An angry gash seared across his forehead and had been clumsily

84

patched up with chunky stitches. Smears of dried blood remained across his temples and nose, whilst the left side of his face had swollen from his cheek bone to his eyebrow, doubling the size of his face in a grotesque contortion. Nobody had thought to clean the splatters of mud from his features.

She waded through the strangers standing around his bedside and took the empty seat near the pillow end, which she presumed had been left unoccupied for her arrival. She grasped his hand and he gave her a groggy smile in return.

"Look at you," she sniffled. With her free hand, she reached into her bag and retrieved a tissue to wipe her eyes, grateful that she hadn't bothered to put on any mascara that morning. "You look like you've gone five rounds with Frank Bruno. Your poor little face. What happened?"

"Diablo," Sam muttered sleepily. Abigail frowned and waited for more, but nothing was forthcoming.

"The devil?" She responded, drawing on her basic knowledge of Spanish.

"I was winning. Bloody horse." With that, Sam obviously felt he had explained everything and closed his eyes with the effort of talking. Abigail glanced around the others in the room for help. There was a tall, well-dressed man who looked to be in his fifties or early sixties. His smart tweed blazer suggested he worked for the racecourse.

Leaning against the wall opposite was a skinny lad about Sam's age. Instinctively Abigail knew he was a weighing room colleague, probably the jockey that had driven his car over. He saw her glance at him and leaned over the bed to shake her hand.

"Abigail, nice to meet you. I'm Eddie."

She raised her eyebrows at him in hope of a better explanation. "He's right - he was winning," Eddie confirmed, smiling affectionately in Sam's direction. "Which is a shame, because if he was at the back, he wouldn't have taken such a kicking! We're not too sure what happened, though, whether the saddle slipped or Diablo jinked, but about a furlong out, Sam's suddenly under a flurry of hooves."

Abigail shuddered. She could recall the thundering sound of a dozen horses galloping at forty miles an hour and imagined the damage those hooves could do.

"Did you walk here?" Sam asked, opening his eyes momentarily. Abigail hoped he was joking.

"No, Sol brought me."

"Oh. Hello Sol."

Abigail was about to explain that Sol wasn't in the room, that he had dropped her off and insisted on getting straight back. She was grateful for the privacy he afforded her.

85

"Fortunately, there's nothing broken," a young pimple clad man explained from the foot of the bed. His white lab coat with the breast pocket bulging with pens, along with the stethoscope and lanyard around his neck indicated that he worked at the hospital. "The gash is just a superficial wound so should clear up OK, but may leave a bit of a scar. It's just the concussion we were worried about so you'll need to keep an eye on him."

Abigail was bombarded with literature on concussion, danger signs to look out for, and tips on his care over the next forty-eight hours and beyond. She felt a pang of guilt at leaving him with Molly, but when she had telephoned earlier to fill Molly in on the situation, she was insistent.

"You can't miss MODA," Molly urged. "You've put so much into this. We'll be fine. I'll make sure Sam follows orders." Abigail tried not to think about Sol's earlier insinuation and thanked Molly gratefully.

It took a frustrating length of time to get Sam discharged, and grim darkness had set in as much as the rain by the time Eddie and Abigail helped Sam into the car.

"Thanks Eddie," Abigail acknowledged, as he handed over the key fob and explained that Sam's kit was all packed in the back.

"Not a problem," he smiled. "I know Sam would do the same for me." He hesitated. There was something else on the edge of his lips and Abigail wondered whether he was about to ask her if she would let Sam go on the boy's trip to Vegas.

"Just keep an eye on his weight," Eddie added. "I caught him flipping earlier."

"Oh." Abigail tried not to look fazed. It was not what she had expected him to say, and had no idea what flipping was. She'd have to ask Molly rather than look silly in front of Eddie. "Will do."

Tiredness began to set in as soon as she took the driver's seat. The warmth of the car and the rhythmic thud of the wipers caused Sam to snooze as soon as they were clear of the hospital grounds, and Abigail put music on low volume to hum along to keep her awake. With a deep breath she dared to look forward to tomorrow.

19

As a new day dawned, the UK's largest fashion trade fair got underway. The size of the hall at the exhibition centre was breathtaking. Stretching several hundred metres long and ten trade stands wide, Abigail buzzed with excitement when she saw the potential. This was just the womenswear section! Another hall contained lingerie and swimwear, there was another exhibition space full of menswear and a gaping side section was set aside for accessories. Many exhibitors had set up the previous day, but Abigail had no choice but to load the car up in the eerie stillness of 4am, and set off from the New Forest in the pitch black. Three hours later she arrived at the venue, where she wasn't the only exhibitor to be leaving the setup to the last minute.

As a smaller plot, Abigail's stand was tucked on the side, but she was close to the entrance and anticipated good footfall. Any weariness she felt from the stress of the previous day, and her early start this morning, evaporated as she entered the exhibition hall. She had brought as much as she could, but she was aware that the professionals around her had put much more time and effort into their displays.

"This is epic!" enthused Kate, tracking down Abigail as the doors opened just after 9am. She dumped her handbag on the ground and hugged her friend. It had been a few months since the pair had seen each other, and Kate had shed a few more pounds thanks to being the girlfriend of a personal trainer. "This is looking good." She cast her eye around the wares, touching dresses and inspecting the row of handbags on the shelving unit.

"I wish I had some pull up banners to say who I am," replied Abigail wistfully. "I'll have to get some for next time."

"Exactly, that's the point of coming for the first time. You can steal ideas from other people."

It wasn't long before the visitors started drifting through the doors, consulting their showguides and working out which stands provided the best trade opportunities for them. Kate and Abigail hovered with welcoming smiles for everyone passing by. It was certainly a distraction from the worry of what may be happening at the Twin Oaks Equestrian Centre 130 miles away. Sam had seemed quite stable as she left his gentle snores that morning, and Molly was stationed on the sofa should he need anything once she was gone. It was a big day for Molly, with Sol's media colleagues descending on the stables for the dummy run of the corporate event.

"So how did it go today?" Abigail asked Molly gingerly as she telephoned home from the hotel room that evening. She was thoroughly exhausted, her feet ached, body longed for bed, but she was happy with how the first day had gone. There were still two more days, and having chatted with the stallholders around her, she learnt that there would be corporate guests from larger businesses on Monday and Tuesday. The opening day was very much about smaller concerns that closed on Sundays, allowing their proprietors to come along and negotiate new business deals. Abigail had taken numerous business cards of people who would be invaluable sourcing new fabric and trims, helping with publicity, manufacturing, and she'd chatted to members of the press, hoping for any scrap of publicity. Her most exciting opportunities came from owners of exclusive clothing boutiques who were prepared to place orders for items from both her spring / summer collection, and advance orders for some of the prototypes of the autumn / winter collection.

"What about the skirt you're wearing?" asked a wiry lady dressed entirely in clashing tartan colours. She didn't look out of place amongst the weird and wonderful outfits of the attendees. Abigail glanced down at the crocheted ra-ra skirt. She hadn't planned to include it in her collections, but it always got a reaction. "I can't see it here on display?"

"I only have the one sample," bluffed Abigail, "which is the one I'm wearing, but I would be happy to talk colours and prices if you were interested."

"Great," nodded the lady, opening a black notebook, and heading for the bistro table where Abigail planned to do all her business deals. "Let's talk unit prices."

Flopping into the chair in the hotel room, she mentally added up all the order values and realised the total had just about covered the costs of the exhibition, accommodation and she could afford to buy Kate dinner tonight. There would certainly be a delay before the income came in and she could repay Sol's generosity, but the day hadn't been the disaster she feared.

"Oh Ab, we had an amazing day!" gushed Molly from the other end of the phone. "Sol's work mates were really funny, and they all got into the swing of it. Sam wanted to help, and I insisted that he couldn't, but you know what he's like, and it was probably better for him to be outside with me where I could keep an eye on him, than indoors where he couldn't get help if needed it, so we wrapped him up really warm and he came outside and sat on a chair watching. Then he had this great idea about filming parts of it and getting some clips for YouTube, so I put him in charge of that and none of the party had any objections..." Abigail tuned out slightly, happy that Molly sounded pleased with the day's activity.

Kate grinned at Abigail from across the room; she could hear the muffled tones of Molly's storytelling. She pulled a bottle of wine from her case, and wiggled it at Abigail, who nodded enthusiastically. Meanwhile, Molly had barely taken a breath. "We've put the last event live on the web, and included all the hashtags and shared it on social media, where it's been shared tons, and it's got loads of views already - how many views, Sam?"

"Do you want to put Sam on?" Abigail suggested, feeling that she'd never get off the phone otherwise. Kate poured the lukewarm white wine into the plastic cups provided in the bathroom of the budget hotel, and handed one to Abigail, chinking cheers silently.

"Evening darling," muttered Sam. He sounded weary, and it wasn't clear how much of the exertion had been simply putting up with Molly. "You can probably tell we've been OK this end. How has your day gone?"

Abigail regaled Sam with the day's activity from the trade fair, where she felt some blossoming relationships could emerge from the contacts she'd made.

"All good?" Kate enquired as Abigail hung up.

"Thankfully, yes. The dummy run seemed to go off OK, and Sam seems no worse for wear."

She sank down onto the single bed and finally allowed herself to relax. She took a glug of wine, then glanced over at Kate who was regarding her intently from here she reclined on the twin bed.

"What?"

Kate shrugged. "You don't quite seem yourself. Are you really OK?"

Abigail sighed. "I think the tiredness is kicking in. I've not had the best twenty four hours. Sam's timing was impeccable."

"But you've done brilliantly today," Kate responded. She was a supportive friend, always finding the positive words of encouragement when most needed. "Sam will be fine, it was just a bump. God, when I think of all the times Callum injured himself..."

If anyone knew how Abigail was feeling, it was Kate, whose husband as a jump jockey came with far greater risk than Sam's races on the flat.

Callum's name hung in the air like a bad smell: his infidelity and attack on Abigail was still less than a year ago and raw for them both. At least he had taken baby Aidan off of Kate's hands for the week, freeing her up to come and spend time helping Abigail.

"We had a row before he left for Lingfield," Abigail lamented. "He accused me of being premenstrual and I told him to piss off."

Kate waved her hand dismissively. "Don't worry about it," she instructed. "I'm sure it's all water under the bridge. You need a top up," she observed, rising from the bed to fetch the bottle from where it sat next to the plastic kettle and pots of UHT milk portions.

Abigail looked at her plastic beaker in surprise, and didn't object as Kate filled it back to the rim. It was warming her stomach and she realised that she'd barely eaten that day.

"I know what I meant to ask you," Abigail remembered, as Kate settled back onto the bed. "What does "flipping" mean?"

Kate's eyes widened and she pulled a face to indicate her disgust. "Flipping?"

"Yeah, Eddie said to me at the hospital to keep an eye on Sam as he'd caught him flipping."

"It means he's making himself sick to get the weight off."

Abigail looked horrified.

"It's not uncommon for flat jockeys," Kate explained, "and if it's just happening occasionally to make the weight for a particular race then it's deemed acceptable. You just need to start worrying if it happens more and more, as it can be a slippery slope when combined with all the other tactics they can use to shed pounds. You know, laxatives, appetite suppressing drugs, excessive sweat treatments. I expect Eddie was concerned as there may be questions over whether the fall may have been a result of him being weakened or dizzy."

Kate sounded like she knew a lot about the subject, and much as Abigail hated breathing Callum's name, she asked whether he had ever resorted to such tactics.

"Not that I know of, but he only nibbled at food. It's easier for the jump jockeys as they get a more generous weight allowance." She put her beaker down on the bedside table and grabbed her handbag. "Anyway, let's forget the men for the moment. I have something for you." She pulled a crumpled envelope from her handbag. "I feel really guilty because Penny from the farm gave this to Dan in January for me to post to you because she didn't know your address, and I put it on the coffee table and, well, it kind of got buried." Sheepishly she handed over the pink envelope. Abigail knew what a pigsty Kate's lounge was in, and could imagine exactly how newspapers, bills, vouchers and coasters would have been piled on top of the envelope. It was a wonder that it only took month for it to be unearthed.

Abigail read Penny's thank you letter with a smile on her face, then handed it to Kate to read.

"She's such a sweetheart," Kate agreed. "Not many twelve-year-olds would handwrite a thank you letter these days." She handed it back to Abigail to store away in her belongings. "One more thing before we go and eat. We need to plan for London. It's only four weeks away, you know."

Abigail's heart quickened at the thought of her upcoming appearance on "*Where in the World*". As Kate had kindly driven her and Mrs Angel to the audition in Bristol, she felt she had a vested interest in the process and insisted on accompanying them both to the filming in London next month. A family room had been booked in a smart hotel on the outskirts of Borehamwood, where Kate had been able to secure the essentials for travelling with Mrs Angel - a room near the lift and free parking. "And what's more, I have managed to track down Mrs Angel's granddaughter!"

"You're joking!" Abigail was impressed. The pair had spent months trawling through search engine queries trying to track down Isabella in order to get a photo to go in the frame Kate had bought Mrs Angel for her birthday. Sadly, they'd drawn a blank and given up hope of being able to fulfil their objective by Christmas, but the search intensified with the thought of being able to get Isabella to London to surprise Mrs Angel at the recording of "*Where in the World*".

"Dan's mum was able to come up with the missing surname, so I put it into Facebook and voila! Isabella Douglas from Edinburgh was the top result." Kate tapped her phone and held up the profile of the beautiful, mysterious Isabella.

"Incredible - we should message her and tell her about London," gushed Abigail.

"Already done it. She messaged back and said she would check dates and get back to me."

"That calls for a celebration," said Abigail, feeling a second wind of energy coursing through her. "Let's go and get some dinner."

20

Sol hadn't promised when the piece would go into the paper, but Molly woke early that Monday morning with a sixth sense that it would already be in print. She crawled out of her sleeping bag on the double bed that she was sharing with Sam and roused him with a cup of coffee. After a brief exchange, she was confident that Sam was well enough to be left alone for an hour, so she walked Bessie to the newsagents in the nearby village and bought a copy of *UK Today*. She'd never bought a broadsheet newspaper before and was surprised at how thick and heavy it was. Walking back up the lane, she tried to skim through the pages, but the wind conspired against her and she had to concede defeat and wait until she returned home where she could spread the pages out across the kitchen table.

"I can't see anything," Molly told Sam sulkily, turning the pages from beginning to end for a third time.

"Give them some time," laughed Sam, from where he sat cross-legged on the sofa. A copy of the *Racing Post* covered his lap, a luxury that he had delivered on a daily basis. He was curious to see which of his weighing room comrades had picked up his rides that day. A diagnosis of concussion sucked as it meant he had been officially signed off and wouldn't be allowed to return to racing until he had jumped through a series of neuro-psychological tests to satisfy the horseracing authorities that he was well enough again. Deep down he knew it was in his interests to have time off and fully recover, but he couldn't help feeling frustrated that he was missing out on some brilliant opportunities. He should be riding three favourites on the all-weather course at Wolverhampton today. Instead he'd be trailing around after Molly, insisting he was well enough to do some small jobs around the yard, whilst she refused to allow him to help and he'd have to suffer her constant chatter.

"Maybe it's made the online edition first?" Sam suggested, attempting to soothe her irritation. "They wouldn't have had time to write it up before the print deadline I bet."

"Good thinking!" Molly discarded the newspaper to one side and opened up the laptop. Sam knew he'd have a few moments of peace, as Molly's ability to talk whilst she concentrated on a task was minimal. He wished she'd concentrate more often.

"Oh, hang on," Sam broke the silence a few minutes later. A small snippet had caught his eye in the corner of the features page in the *Racing Post*. He sat upright and made sure Molly was paying attention.

"Moody Muppet shines in new role," he read aloud. "The ex-race horse Moody Muppet has found a new niche in helping jockey Sam Ashington teach equestrian skills to corporate executives. A YouTube video released yesterday reveals the feisty grade one winner being used to give the victors a lap of honour in her new yard in the New Forest. The mare was banned from racing in 2016 after refusing to race on several occasions, but the video clip showed the seven-year-old looking keen and cooperative. Maybe a new name should be on the cards."

"I don't understand," Molly responded, joining Sam's side to read the feature for herself. "How come the *Racing Post* got to report something but *UK Today* hasn't."

"They've obviously picked up the video I posted on YouTube," Sam replied with a self-satisfied smile. "Maybe this marketing thing isn't as difficult as Abigail makes out!"

As if to prove his point, the telephone rang with the Equestrian Centre's first enquiry.

Further north in Birmingham, MODA had a different feel on a Monday than the previous day. Visitors seemed more traditionally suited and booted compared to the individualist styles of the previous day. The exhibition hall was still packed with people, and Abigail felt the adrenaline pump through her as she and Kate took their place for day two.

She was blissfully unaware that the YouTube clip was gathering hundreds upon hundreds of views and being shared on countless social platforms. It hadn't been a plan to use the Moody Muppet at all. Given the mare's unpredictable history, it was an absurd risk to put novice riders on her back, but at the end of the session, it had felt hollow and unfinished to just name the winning team and send them on their way.

"What do we win?" Sol had asked. Along with his colleagues Andy and Steph, he had accumulated the most points through the day.

"Oh, er," Molly glanced at Sam for support. "You all get a rosette, and how about your photo taken with a famous racehorse?"

"Would that be the Moody Muppet that I've heard so much about?" asked Sol.

"The very same." Molly glowed with pride at her initiative. It was an attractive prize and wouldn't cost the yard anything.

"As we've proved ourselves to be the top horsemen - and woman - this afternoon, couldn't we have a lap of honour on said racehorse?" Andy argued.

"There's no way I'm sitting on Moody Muppet," Sol said decisively. He'd heard too many disparaging tales from Abigail to find a ride on Muppet an attractive proposition. Steph, on the other hand, rode ponies from an early age and still took part in riding events around Berkshire. She was up for the challenge of trotting around the field on Muppet, whilst Sol and Andy jogged alongside.

Sam hesitated. To say no would disappoint the group and could result in an unfavourable write up. Agreeing to this would set a precedent and could lead to an injury that definitely would affect the write up. But the participants had all signed a disclaimer.

Before he knew it, he had agreed and Molly tacked up Muppet. He got their consent to film the finale and the pair watched nervously as Steph mounted and set off at a gentle trot around the paddock. Sol and Andy jogged alongside, gleefully waving their winner's rosettes in the wind.

Despite their apprehension, the Moody Muppet behaved impeccably. With pricked ears, she trotted steadily and glamorously, showing off the grace and pride expected of a racehorse. Steph was bubbling over with praise for the mare as she dismounted.

In Birmingham, blissfully unaware of the impact of the video, Abigail was feeling relieved. The third day was drawing to a close and she'd had a productive time. Relaxing at her stand, she smiled politely at potential customers and clients, chatted to fellow vendors and jotted down contact details of representatives that could be useful to her going forward.

"Right, well, I'm going to nip to the loo and then it looks like we can start to tidy away a few things," Abigail told Kate, noticing that the stall holders were starting to make moves to pack away, now that the show was in its final half hour. The halls had emptied out of customers, and a collective exhaustion rang out from everyone involved in the exhibition.

No sooner had Abigail bustled off to make the quarter mile hike to the toilets, than a tall man with receding hair and a Beano tie paused at the stand and double checked his show guide.

"Might you be Abigail?" he asked Kate, flicking his eyes vaguely between the stand and her.

"Oh, no, she's just been called away," Kate apologised, stepping forward and holding out her hand. "I'm Kate, her assistant."

"Hmmm," his eyes darted around the stand dismissively before realising that he should shake Kate's outstretched hand. "Eric Callendine, from Teen Zero. I must be mistaken. I was expecting more items for the youth market."

"Oh." Kate was flummoxed. She couldn't think of anything on Abigail's website or in the show guide that would have given him the impression that "April Smith Designs" specialised in children's clothing. "We offer ranges in ladies occasion wear mainly, but some of the designs have been reproduced for a younger clientele. Was there anything specifically that has caught your eye?"

He reached into the breast pocket of his crisp navy shirt and produced a business card. "It's probably best I speak directly with Abigail," he concluded, handing over his card. "If you could tell her to give me a call."

Kate confirmed that she would, and watched, bemused as he receded from the stall towards the exit. She gazed around the silk and taffeta hanging around her, wondering why he thought any of Abigail's designs would suit the Teen Zero market. She thrust the business card into her handbag so that it wouldn't get misplaced, and started to gather up the rubbish that had accumulated around the space. By the time Abigail returned, both Mr Callendine and his business card had been forgotten.

21

Over the next few weeks, Abigail felt virtually confined to the spare room where she worked tirelessly to fulfil orders from the current and upcoming collections. She was frustrated at how gradual her success was in coming. She didn't feel as though she was close to reaching the big time; the dream that she'd fantasised about since graduating from fashion college.

She knew she would have to take baby steps, but the more she tried to stretch the business, the more financially unstable she became. With the world of shipping out orders before payment - whether bulk or individual – she was put in a precarious position. As a new business, her cash reserves were non-existent and the ebb and flow of income was increasingly uneven with the mismatch of seasonal orders. She was thankful that she had few overheads, but it meant having to take on the burden of the work herself, which resulted in long hours and little time for anything else.

Ironically, after months of praying that the telephone would ring with enquiries and bookings for the stables, it was now happening, but was an irritant as Abigail was interrupted throughout the day. Not every enquiry would result in a booking, and those that did could be seeking a date that was months in advance. This meant that Sam suffered the same cash flow issues with the equestrian centre as Abigail was experiencing with April Smith Designs. Horses needed feeding, shoeing, veterinary care and equipment whilst time passed waiting for customers to come and then, more importantly, to settle their bill.

UK Today finally carried a write up of the team building day. Molly had stopped buying the newspaper, so it was a text from Sol to Abigail that alerted her.

"Sol says it's on page twenty five," Abigail told Molly as soon as she returned from the newsagent. Abigail could tell she had run all the way back as her cheeks were flushed and Bessie was panting. She spread the paper out on the kitchen table and flicked over the cumbersome pages as quickly as she could.

"It's a shame Sam's not here to share this moment," Molly observed. Sam was back on the racecourse again. His forehead now bore a small scar as the gash healed, and his swollen cheek had deflated back to its normal sunken state. His absence wasn't going to stop the girls from having first look at the article, though.

"Oooh, here we are," Molly stabbed the article with her finger and glanced up to check Abigail was paying full attention. "How many journalists does it take to bring a racehorse out of retirement?" Molly paused and tilted her head in confusion. "What an odd headline. But then I suppose it's a posh paper, you know one of those intellectual ones. If this was in The Sun it would probably talk about my tits or something." Molly laughed at her own humour. "It's been written by Steph. Oh, you weren't here, were you, but Steph was the one who was on the winning team - probably because she was into horses, so got to ride Muppet at the end."

Sam had already confessed to Abigail about using Muppet in the finale. Abigail wanted to be resentful and felt protective towards Muppet, but deep down she knew that she was neglecting the poor mare enough, so it was good to utilise her in this way.

"Anyway, I'll read the article," Molly finally stated, returning her attention to the paper. "Three. In a field on the edge of the New Forest, a team of three *UK Today* journalists proved their equestrian skills by winning the corporate games at the Twin Oaks Equestrian Centre. Our prize? A rosette and a gallop around the field on the infamous grade one hurdler, Moody Muppet, who now resides at the centre." Molly lowered the paper and looked at Abigail. "I'd hardly say they had a gallop. More like a dainty trot, which is just as well because if Muppet started to gallop, goodness knows where they'd have ended up!"

Abigail smiled weakly, and Molly turned her attention back to the article. "It's all the brainchild of jockey Sam Ashington, who was forced to sit on the sidelines, having been thrown from his mount at Lingfield the previous day. Sam is assisted at the equestrian centre by his partner, the gregarious Molly Packer, who happens to be the sister of jump jockey and Grand National hopeful, Luke Packer. Together, the pair put us through our paces with team building games that tested our communication, balance, and ability to plait a mane neatly. It was an enjoyable day that bonded us in competition, but the icing on the cake was the appearance of the Moody Muppet, whose retirement from competitive racing means the mare had as much pleasure as we did."

Molly straightened up and gave a satisfied nod. "It's a bit short, but they didn't say anything nasty about me."

Abigail suppressed a smirk. She suspected that the word "gregarious" was not necessarily meant in a positive way.

"You don't mind about the word 'partner' do you? They just mean business partner, obviously."

Abigail had no time to answer, as her mobile rang, distracting her.

"I just don't know why they want me to be in the piece," Abigail moaned to Sam later that evening. They had retired to bed unusually early, with Sam exhausted by a long drive back from Southwell, and Abigail unable to concentrate on anything since receiving the call from *Raceday One*, the main satellite channel for horse racing fans. They lay together, snuggled under the winter duvet, limbs randomly entwined. "It would make more sense for you to be riding Moody," she continued. "You're the one all the viewers know; you're the big name in all of this."

"I guess they think it's more of a story to have someone that isn't from the horse racing world looking after the famous superstar."

"They just want to film me falling off," Abigail replied. She had been taken aback by the call from the TV station, asking whether they could come and film a piece, updating Moody Muppet fans on what the mare's new role was. It was evident that they had read the *UK Today* piece, and were curious to see how Moody's new life away from the racecourse was shaping up. When Abigail asked what it would entail, the producer explained they would like to get shots of Abigail grooming and tacking up the racehorse, and then they would also interview her and film her riding around the paddock.

"You know, just a bit of cantering and jumping over some small hurdles," the lady explained as though that was the simplest thing Abigail could do. She couldn't bring herself to admit that she was still a novice rider, that she'd never jumped before, and that quite frankly, she was scared shitless of the mare. Instead she found herself reaching for the diary and agreeing a date towards the end of March for the film crew to descend on the stables. That gave her three weeks to become a competent rider, make Moody do as she was told, and convey bags of confidence on screen.

Oh shit.

22

There was the merest hint of spring in the air. A milky sun penetrated beyond the wispy clouds of late afternoon, and Abigail had already noted that the evenings were drawing out. If they were lucky, they could stay out until around six o'clock before the sun sank over the western horizon tonight. She was still wrapped up in her raincoat with the fleece lining, more as a comfort blanket than for practical necessity.

By contrast, Sam and Molly came from tougher stock, with Molly in her dirty hoody and Sam just in a micro fleece base layer.

Whilst Abigail didn't relish the task ahead, it was nice for the three of them to get out together. Sam hadn't had any race meetings that day, and was able to help out with the first proper corporate session, complete with paying customers. It had ended half an hour ago with a jubilant team of stock brokers parading on Moody Muppet with Molly firmly grasping a leading rein. She had been shocked at how childishly they had behaved throughout the day. From the start, they made inappropriate jokes, were laughing at the size of the male horse's penis when it had a piss in the yard, and poked each other like a gang of preschool kids. She wasn't ready to trust this particular team with Moody Muppet.

Since the mare was already tacked up, Molly dashed into the cottage where Abigail was putting the finishing touches on a large order, and suggested that now would be a perfect time for her to have a jumping lesson ahead of the film crew's visit.

There was no getting out of it, and she now sat aboard the Moody Muppet whilst Sam and Molly walked alongside, heading to the small paddock where the jumps were still laid out from the afternoon's activities. She sensed the mare was not in the mood to behave. Her ears were pricked forwards and she held her head high, swinging it from side to side as though looking for trouble.

"Right, I'll put that pole on the ground as a starting point. Just trot Moody round and take her straight over it," instructed Molly, breaking out into a run to get over to the jump before Abigail and Moody got there. Abigail pointed the horse to the westerly hedge and nudged her into trot. The first three strides were fine until Moody decided she preferred to dance sideways, twisting her rear end towards the centre of the paddock and side stepping her way towards the hedge.

"Don't start this," hissed Abigail, watching the horse's ears flicker in reply. She put pressure on the left rein, and Moody twisted her body the opposite way.

"Maybe we should re-train her as a dressage horse," joked Sam from where he was watching in the centre of the field. Abigail managed to get her back in a straight line and aimed her directly at the pole.

"That's it," Abigail told the mare soothingly, trying to encourage her to keep the line and just trot over the obstacle. "Keep going girl."

Just as they approach the pole, the Moody Muppet sped up her trot and veered off sharply to the left to bypass the jump.

"Keep her focussed," nagged Sam. "Go around again and keep that right rein nice and tight.

Sighing heavily with defeat and humiliation, Abigail guided her round the paddock full circle and lined her back up towards the jump. Keeping Sam's advice in her head she shortened her right rein, ready to force Moody's head towards the jump and not change her direction at the last minute. Moody's ears were flickering as she approached. She kept straight but a few strides from the jump slowed herself down to a walking pace. She plodded over the pole, kicking it with a clang on her back leg.

"Oh my God, Moody, you're like a stroppy teenager," scolded Molly. "You're not getting away with that. Trot her round once more and make her get over this at a trot."

"She hates me," replied Abigail. "She's doing this on purpose." She kicked Moody back into a trot and around they went again.

"Show her who's boss, keep nudging her on," Sam advised. "That's right, keep kicking."

Abigail struggled to maintain the rising trot whilst still nudging Moody on with her heels and keeping a tight rein to stop her making up her own trajectory to the side. There was just too much to remember, and it didn't come naturally to her.

This time, Moody kept on trotting and despite a momentary slowing, she reluctantly skipped over the pole and continued to trot. Molly and Sam let out a cheer, but Abigail knew this was just the start of a very long process.

"Well done!" Molly sang, darting over to the pole. "This time I'm going to raise it to the first rung. There - it's not very high, but you will need to take this at a canter."

Abigail's heart began racing. Now there was yet more to remember; yet more potential for disaster. The jump was barely a foot off the ground and Muppet wouldn't need to put much energy into the jump, but Abigail sensed she would pull out something from her bag of tricks. She urged the mare into a canter, which surprisingly Muppet did willingly, and as they lined up to approach the obstacle, Muppet's canter got faster. Abigail had no time to think about what she was doing with the reins, steering, or controlling speed as the pair sailed over the jump at close to a gallop. Abigail was thrown forward onto Muppet's neck on landing and lost a stirrup, but thankfully she managed to wriggle her way back into the saddle and pull Moody up before too much damage was done.

"Not quite the graceful jump we were aiming for, but it's a start," Molly observed. "Just as well *Raceday One* weren't filming that!"

Abigail felt her hackles rise. She wanted to retort that at least she had got over it, but held her tongue.

"Do you want to try that again?" Sam asked, more as a command than a question. "This time, remember to keep your seat deep, and watch that your lower leg doesn't slide backwards otherwise you're encouraging her to speed up. Move your hands a bit further up her neck as she jumps and try to lift slightly out of the saddle as she takes off." More instructions, more words whizzing around Abigail's brain like breadcrumbs in a food mixer.

"Come on then, Moody," Abigail urged, nudging her back to work. "Let's do it gracefully this time."

The mare's ears were pricked and she struck up her regal racehorse canter. Abigail wished she could enjoy this feeling, but she was continually suspicious that Moody had something up her sleeve to spoil it.

"Looking nice!" called Molly patronisingly from the sideline.

"Come on girl, let's do this," Abigail urged quietly, more to herself than Moody. The jump was getting closer, Moody's gait was regular and rhythmic, and over she went, calm and steady. By some miracle, Abigail maintained her posture and felt a surge of relief and accomplishment.

"Yay, that was textbook!" Molly confirmed. "Well done. Let's try the next rung."

Abigail had been hoping they could call it a day there. Her legs were already aching, and she wondered whether her blood pressure could take much more. She looked back at the jump and realised she was going to have to get confident over higher jumps otherwise she would look pathetic when they came to film for *Raceday One*. That might even be their objective,

Abigail thought suspiciously, to make her look incompetent in the hands of the nation's favourite ex-racehorse.

"OK? It's not too much higher, so just do the same again," Molly instructed needlessly. "Keep her nice and steady." Abigail wished she'd just shut up for a few minutes and let her concentrate.

The Moody Muppet gave an audible huff as Abigail asked her to pick up to a canter again. This time it was a reluctant canter, her lolloping gait. Her ears were back and Abigail knew this wasn't going to go to plan. She urged her on towards the jump, trying to remember everything, but it was like learning to drive a car for the first time. Gears, brakes, steering, biting point. At least cars had an element of predictability to them. As they reached the jump, Moody swerved sharply to the left and decelerated to a trot, sending Abigail sliding onto her right flank.

"Ah, you forgot to keep that right rein tight," scolded Sam. Abigail felt her face flush, both from physical exertion and humiliation. "Try it again."

Wearily, Abigail and Moody circled once more, and at the top of the field Moody got her enthusiastic canter back. This was better, if not a bit too fast. Deep seat, heels down, check. Don't move the lower leg back. Her hooves thundered down the straight towards the jump and Abigail prepared for the feeling of a break in stride to hop over the bar, ready to slide her hands up the neck further and lift from the saddle. Instead Moody put her brakes on, lowered her head and Abigail found herself plummeting towards the ground before she could even process what was happening. There was a clatter as Abigail's shoulder crashed through the uprights of the jump, sending the wood flying in all directions.

"Are you OK?" enquired Sam, making his way over to where Abigail had sat up, wondering the same thing.

"I think so," she replied, getting to her feet and wiggling her limbs to check they could all move without any searing pain. The adrenaline was currently masking the discomfort of what would come out as bruises in strange places by the morning. She had an overwhelming urge to slap Moody, who stood nonchalantly a few feet to the side of the carnage.

"We've all been there and done that," Molly laughed, wandering over and grabbing Moody's reins. "Do you want my crop, then if you feel she's going to do that again, just give her a sharp slap on the shoulders to remind her you're in charge."

"Oh, I am *so* not in charge," Abigail replied, dreading the thought of trying to keep hold of a crop on top of all the other instructions in her head. "Maybe we should just call it a day."

"Come on, jump back on," Sam ordered. "You know what they say, you've got to get back on the horse."

Molly began the task of rebuilding the shattered jump as Sam helped a reluctant Abigail remount Moody. As she kicked her back into a trot, Moody resumed her playful dressage technique, trotting sideways. This didn't bode well. Abigail struggled to get her to approach the jump in a straight line, and didn't bother to fight her as she skipped around the jump.

"Here - take my crop," insisted Molly, jogging over to meet the pair at the gate. "Give her a tap if you feel she's not concentrating."

Abigail didn't have the strength to argue, and took the leather whip from Molly, holding it clumsily in her right hand. Moody's ears went back and it was as if she knew a threat hung over her. Obediently she broke into a dainty canter, kept a straight line and hopped over the jump perfectly. Abigail banged around in the saddle like a sack of King Edwards but stayed upright, and felt a small rush of pride.

"Excellent, keep going!" urged Molly. "Lean slightly forward and rise as she takes off and then keep that lovely deep seat of yours. Practice makes perfect."

Abigail had been hoping that a successful jump meant they could all stop there and go and have a lovely celebratory dinner together. Moody clearly was hoping for the same and tried to slow to a trot as they rounded the end of the field closest to the path leading back to the stables. "Once more, Moody," Abigail encouraged the mare, nudging her on with her heels. She wondered whether she dare give her a tap on the shoulders with the crop, but Moody accelerated back an obedient canter. They lined up with the jump and Abigail ran through the ever-growing checklist in her head. Reins, keep her straight, anticipate her stopping, lower leg, crop at the ready, nudge her on, rise out the saddle. In reality, it was luck rather than skill that resulted in Moody jumping the obstacle for the second time. Abigail tried to remember to lean forward and rise as Moody took off in flight but the movement of the horse was still so alien to her that she still thudded back into the saddle on landing, slid around and wobbled momentarily before regaining her composure.

Relief flooded through her and she pulled Moody back to a walk.

"Right, let's get that baby a bit higher, shall we?" Molly announced, making her way towards the jump.

Abigail stared at her incredulously and pulled Moody up. "Oh Molly, I'm shattered. I don't think I can manage much more."

This time it was Molly's turn to pause and regard Abigail in confusion. "But you've barely got started. There's loads more rungs higher we need to go to build up your confidence, and we really need to work on your jumping posture, don't we Sam?"

The pride Abigail had felt a few moments earlier at having completed a couple of successful jumps in a row soon evaporated. She was rubbish at this.

"Unless you want to make a tit of yourself when the *Raceday One* crew turn up, then I think you need to carry on," Sam agreed. Abigail felt a sting of hurt as her boyfriend sided with Molly. It was as though they were conspiring to push her to the limit. She knew she was onto a losing battle by continuing to whine.

"OK, once more," she conceded, asking Moody to strike up again. She could feel Moody's displeasure in her gait through to the unnecessary snort as she rounded the end of the field. Molly had raised the bar to thigh height. A piece of cake for her to jump, no doubt, but it looked a scary prospect for Abigail as she approached. The colourful red and white stripes on the pole made it look deceptively jolly, like an oversized piece of seaside rock. Despite Abigail's urging, Moody stopped abruptly in front of the pole and by some miracle, Abigail managed not to slide over her head. However, before she had chance to settle back into the saddle, Moody decided that it would be a good idea to spring over the jump from a standstill. Like a bucking broncho firing off a spring, Abigail had no chance and could feel the loss of contact between her and the horse and gravity sucking her downwards into the blur of wooden pole and hooves.

"Oh, for fuck's sake," Abigail spat, slowly pulling herself up into a sitting position and waiting for any signs of shooting pain. The adrenaline was pumping, and she wasn't sure whether she was angriest at Moody for humiliating her again, for Molly at insisting they carry on, or at Sam for supporting the decision. Either way, she could feel the blood boiling in the pit of her stomach.

Moody had skipped down the field, clearly pleased with herself, her reins flapping loosely on her flanks and stirrups jiggling around on their own.

"You OK?" To his credit, Sam appeared genuinely concerned as he pulled her to her feet.

"Oh fabulous." The sarcasm came easily. A tense silence hung between them momentarily as Abigail inspected the smears of mud on her coat and wiggled her limbs to check they all moved as they should.

"Just a tip for you," Molly's voice came drifting over the field as she led an alert Muppet back over towards them. "Try to keep hold of the reins if you feel yourself falling. If you can. You know, to stop her shooting off on her own."

"Oh, I'm sorry," Abigail retorted. "I was slightly preoccupied with whether I was about to break my neck to remember to keep hold of the reins."

"Yes, well, no harm done. On you jump." Molly indicated the empty saddle.

Abigail folded her arms like a petulant child. "No, I think I'll call it a day before Moody kills me once and for all."

"Don't be silly," Molly laughed. "You can't let a couple of little falls put you off. You need to stop being scared and take control. When I was at racing school, I had to put every tumble behind me and just get on with the job..."

"Until you were kicked out, right?" Abigail retorted. "Well, when I need the advice of a racing school dropout, I'll ask for it, but in the meantime, you can shut the fuck up."

Abigail shoved past Sam and stomped towards the gate, shaken by her ability to be so rude and ungrateful. She expected one of them to run after her, or at least call her name, but she had gone twenty paces and there was still nothing but silence behind her.

She longed to turn and see what was happening, but pride led her to continue through the gate and head down the path towards the stables without the slightest turn of her head.

Once safely encased between the blackberry bushes that lined the path, she paused and stood on tiptoe to glimpse what was going on in the field. Glumly she observed that Molly had mounted Moody and was now charging her towards the jump that Sam had raised to waist height. Horse and rider arced over the jump in perfect unison and landed perfectly. She heard Sam applaud the textbook demonstration. Abigail felt a stab of jealousy and misery, and found herself heading straight for the pub.

23

Night had fallen and only the dim moon that peeked out from wispy clouds lit the gravel driveway between the pub and the cottage. Abigail's footsteps broke the silence as she crunched towards the building. The double brandies that Sol insisted she drank warmed the pit of her stomach, fuelling much needed courage for the task ahead.

She stopped outside the wooden door to Molly's side of the cottage and took a deep breath. She hadn't had time to work out what she was going to say, but before she could overthink the task, she rapped at the door. Her knuckles stung as she did so, revealing another injury from her earlier falls that she hadn't noticed until now. She'd scraped the skin from three of her fingers, leaving her middle finger red raw.

The door swung open and the smile on Molly's face fell instantly.

"Oh, it's you," she said needlessly.

"Why, were you expecting Brad Pitt?" Abigail tried to lighten the mood, but the realisation that Molly must have expected Sam created a wave of bitterness that swept over her again.

"What do you want?"

"I've come to apologise, but it's not easy stood here. Can I come in?"

Wordlessly, Molly stepped aside to let Abigail through the door. She hadn't set foot in this side of the cottage since Molly first moved in and had forgotten how cramped the converted garage space was. The main room served as Molly's bedroom and living space all in one. The double bed that they'd bought from the charity shop in Salisbury dominated the space, with a bedside cabinet alongside it to house Molly's possessions, which seemed to be a clock radio, a tatty copy of the *Racing Post*, a packet of chewing gum and her bag. A door at the back of the room led through to a tiny space containing the shower, sink and toilet. Considering it was a run-down double garage originally, it was a transformation, and suited Molly's needs, even if it meant her invading Sam and Abigail's side of the house for food, company and TV.

"Excuse the mess," Molly mumbled, scooping up a discarded pair of jodhpurs and riding crop from the bed and stashing them in the corner. She smoothed down the duvet cover and waved vaguely towards it. "Take a seat."

Abigail rested a bum cheek on the edge of the bed and waggled the bottle of chardonnay. "I brought a peace offering."

The wine had been Sol's idea. Over the past two hours he'd had the full run down of everything that had happened in the field with Moody. As soon as she had stormed through the door of the Twin Oaks pub, he knew something was wrong. It was unusual for a woman to burst into the pub alone, but as soon as he saw the mud splatters on her coat, the tension in her posture and unspilt tears in her eyes, he leapt up from his pint of real ale and middle-class monthly travel magazine. He'd been halfway through an article on the wildlife of the Inner Hebrides, but this was more important.

"Abigail, whatever's the matter?" He knew it couldn't be another accident involving Sam. He'd heard from Anna about the corporate session that took place earlier that day. Besides, Abigail was clutching her riding hat. "Anna, can we have a brandy for the lady please? Best make it a double."

Abigail wasn't even sure that she liked brandy, but wasn't in the mood to argue.

"Come on, sit over here." With an arm around her shoulder to guide her, he placed her on his vacated bench alongside the fireplace, and slid in beside her, knowing that Anna would bring the drink over to them. Not only was it a quiet time of day, Anna would want to be part of the gossip.

"Thank you," she mumbled as Anna placed the brandy in front of her. She took a sip, and pulled a face as the brash heat hit the back of her throat. Two pairs of expectant eyes regarded her. She took another gulp of the drink, enjoying the warmth travelling down to where her stomach was still in turmoil.

"I fell off. Twice."

She recounted the tale of Moody's unpredictable behaviour and how Molly and Sam conspired together to force her to keep going time and time again. It sounded a bit pathetic when she described slithering off Moody. It was hardly a death-defying experience, however much it frightened her.

Anna didn't seem concerned and drifted back to serve at the bar. Abigail removed her coat, warmed now from the fire and the alcohol.

"You've got a war wound," Sol observed, running a finger gently over a graze on the base of her neck. His touch sent tingles down her spine.

"I've probably got several more that I'll find once I undress later."

Sol grinned in the cheeky way that made Abigail's stomach flip. "Stop imagining me with my clothes off!" she protested. Despite his perving over her, he was cheering her up in a way that Sam never could. Spotting her glass empty, Sol got another round in and sat back down, regarding her. Something in his expression had changed.

"So, after you told Molly to fuck off, you stomped off, leaving the two of them together?"

Abigail nodded, suddenly feeling like a child being scolded.

"And neither of them came after you." It was a statement, not a question.

"No, they carried on riding, and seemingly enjoying themselves."

A silence fell between them.

"You need to apologise to Molly."

Abigail nodded. Now that she had calmed down and recounted the experience out loud, she realised that she had acted petulantly.

"I probably shouldn't say anything," Sol began, lowering his voice conspiratorially, and leaning in towards Abigail, "but Molly was in here the other day asking Anna whether she had any bar work that you could do in the evenings. She's worried that your cash flow is …er.. fragile."

Sol sat back upright and checked Abigail's expression, which changed from confusion to indignation.

"Molly was trying to find me a job?" Abigail checked she'd understood correctly. Sol nodded, a hint of a smirk on his lips.

"Meddling little bitch, my finances are none of her business!"

"But you are short of cash?"

"Yes, but if I want another job on top of my exhausting twelve-hour days, I'll find my own position!"

Sol covered Abigail's hand to calm her down. "Please don't say anything to Molly, otherwise she'll think Anna has told you, and she instructed Anna not to say anything … unless she did have some work for you, then to ask you like it's her idea."

"I still can't believe she'd do that! So much for an apology, she deserves a word or two of another kind."

"Look, please keep this between ourselves," Sol pleaded. "She was just trying to help. I think it's quite sweet of her."

They sat in silence momentarily. "Unless she's got an ulterior motive of course," Sol added as an afterthought. His tone was light and dismissive, but after their conversation en route to the hospital last month, Abigail was grateful for the insight from an outsider.

"What do you mean?"

"Maybe Molly's trying to get rid of you in the evenings. That way, she can have Sam to herself."

Sol grinned at Abigail to show he was joking, but suddenly his words made a lot of sense. Why else would she ask Anna whether there was any work for Abigail, and why ask Anna to keep it quiet? She mulled it over. If there were any truth in his words, Sam and Molly would be together now. She could catch them red handed. Abigail leapt to her feet.

"I'm going to see what they're up to," she declared. She tugged on her coat, her fleeting bravery fuelled by brandy and driven by paranoia.

Before she could take any steps towards the door, it swung open and Sam stepped inside, instantly disproving the theory that the pair were together. He glanced across at Abigail and Sol with displeasure. Now she felt like the guilty party and a flush of embarrassment swept across her face.

"I thought you must be in here," Sam mumbled, making his way to the bar rather than to their table.

"Hey, Sam, can I get you a drink?" Sol jumped to his feet, always the gentleman on such occasions.

"I'm not staying, I just came to settle up with Anna for the lunches today."

Abigail padded across to his side so that she wouldn't have to raise her voice across the bar.

"I was just on my way to apologise to Molly," she explained.

He nodded glumly and she realised she was still in the doghouse. "You should."

She would have to grovel to Sam later, she realised as she headed for Molly's quarters, although one thing at a time.

Molly regarded the bottle in Abigail's hand. "I haven't got a corkscrew," she responded.

"It's screw top. You don't think the Twin Oaks pub is posh enough for wines with a cork, do you?"

Wordlessly, Molly scratched around on the floor under the bed and pulled out a couple of tumblers. She regarded them with a frown before disappearing into the cramped bathroom to rinse them out. It was the longest Molly had ever gone without saying a word to Abigail in her company.

"So," Abigail began once the wine was poured and Molly had perched on the other side of the bed. "I just wanted to clear the air. I shouldn't have lost my temper with you earlier and I'm sorry for what I said."

"Yeah, well, I was only trying to help you." Molly sipped at her wine and seemed to shed her veneer of hostility in seconds. "I've never seen you lose your temper before," she grinned at Abigail. "Moody really knows how to push your buttons. She's such a temperamental mare."

Abigail smiled back, finally relaxing now that she appeared to be forgiven.

"Don't forget the voucher I gave you at Christmas; it's still valid so if you want any lessons - it doesn't have to be on Moody, we can use any of the riding school horses, oh!" Inspiration hit Molly. "Why don't you join in one of the corporate sessions and you can learn all the basics. I think we have a team coming down from Birmingham on Monday, and if they are an odd number, I'm sure they won't mind you tagging along..."

Abigail sipped at her wine and tuned out. Molly was back to normal. Which just left Sam.

By the time Abigail left Molly's side of the house it was gone midnight and the wine was long consumed. She crept into the darkness of the silent kitchen and flicked on the lamp on the threshold of the lounge. The stillness meant that Sam had gone to bed, although Bessie sprang out of her basket in surprise and trotted over to greet Abigail, her tail thumping against the oak table leg. Abigail realised that she hadn't eaten since lunchtime, and raided the cupboards in the kitchen to no avail. There was an out of date crumpet lurking in the bread bin, which she toasted, spread with peanut butter and chomped down in three mouthfuls. The lack of food in the house was standard these days as her finances continued on a knife edge. The farm shop got used to her arriving shortly after they had marked down the goods that were about to reach their expiry date. She became creative with mis-matched ingredients, and fortunately neither Sam nor Molly complained.

She sat at the kitchen table mulling over the evening's events and was surprised to find that she had enjoyed Molly's company after all. Molly had told her all about her upbringing, opening up to describe how her mum had walked out on the family when she was just four, leaving her dad to bring up her, Kelly, the older sister, and big brother Luke. As a single parent, her father had struggled with money and ended up losing the family home, so the four of them found themselves living in a caravan on a farmer's field in return for helping out around the farm.

"It's how we ended up being such good riders," she explained. "He had loads of horses but we never knew why. He never did anything with them, so we took advantage and rode them every day. It got us out of the cramped caravan anyway."

The farmer knew Gordon Amblin, one of Gloucestershire's most renowned racehorse trainers, so Luke had become a work rider as soon as he left school, going on to become his apprentice, then his regular stable jockey.

"I feel sure he's going to win the Gold Cup next week," she admitted. "He's on such a roll in life, marrying Harriet, winning the King George and now riding the favourite for the Gold Cup."

Emboldened by the alcohol, Abigail asked Molly about her career path, hoping to gain more insight on her expulsion from racing college.

"Oh, I'm never going to be light enough to be a jockey," Molly laughed, avoiding the question. "But I want to work with horses so this opportunity you guys have given me is amazing and I can never thank you enough."

"You certainly spend enough time at the races," Abigail commented. It was a bit of a snipe, as she'd noticed how frequently Molly was accompanying Sam to the races these days. Partly she was grateful to have the peace and quiet to be left alone with her work, but the other jealous part of her resented the time Sam and Molly spent together sharing their mutual interest.

"Well, I have a lot of friends in racing, and it beats hanging around here. Oh! No offence!" She realised how rude that must have sounded, but Abigail waved it off. "Besides," Molly hesitated and smiled coyly, "there's someone I quite like, and it means I can see more of them."

"Oh?" Abigail felt the paranoia creep back in. Was she referring to Sam? "Tell me more."

Molly rose from the bed and grabbed a sweatshirt from the floor and tugged it on over her t-shirt. "Ah, it's early days," she replied dismissively. "Nothing to tell...yet."

What had she meant by that? Abigail pondered as she sat in the dim light of the lamp. Molly had made a wish on New Year's Eve to find the love of her life, and two months on, it appeared she was putting her plan into action.

Bessie placed her chin on Abigail's lap, drawing her attention back to the room. "I know," she told the dog. "It's late. I should get up to bed."

As she rose, she spotted her phone on the table. She hadn't even realised she didn't have it on her. She discovered that she'd missed three calls from Kate at various points in the evening, who had obviously given up hope of trying to speak to Abigail, and had texted instead.

"Give me a call - need to make arrangements for Wednesday. Exciting news about Mrs Angel's granddaughter."

Abigail glanced at the clock. It was too late to call Kate now, but she felt a twinge of nerves at the thought of appearing on *Where in the World*. It was still a couple of days away, so she tried to push it to the back of her mind and started her weary journey up the stairs to the bedroom. She could hear Sam's gentle snores as she reached the landing, and with relief undressed in silence and slipped carefully into the sheets without waking him.

24

As the studio lights dimmed, the eight contestants stepped out onto the set of '*Where in the World*' and Abigail bet that all of them felt as petrified as she did. The studio audience were already assembled, mainly pensioners enjoying a free afternoon of entertainment from what Abigail could tell from a cursory glance through the gloom.

Her heart thudded loudly in her chest and for the first time, she was regretting the decision to take part in the show. She could have backed out, but Mrs Angel seemed up for the adventure, and who was she to let down an eighty-nine-year-old?

Like a jury, the eight contestants lined up behind their plinths, which weren't as glamorous in reality as their shiny veneers appeared on TV. Mrs Angel smiled encouragingly at Abigail; she was oozing more confidence than her contestant partner. They were placed behind plinth one, which meant being first in the line-up. A stool was found for Mrs Angel to save her standing for a length of time.

The make-up artists buzzed around like flies, dabbing emergency powder on faces and applying the last-minute touch ups. The warm-up guy was cajoling the audience into practising their clapping, even though most seemed more distracted by fishing toffees from their pockets, or nudging their other half to point out that Henry Harding had just walked on set.

Henry Harding. Middle aged, suave and charming, almost to the point of being creepy. The old dears adored him, including Mrs Angel. He made his way down the line of contestants needlessly introducing himself, and asking the sorts of predictable questions that are thrown around when people are introduced at parties. Each contestant sported a name badge made from stiff cardboard and bearing the glittery blue colour scheme of the programme, so Henry already knew everybody's name. Mrs Angel had continued to insist she didn't want to use her Christian name and that she should be referred to as Mrs Angel. The producers argued that it was the policy to use Christian names only, so after much negotiation, Mrs Angel conceded to being called just "Angel". It suited her, and highlighted the point to Abigail that even she had never discovered her real name.

"And are you related?" Henry asked Mrs Angel and Abigail when he reached them. Abigail's mouth felt dry and she wondered whether she'd be able to get any words out once the filming began.

"Yes, we're sisters," joked Mrs Angel, provoking a hearty laugh from Henry.

"Just friends," Abigail managed to say in the intervening pause.

"Splendid," beamed Henry. "We'll be getting underway in just a moment, so good luck to both of you."

Five minutes later Henry was on his spot waiting for the opening titles to come crashing through the speakers. The lights dimmed and the audience hushed in anticipation. Abigail felt sick. Like a wave crashing onto the shore, the theme tune jolted the studio into silence, and the audience were prompted to applaud and cheer as the closing bars faded away. Black clothed crew dashed silently around the set like bats, moving cameras, operating booms and jumping up and down to motivate the audience.

As the applause died away, Henry beamed at the camera and gave the same opening spiel he recited each episode. Abigail and Mrs Angel could have chanted along with him. The first round was announced.

"As you know, in this round, the four pairs of contestants must work together to build up the jackpot by getting as many correct answers as possible," Henry explained to the camera. "One question each, and two hundred and fifty pounds for every correct answer. Beware though, a wrong answer or a pass means a deduction of two hundred and fifty pounds. If we're ready, let's begin."

A three second sting rang out from the speakers and the lighting changed. The spotlight was on them.

"Starting with Angel. What nationality was Chopin?"

"Polish," Mrs Angel fired back confidently.

"Correct. Abigail. Jamaica Inn is a novel set in which English county?"

"Oh, er... Cornwall," Abigail blurted as her panicked brain grasped the recollection.

"Correct."

Abigail relaxed a second and barely heard the answers of the other six as the questions worked down the line. Then Henry was back facing them.

"Angel. Which ocean is home to the island of Bora Bora?"

"Oh," Mrs Angel paused thoughtfully. "I'd imagine it's the Indian Ocean."

"Correct. Abigail, The Beatles played at the Cavern Club over 300 times… in which city?"

"Liverpool."

"Correct."

As questions fired down the line once more, Abigail realised that this was just like being at home and watching the show. She needn't panic, she knew the answers, and nobody was out to trick her. Just as the circuit of questions swooped back to the start of the line, the buzzer sounded to denote the end of the round.

"Congratulations! Only Tony tripped up there, losing you money, but otherwise you earned three thousand five hundred pounds!" The audience were encouraged to cheer. "We'll add that to yesterday's rollover jackpot of twelve thousand five hundred pounds, taking today's jackpot total to sixteen thousand pounds!" This prompted more whooping from the audience, a sting of sound and a change again in the lighting.

They took a short break whilst the make-up artists swarmed once again, and crew tinkered with elements of the set. In the audience, discussion and laughter broke out, along with synchronised rustling of sweet wrappers.

"So round two," announced Henry into the lens, "is on the buzzer. It's a point building round, where you can score fifty points for each correct answer, but you'll lose one hundred points if you buzz in and give an incorrect answer. At the end of the round we will have to say goodbye to the two pairs with the lowest scores."

Abigail's hand hovered over her buzzer. At home, she and Mrs Angel could be quick as lightning shouting their answers at the television set.

"Our first category is cuisine." Henry paused and glanced at the contestants to make sure they understood. "In Spain, a meal comprised of several small dishes to be shared is called what?"

Abigail's hand slammed on the buzzer at the same time as three other contestants, but miraculously her reaction time had been fractionally quicker and the question was hers.

"Tapas," she replied, remembering fondly the times that she and Nadine had shared dishes together at a charming Spanish cafe on Broadway Market. It was hardly Barcelona's Las Ramblas, but they liked the place.

"Correct. That's fifty points to Abigail and Angel. Our next category is history. What year was the Great Fire of London?"

Mrs Angel slapped the buzzer but a dizzy looking girl with platinum hair was quicker.

"Was it ten sixty-six?" she asked vaguely, as nonchalantly as querying the price on a loaf of bread.

"I'm afraid not, Cara. You and Tim lose one hundred points. The next category is art."

Mrs Angel straightened up. Art and music were definitely her bag. "In which country does the Bayeux tapestry hang?"

Mrs Angel almost shouted out the answer before remembering to slam her hand on the buzzer.

"France," she answered, and then nudged Abigail as Henry confirmed she was correct and the pair had now accumulated one hundred points in total. Abigail glowed inside, but realised that one false answer could wipe their score.

The next question concerning the capital of Malta, was incorrectly answered by Tony, who consequently lost one hundred points for his pair, then Leigh beat Mrs Angel to the buzzer to correctly answer that Bath used to part of the county of Avon.

"Our next category is fashion," announced Henry, glancing momentarily at Abigail. She had to get this right, surely? "What am I? I am a long, loose-fitting unisex outer robe with full sleeves, worn in North Africa. I am generally made of two types of material, cotton for summer wear and coarse wool for the winter."

Tentatively Abigail struck the buzzer. "Is it a Djellaba?" she asked as timidly as Cara had done a few questions ago. She could visualise the garment, but wasn't one hundred percent certain of its name.

"It is indeed. Well done!" Henry replied admiringly. Mrs Angel beamed at her. With one hundred and fifty points, they were well ahead of the other pairs now.

"Our next category is sport," Henry said. Abigail and Mrs Angel groaned inwardly. Neither of them knew much about sport. "Which racecourse hosts the Ebor festival each year?"

Abigail couldn't believe her luck and her hand slammed on the buzzer before any of the other contestants could process the question. Sam hadn't stopped boasting about his wins at the four-day race meeting last August.

"York," she announced with a laugh, disbelieving the way the round was playing out.

"Very well done. You're a step closer to going through to the next round."

Nigel got a question correct concerning the nationality of the Dominican Republic, whilst Tim pulled back one correct answer about German sausages. Abigail could sense the time limit of the round would be drawing to a close shortly, but they should stay safely in the lead.

"Our category is language," Henry continued. Neither Abigail nor Mrs Angel had strong foreign language skills. "What does the Spanish word 'Diablo' mean?"

Abigail's reflexes slammed the buzzer. How could she forget the horse that had thrown off Sam at Newmarket last month?

"Devil," she replied, as the gong sounded to denote the end of the round.

"Well, this is easy, isn't it?" Mrs Angel confessed to Abigail once the cameras had stopped running to give them a break between rounds. Poor Cara and Tim, and Tony and Mary were heading home after scoring negative points. That left Mrs Angel and Abigail to face Leigh and Nigel in the third round. Only one pair could survive to the final round.

"OK, to the third round," Henry announced. "Angel and Abigail are taking on Leigh and Nigel in the picture round to try and get that place in the final to be in with a chance of winning the jackpot of sixteen thousand pounds." The audience cheered on cue. Sixteen thousand pounds would be a dream for Abigail right now.

As the highest scoring pair, Abigail and Mrs Angel went first to identify a location from a photo that flicked up on the monitor in front of them. They were allowed to confer and it was a race to see which pair could get three pictures identified correctly first.

Their picture showed a huge red-bricked dome. It almost seemed too obvious.

"That's the Royal Albert Hall," said Mrs Angel without bothering to confer with Abigail.

"It is indeed. Nigel and Leigh, here's your picture."

An image appeared of an impressive waterfall, with a rainbow streaking across the image. "I think that is Victoria Falls," Nigel murmured to Leigh. She cocked her head and looked doubtful. "I think that's too obvious. It could be Iguaçu Falls in Brazil."

Nigel shrugged. "I have no idea what Iguaçu falls look like, but we can go with that if you want."

"We think it's Iguaçu Falls," Leigh said to Henry.

Henry teased the pairs with an agonising pause, and then cocked his head with a sympathetic smile. "Oh, I'm sorry. Nigel was right, it was Victoria Falls, but I have to take your answer Leigh. That means Angel and Abigail lead one nil. Here's your next picture."

The image on the screen was taken from inside a large glass domed roof, with a pond full of pancake shaped water lilies floating on the surface.

"Oh, isn't that beautiful?" sighed Mrs Angel.

"It is indeed," replied Henry, "but do you know where it is?"

It looked familiar to Abigail; a place that she visited as a child. Maybe she'd been there on a school trip. She had vague memories of being hot and bored, the air stuffy and oppressive under the glass.

"Could it be Kew Gardens?" murmured Mrs Angel to Abigail. Yes, that was it. The school trip to Kew where fifty sulky teenagers had trudged through immaculately manicured lawns, admired patches of snowdrops, and bickered irritably with each other before spending all their lunch money on sweets in the gift shop.

It was Kew Gardens, and that put them two nil up. The next picture showed a waterfront flanked with a brightly painted terrace of tall buildings. The blue of the water contrasted with the vibrant red, orange, yellow and turquoise of the facades. Abigail was glad it wasn't their picture, as she had no idea where it was taken. Fortunately for Leigh, she recognised it instantly.

"Oh, I went there last year; it's Copenhagen. It's a wonderful City."

"That's right, Copenhagen it is, getting you back in the game. It's two one, so if Angel and Abigail get this next one correct, they are through to the final."

Abigail had seen enough episodes to know that the fifth picture was always tougher. Her heart rate increased in anticipation. The picture flashed up and she gave an involuntary gasp. Racehorses were in the foreground, captured in full gallop. The picture was taken at night, and in the background vast glassy lights shining out from the grandstand lit up like a beacon against the inky sky.

"To take you through to the final round, can you tell me where in the world is that?"

"Is that Ascot?" Mrs Angel asked Abigail, peering closer to the screen.

"No, no..." Abigail hushed her. She had to get this right. "They don't run in darkness at Ascot. It's not in the UK... that grandstand is really flashy, but it's not America because they're not running on the dirt... At least, I don't think they run on grass anywhere in the States, but I could be wrong."

She racked her brain, willing inspiration to come to her. It could be Paris. She had no idea what the grandstands were like in France, but she didn't recall Sam watching any of the big races in darkness. Or could it be Melbourne?

"It must be somewhere hot for them to run at night," offered Mrs Angel.

"Oh!" The desert, she thought. Money, flashy, it had to be Dubai. She just had to remember what the racecourse was called. Sam had been talking about it this week, the Dubai World Cup was next Saturday night. There had even been a headline on the front page of the *Racing Post* yesterday about Dan Costler, the current champion flat jockey, it read "May Dan shine in..."

"Meydan!" She gasped with relief. The headline had been "May Dan shine in Meydan".

Oh, thank God.

Henry's eyebrows shot up in admiration. "Is that your final answer?"

"Yes, it is."

"Well, congratulations, you're absolutely right and that takes you through to our grand final!"

Ten minutes later Abigail sat in the glass booth, perched on a plastic stool, listening to cheesy pop music being pumped through headphones that she feared would ruin her hair. She wore chunky dark glasses but it wasn't necessary to blindfold her, as she had closed her eyes to try and calm her nerves. Mrs Angel was out with Henry answering questions about herself. In a few moments it would be Abigail's turn to try and match her answers to win the sixteen-thousand-pound jackpot prize. In her head Abigail had already worked out where the winnings would go. Between debts, bills and new stock, her share of eight thousand would be eaten, but Abigail suspected Mrs Angel would insist on donating her half too. She could hear Mrs Angel's voice in her head, 'What am I going to do with eight thousand pounds? You take it, you can use it more than me." Abigail would protest, but it would be futile. She'd take it, and make Mrs Angel a present to say thank you. Probably a nice scarf.

"Abigail, come and join us!" Henry's voice in her headphones made her jump.

The audience clapped politely as she emerged from the glass booth, and stood with her back to Mrs Angel facing Henry.

"There are just three questions standing between you and sixteen thousand pounds," Henry recapped unnecessarily. "I asked Mrs Angel three questions and she gave me her answers. All we need you to do is to match those same answers. Ready?"

Abigail nodded.

"I asked Angel where she went for her first foreign holiday. Did she say Paris, did she say that she's never been abroad, or did she say Las Vegas?"

Abigail grinned at the thought of Mrs Angel in Las Vegas. She allowed herself to relax a little; she knew this one.

"She said she's never been abroad." The audience erupted into applause.

"That's correct. For the second question, we asked Angel where her favourite beach was, and why. She said it was Margate, but can you tell us why?"

Abigail remembered being told the story. She smiled in memory. "Because that's where her husband proposed to her." The audience's reaction told her she was correct again, even before Henry confirmed it. There was now a tense atmosphere in the studio as Abigail was one question away from winning sixteen thousand pounds.

"So, Abigail, we arrive at the big one. This is your third and final question. We asked Angel where she would choose to visit - if she had to pick between Venice, San Francisco or Sydney. What did she say?"

The silence was excruciating. Abigail wasn't sure, but she dismissed San Francisco straight away. Mrs Angel had a low tolerance of American people and the hills would be a nuisance. She suspected that Mrs Angel would consider Sydney too far away. A twenty-four-hour jaunt on a plane is unpleasant for people her own age, let alone a woman approaching ninety. Which left Venice. Yes, thought Abigail, Mrs Angel would enjoy the art and culture, and travelling along the canals. Surely, she had said Venice?

"I think she chose Venice," stated Abigail confidently, expecting to hear the audience burst into applause. Instead, there was a collective groan, and Abigail knew instantly she'd messed up. Bugger, bugger and bugger.

"Oh, I'm so sorry, Abigail. That's not the right answer."

Mrs Angel turned around to face Abigail and gave her a hug as they'd witnessed so many losing contestants do in the past.

"Never mind, dear," Mrs Angel whispered in her ear, as carefree as if Abigail had apologised for getting a bit of mud on the carpet. Not letting sixteen thousand pounds slip through their fingers.

They turned to face Henry.

"Angel said she'd like to go to Sydney so that she could hear a concert at the Opera House," he confirmed, as if it mattered. Abigail felt foolish and wanted to run backstage and kick something. Hard. Instead she forced a smile on her face.

"Well, I'm so sorry you didn't win today's jackpot, which will roll over to tomorrow's show. Have you both had a nice time?"

"It's been lovely, we've had a great time," Mrs Angel replied, and Abigail nodded dumbly at her side. She couldn't trust herself to speak and could feel her bottom lip wobble. All she could think about was how she was going to clear her debts now.

25

Abigail, Kate and Mrs Angel arrived at the hotel each with very different state of mind. Abigail felt peevish, but was unsure who to direct her anger at. It wasn't Mrs Angel's fault that she had said Sydney, and it wasn't her own fault that she'd guessed incorrectly, but it was so frustrating that they came so fucking close to winning the jackpot. Henry had wrapped up the show with his well-rehearsed spiel, being jolly and optimistically inviting the viewers to tune in again tomorrow.

As for Mrs Angel, she was still riding the exhilaration that came from a break of routine. She'd had a thoroughly enjoyable afternoon out, although she was beginning to tire now. They'd been on the go since the crack of dawn, getting her suitcase into Kate's tiny boot, then having to walk from the public car park to the studio. There had been a lot of waiting around at the studio, and shuffling around the set. Then the walk back to the car to get them all to the hotel. If Kate had struggled to transport two cases, as well as a wobbly nearly-ninety-year-old lady, she didn't complain.

By contrast, Abigail had travelled up from the New Forest into Waterloo and breezed across London's tube network to meet them. She was back on home turf, and realised suddenly how much she missed the energy of London.

There was just time for a quick bite to eat at an overpriced fast food cafe before heading to the studios. For a thirty-minute show recording, the trio spent most of the day in the building, so Kate nervously glanced at her watch as she checked them into the hotel afterwards. It was nearly six o'clock and she had arranged for Mrs Angel's granddaughter, Isabella, to come and surprise her gran at the hotel's restaurant at seven. Mrs Angel knew nothing of the arrangement, so Kate hoped nothing was going to disrupt her careful planning.

"Oh, this is lovely!" Mrs Angel gushed, taking in the neat family room. Kate and Abigail had agreed to share the double bed and Mrs Angel take the single, which was closest to the bathroom. Kate wheeled the cases to the window, where there was more space and Abigail tossed her backpack onto the bed and kicked off her shoes.

"So, we've got about forty five minutes before we need to head to the restaurant," Kate reminded the group. She'd taken on role as Mum.

"I think I'll have a shower, if no-one minds," said Mrs Angel, peering approvingly into the bathroom. Kate glanced at her watch anxiously but both girls nodded.

"Have you had any update from Isabella?" Abigail asked Kate when the sound of the running water told them it was safe to talk about the secret plan.

"Nope," sighed Kate. "The last text I had from her was last weekend and she just said 'let me know when and where and I'll try and make it.' There was no acknowledgement from her when I sent through the details. I've tried ringing her a couple of times but it just goes to voicemail, so I've left messages with the details again, you know, trying to keep it all light and breezy so she doesn't think I'm a weird stalker or anything."

Abigail pulled a face to indicate that she had little hope that Isabella would show up. "If Mrs Angel was my grandmother, I'd walk over hot coals to see her." She pulled out a clean top from her bag, a new creation that she needed to get onto her website before the season ended. "I can't believe she hasn't seen her in over three years, especially now she's living in London. She could easily jump on a train to Gloucestershire."

Kate was grinning at her friend. "I dare you to say that to her face."

"The way I'm feeling now, I might just."

Kate's face fell. "Why, what's the matter?"

Abigail hesitated. It sounded childish, even in her head, but she trusted Kate enough to be honest with her. "I just thought we would win that money this afternoon, that's all. I'm really annoyed at myself." Kate didn't know how to respond, and sat thoughtfully on the bed watching as Abigail tugged on her clean blouse and surveyed the look in the mirror. "I could have done with that money," she continued. It felt good to confide in someone at last. She hadn't told anyone about the debts she was building up. "I borrowed money to pay for the stall at MODA, and as soon as money comes in, it's allocated for the next batch of fabric or the next bill that needs paying. That jackpot would have made a significant difference."

"Oh Abi," Kate sighed. The sound of the shower stopped and instinctively Kate lowered her voice, despite the thick wall between the bedroom and bathroom and the limitations of Mrs Angel's hearing. "I'm sure Mrs Angel would help you out."

"No, no," Abigail was adamant. "She's done plenty. It's my mess; I'll get myself out of it. I just need to work a bit harder and catch that lucky break."

Kate looked thoughtful. "Could you do a bit of temping work, you know just a day or two a week to bring some extra money in?"

Abigail thought of the isolated location of the stables and wondered where the nearest office needing a temp would be. Hampshire was a far cry from London, especially as she didn't have her own transport. Then Sol's words suddenly came back to her. Molly asking Anna at the pub whether there was any work for her. Perhaps that wouldn't be such a bad course of action if there were any jobs going. The pub was right on the doorstep and any work may be cash in hand. Yes, if Sol's insinuation was right, it could drive Molly and Sam together in the evenings, but it could also take the financial pressure off her a little if she could earn some cash to cover the food bills. "I'll give it some thought," Abigail replied as Mrs Angel emerged from the bathroom.

"These dressing gowns are a bit posh, aren't they?" she swooned, stroking the fluff covering her chest. "We may not have taken home the jackpot but at least we got some hospitality out of the production company."

By 6.45pm they were all ready to make their way up to the "Glasserie" - the restaurant on the 22nd floor, housed under a dome of glass and fairy lights with views out over North London.

Mrs Angel gasped as the lift doors opened with a ping and the calm of the restaurant hit them.

"Let's have a drink first," instructed Kate, trying her best to act normal. Mrs Angel was so enamoured with her surroundings that Abigail doubted she would ever suspect anything. 6.50pm. Kate and Abigail both scanned the other customers in the bar, looking out for a lone blonde head that could be Isabella, but it was mainly family groups catching up, and the after-work crowd winding down. After ordering drinks and taking their seats in crushed velvet armchairs, the trio all sighed with a weary relief that their stressful day was drawing to a close.

"Maybe we should apply to go on another TV show," remarked Mrs Angel, flashing a cheeky grin to demonstrate she was only joking. "If they put you up in hotels like this and pay for lovely meals, we could just leave home and be serial game show contestants."

"We might even win occasionally!" Abigail threw back sullenly.

"Oh, don't beat yourself up about it. It was just one of those things that we didn't match answers, the luck of the draw."

A waiter glided to their table, hugging menus to his chest. "Your table is ready when you are," he said addressing Mrs Angel as the eldest of the group. "Would you like to stay here and wait for the other member of your party, or make your way to the table now?"

Mrs Angel frowned momentarily and opened her mouth to contradict the waiter. Kate jumped in. "We'll just wait here a few more moments," she replied.

He nodded respectfully and retreated.

"Sam said he might be able to join us," Kate lied. "He's been racing at...er...nearby, and thinks he may be able to join us."

"Well, I hope he doesn't want to stay the night otherwise your double bed is going to get very cosy," Mrs Angel joked.

Another fifteen minutes passed and hopes were fading that Isabella was going to show. The waiter hovered nearby until the embarrassment was too much for Abigail. She made a show of retrieving her mobile phone from the depths of her handbag and clicking a few buttons.

"Oh, I've had a text from Sam." It was her turn to tell fibs and she hated doing so to Mrs Angel. "He says sorry, but he's not able to join us after all. There's a massive tailback on the motorway so he's just going to head for home instead."

"It would have been nice to see him," Mrs Angel admitted, "but it won't be long until Robin holds the Grand National party. I trust you'll be coming to the village for that."

Before either girl had chance to reply, the waiter's sixth sense kicked in and he reappeared beside them, delighted when they agreed to be led to their table.

Abigail fumed at Isabella all through the meal and lay in bed later that night composing a tersely worded text message in her head. She was still distracted the following morning, especially once she'd hugged her goodbyes to Kate and Mrs Angel and made her way separately across London to Waterloo.

It was a beautiful spring morning, with a cloudless blue sky, so Abigail impulsively jumped off the tube earlier than she needed to in order to walk along the river. There was no hurry to get back to the stables. Sam was no doubt travelling to some far-flung racecourse, and all that awaited her was a silent house and a sewing machine, or a chatty Molly. She wasn't in the mood to face either.

Tourists flooded the South Bank, flocks of young Asian travellers taking selfies in front of the London Eye, and pointing excitedly at the Houses of Parliament and Big Ben. Abigail barely noticed them. She was musing over missing out on the *Where in the World* jackpot, Isabella standing them up, and whether to call in at the Twin Oaks pub and enquire about work. Harriet had to call her name twice before she snapped out of her reverie.

"It IS you," Harriet exclaimed, relived that she wasn't randomly calling to a stranger. Abigail recognised the tall blonde clutching at her arm, but took a moment to place her.

"Hi...Harriet." Relief flooded her as she remembered her name. She hadn't seen Harriet since the wedding last summer. The wedding where she had first met Molly. Wow, time had flown.

"Lovely to see you. Are you here for work?" Harriet asked Abigail, looking at her quizzically.

"No, I came up yesterday and spent some time with Kate." Abigail wasn't sure how well Harriet knew Kate so had to frame the relationship in racing terms. "Kate O'Casey, Callum's ex-wife?"

"Oh ya, I remember Kate. She's got that toddler." Abigail wasn't keen to mention the appearance on the quiz show, and turned the same question back to Harriet before there could be any more questions about what they got up to.

"I've come up to meet Mummy later. We're going to get some outfits for Cheltenham ladies' day, you know, Gold Cup. Talking of Callum O'Casey. If he beats my Luke again, there will be trouble. Say, I'm at a loose end for an hour if you wanted to grab a drink?"

This was Abigail's opportunity to remind Harriet about her offer to photograph her collection, and she had nothing to rush back for.

"Great, I could use a coffee."

"Oh, Abi," Harriet pushed her designer sunglasses to the end of her nose so that Abigail could register the mock horror in her eyes. "I was thinking of something stronger. It's nearly midday!"

Taking command, Harriet led Abigail across Westminster Bridge Road to a swanky cocktail bar. At this time of the day it had barely opened and was deserted, the dim lighting of the interior not distinguishing day from night. Abigail was suddenly struck by the thought of paying for drinks here. She had barely enough cash to scrape together money for a coffee, let alone a cocktail, and any plastic she tried to use ran the risk of being declined. It was too late now, she figured, and prayed that this one was on Harriet.

"Harriet, darling," the bar tender greeted with a foreign accent Abigail couldn't place. "How lovely to see you." Clearly Harriet was a regular.

"You too, Paco," she replied with less enthusiasm. She placed her oversized handbag onto one of the many brown leather sofas and indicated to Abigail that she should take a seat. "I'll have a bottle of the usual."

"Coming right up."

"I trust champagne is OK for you," Harriet said as an afterthought to Abigail. It didn't seem she had a choice in the matter. Harriet took off her red woollen coat and settled into the sofa facing Abigail, gently folding her coat onto the seat next to her. She slid her redundant sunglasses onto her head and leaned forward, assaulting Abigail with a waft of Chanel.

"So, fill me in."

Abigail spoke about the stables, being careful to be tactful about Molly, who was now related to Harriet. Any negative feedback would probably be relayed back to Molly's brother, Luke, who was presumably more protective over her than Harriet was. She paused as Paco placed flutes in front of them and expertly poured bubbles into them using only one hand guiding the base of the bottle. He nestled it into a bucket of ice in a stand next to them and smiled graciously.

"Be a darling, Paco, and stick it on Daddy's account."

"Certainly, Madame."

Abigail mirrored Harriett and picked up her flute by the stem.

"Cheers!" They clinked glasses and Abigail thanked "Daddy" in her head.

"And how's the fashion empire?" Harriet asked.

"I'm building very gradually," Abigail replied, choosing her words with care.

"Oh my God, I've just had THE most amazing idea," Harriett chipped in. "You could make the dresses for Mummy and me! We were going to go to Regent Street to buy them, but you could do something amazing for us, I'm sure. I've seen a few of your Instagram posts, and love your boldness with colour and quirky design. Mummy and I like to stand out."

Abigail's heart raced momentarily. This family seemingly had very deep pockets.

"When's Gold Cup Day?" She asked, feeling that she should already know this. The *Racing Post* littered the lounge daily but Abigail paid no attention to its headlines ordinarily. Except "May Dan shine in Meydan".

"Next Thursday."

Her heart sank. Six days was not enough time to design and execute two dresses of the quality the Whittington family would expect. It must have showed on her face, as Harriet was quick to shrug off the idea.

"No, that's too soon - don't worry. You could make us some for Newmarket Guineas instead. That's in May," she added, sensing the question was about to fall from Abigail's lips. "I guess you don't do the millinery too, do you, but that's OK, if we sign off the colours and material, I can get something to co-ordinate from Carrie. She makes the most wonderfully quirky designs."

Abigail reached for her backpack and squirmed at its tattered appearance in such an opulent setting. She dug out her notebook and began to scribble some notes.

"The other thing you mentioned you might be able to do," Abigail remarked, emboldened by the champagne, "is to get your bridesmaids around and have a photoshoot with some of my dresses?"

She watched as Harriet took a ladylike sip and pondered. "Oh, my goodness, you're absolutely right. I did say that, didn't I?" She placed her champagne on the table and picked up her phone - sparkling in its diamond encrusted case - and flicked through a few screens. "I'm so up for that. It'll be such a scream. Right, my hens are coming to Daddy's place for a clay pigeon shoot at the end of April. We can get some of the hunters together and do a photoshoot of the girls draped over the horses. How does that sound?"

It sounded just what Abigail needed, and the girls agreed a time and date. By the time Abigail left the bar to catch her train she was floating. Whether that was from the fizz or the business progress, she couldn't be too sure.

26

"Welcome to Twin Oaks Equestrian Centre," Molly sang to the group assembled in front of her in the yard. It was a beautiful spring morning, with blue sky and birdsong, and Abigail had decided to cash in the Christmas voucher to attend a corporate session. The date of *Raceday One*'s visit was getting even closer, and Abigail realised she had no idea how to groom or tack up. She stood at the end of the group in her barely worn Christmas jodhpurs, clutching her flawless helmet. Her riding boots were a little more worn. She'd found them useful for the muddy dog walks and wading across the many streams and brooks that crisscrossed the undulating land of the New Forest.

It was three days after the disappointment of losing the *Where in the World* final, and the frustration of being stood up by Isabella, but time had made Abigail calm down and take it on the chin. She focussed on getting her collection ready for the photoshoot with Harriet and her hens, and when her fingers wandered to her phone ready to compose a terse text to Isabella, she forced herself to abandon the idea. It was none of her business. She had other challenges to overcome.

"My name's Molly and I run the centre along with top jockey Sam Ashington. Unfortunately, he can't be with us today as he's racing at Southwell this afternoon..." There was an audible groan from a few of the group, which impressed Abigail. She still underestimated the fame her boyfriend attracted within the small set of race goers around the country. "...but not to worry, as you're in safe hands with me." She chuckled at what she thought was a joke, and a few of the group smiled along supportively. Molly had a way of instantly engaging people, Abigail noted. Her face lit up when confronted with an attentive audience and she clearly relished being able to take charge and command respect.

She outlined some of the activities of the day and split the group down into three smaller teams. Abigail found herself with a bald engineer called Ken, a skinny pale girl called Ali and a forthright Asian lady who insisted everyone call her H because "no-one can pronounce my name properly and it gets embarrassing watching people try".

"The first thing we're going to do is a basic groom, then plait a mane, and we'll see which team win the prize for the best turned out horse."

"It's like the generation game, this," quipped Ken. "I wonder if we win a cuddly toy?"

Molly ran through the safety aspects, then introduced the range of brushes and what they needed to be used for. She proceeded to lead out Womble and systematically demonstrated to the group how to brush and comb the horse. The group watched in rapt silence as she proceeded to plait the mane and create a chequered effect on Womble's hind quarters. She then led out a horse for each group and set thirty minutes to complete their creations.

"Would you like to take Muppet?" She asked Abigail's group. This meant nothing to the guests, but Abigail knew that it was directed at her. "It's a good way to bond with a horse," she explained, as she led Muppet from the stable on the end. The mare was caked in dried mud and had a woodland mix of twigs tangled into her mane.

"So, decide amongst yourself who's going to do what. We need someone to hold her, two people to do the brushing and someone to comb and plait the mane."

Ken volunteered to hold Muppet's rope, the easiest job, whilst Ali said she was artistic and would like to plaint the mane. Abigail took the first round of brushing, and found it surprisingly satisfying to dislodge the mud and see plumes of dust flying off her coat. To Abigail's relief, Muppet appeared to be in an obliging mood and stood patiently as the amateurs worked on her.

"Most horses enjoy being brushed," Molly reassured the group. "It's like a massage for them. And we all feel better after a trip to the hairdressers, don't we ladies?" Molly giggled, but Abigail couldn't imagine Molly ever going to the hairdressers. She had a recollection of discovering Sam and Molly cutting each other's hair in the kitchen one evening, but suspected that Molly's unruly mop of hair had never experienced the professional touch of a qualified stylist.

Within thirty minutes Muppet was transformed from scruffy nag to glistening thoroughbred. Abigail felt proud to think that the horse belonged to her. Each group then voted on which team should win the grooming round, and Abigail felt a swell of elation when all three groups chose their efforts as the winning one.

The next task was cleaning tack. "This is genius," thought Abigail, observing the paying guests competing to win the shiniest saddle round. The business was getting income from people carrying out tasks that would normally require paid staff to do. Molly had a couple of students coming for riding lessons tomorrow and the ponies were pristine and you could eat your dinner off the tack. Maybe they could incorporate a dressmaking challenge, she thought with a smile.

At lunchtime, the group traipsed up to the Twin Oaks pub where Anna led them through to the function room. A long table was set with places for them all, generous ploughman's lunches already awaiting the guests. Abigail took advantage of a good meal, knowing there was little in the cupboards for later.

"Looks like you enjoyed that," Anna commented as she collected up the plates. Abigail rose from her seat and started to collect up the other plates from around her. She could at least prove helpful in return for the free meal. "Mind you, that ham from the farm shop is delicious, isn't it?" Abigail sensed now was a good time to enquire about work at the pub. If Molly had already broached the subject with Anna as Sol claimed, the question wouldn't come as a surprise to her.

"It's great," agreed Abigail, following Anna out towards the kitchen. "I just have to stop Bessie stealing it off the plate when I'm not looking." Navigating past the row of chairs, the pair entered through to the confines of the kitchen. Abigail was surprised how small it was for churning out dozens of meals.

"Just stack the plates by the sink," Anna instructed. "There's no such thing as a dishwasher I'm afraid... well, we do have one. It's called Paul, but it tends to be unreliable!"

Her comment was the perfect prompt.

"I meant to say," Abigail began casually, "if you were ever looking for an extra pair of hands to work in the pub, or kitchen, would you consider me? It would get me out of the four walls of the house at least."

Anna looked surprised, and hesitated in her answer. In that split second a whirlwind of paranoid thoughts span through Abigail's mind. Maybe there was a job available and Anna didn't trust her, or worse still, she was aware of Sam and Molly carrying on and didn't want to be responsible for creating more opportunity for them to be together...alone.

"Well, I'll bear it in mind, love, but between Paul and I, we can usually manage."

Ah. Maybe there was never any possibility of a job. Abigail shrugged, as though it wasn't important, but her heart sank. No cash in hand, no extra pin money to tide her over.

Before she could give it any more thought, Molly came crashing through the kitchen door. There wasn't space in the cramped kitchen for her to come any further, so she hovered in the doorway.

"There you are, I'm just herding people up to head back to the stables. We'll do the tacking up next and take the horses down to the field for the riding games. Although that guy in the red t-shirt is a bit of a worry, I don't know how he's going to mount a horse."

"Yeah, I'm coming," Abigail replied. "I was just asking Anna about any jobs going here."

"Oh? Who for?"

Abigail took a second to register the expression on Molly's face. "Me."

"Blimey, you glutton for punishment. You already work long, hard hours on your dresses, and keeping the stables running, and doing all the promotions and accounts. You haven't got time to work here too."

Abigail smiled in thanks at Anna and followed Molly out of the kitchen and into the bright sunshine. Molly's reaction seemed genuine, leaving Abigail was more puzzled than ever. Her words didn't sound like those of someone who had already asked Anna about jobs at the pub. But Sol had seemed so certain he heard correctly. Someone was clearly lying, but who? Abigail was too scared to find out.

27

"You know you mentioned a holiday," Sam said casually that evening as he took a soapy dinner plate from the draining board. He thought he was helping by drying the dishes that Abigail had just washed, but he was being so slow about it, Abigail wished he'd just leave them to dry on their own. It had been another makeshift meal cobbled together from an out of date packet of super noodles, with fish fingers and peas that she found lurking at the bottom of the freezer. Abigail placed the last saucepan onto the pile of plates on draining board, its suds sliding lazily across the surface and popping into thin air. Abigail couldn't remember mentioning a holiday. It was the last topic she would wish to raise after admonishing Sam for wanting to go to Las Vegas with his winnings a few months ago.

The prospect of a holiday was appealing now, though. Although her own finances remained precarious, the bookings were starting to become more regular for the corporate sessions, and Sam had accumulated a decent amount of prize money on the racecourse over the past few weeks. Ironically, just as Sam was supposed to be considering his retirement from racing, so his ranking as a jockey increased. Like premiership footballers, the more wins you clocked up on the racecourse, the more in demand you became, attracting the attention of elite trainers with better horses that would bring in more winners. And so the virtuous circle continued, trapping Sam in its grip.

Abigail wiped her hands on the towel and turned to give Sam her full attention.

"I did?" She wasn't going to contradict him if this conversation was about to lead to the prospect of sipping cocktails on sun drenched loungers listening to the Mediterranean lap the shore. The volume of work she'd absorbed over the winter months was taking its toll on her, and a holiday sounded the perfect remedy.

"Well, I was thinking we could book a posh hotel in Newmarket for our birthday night."

Every ounce of optimism drained from Abigail in an instant. She should have known that Sam's definition of a holiday would involve a bloody racecourse. Sharing the same birthday was always going to mean compromise, she realised. Their previous birthday had been spent at Ascot. Admittedly, she officially became his girlfriend that day, and it was a brilliant day, but this year she hoped for more.

"Sounds great," she replied sarcastically.

"It's the Newmarket Festival," Sam continued, oblivious to her tone. "I'm riding Flora for Dad in the 1000 Guineas, who has a brilliant chance, and then guess who might be riding the Queen's mount in the 2000 Guineas?"

"Bloody hell, Sam," chirped up Molly from the sofa. She put down the dog-eared copy of Heat magazine, and swivelled around to face the pair. "You've been asked to ride for Her Maj? That is bloody epic, mate."

Unimpressed, Abigail filled the kettle to make a pot of tea.

"Well it's not official yet," Sam replied modestly, addressing Molly. "Ryan should normally take the ride but it's looking like he'll be heading to the Kentucky Derby, so I'm next in line. But if that doesn't come off, I have a few other irons in the fire, as they say."

"I can just imagine the Queen having that conversation with her trainer." Molly cleared her throat and attempted a poor impression of the Queen. "I say, I rather like the way that young boy Sam Ashington rides. He's not bad at all... for a *ginger*."

They both giggled, and Abigail realised that this conversation was straying way off track. It had started out as a promise of a holiday.

"Queen or no Queen, I really don't think it's much of a holiday treat for me," Abigail stated. She was aware she sounded petulant, but couldn't care less. Newmarket, honestly! The kettle clicked and gratefully Abigail turned away and began to make the drinks.

"But it'll be a really posh hotel, you know," Sam persisted, "one with a spa and a five-star restaurant."

Abigail jettisoned a soggy used teabag into the bin with peevish force that caused Sam to pause.

"Sam, if you're racing, you won't be drinking alcohol, so I'll be supping the booze on my own, and we'll barely making the most of the restaurant as you nibble on less than a thousand calories a day. Then you'll swap your smart suit for jogging bottoms and a hoodie whilst you run around Newmarket trying to sweat out a few pounds to make weight..."

"But you can dress up in all your girly finery and watch me storm over the winning line to the roar of the crowd.."

"And the cheer of Her Majesty!" Molly quipped unhelpfully. "God, I'd give my right kidney to go."

An awkward pause fell over the trio and Abigail finished making the tea and carried it over silently to the sofas. Sheepishly Sam wiped the last plate on the pile and hung the damp tea towel on the rail before joining them. Molly went back to turning pages in her magazine, but Abigail swore she caught a glimpse of a momentary look passing between them as Sam sat down.

"It's just not my idea of a birthday treat," continued Abigail in what she hoped was a more conciliatory tone. "I think I'll stay here, and maybe you and I can take a break somewhere once the festival is over? Courtesy of your winnings on Her Majesty's mount?"

"Whatever," Sam responded, defeated. He reached for the remote control and turned the telly on. The theme tune to Mastermind blared out and indicated that the discussion was over.

28

A few days later, and the *Raceday One* filming was approaching fast. In an attempt to further bond with Muppet, Abigail was spending more time with the mare. She rubbed the patch on Muppet's forehead where the chestnut hair gave way to her distinctive white star. It was an identical marking to Muppet's father, a Kempton favourite called Moody Master, now sire to hundreds of thoroughbreds across the country. Abigail felt that Muppet was finally starting to build a rapport with her, and she would now trot over to the fence to greet her when Abigail approached. Molly said that this was probably more to do with the hope or expectation that there could be some food treats lurking on Abigail's person.

"I wish I had the courage to ride you on my own," she murmured to the mare. It was Good Friday and they were alone again, with Molly joining Sam at the Lambourn Open Day, where the racing community came together to raise money for charity. Abigail had been tempted to join them for a change of scene. The tales of jockeys competing in showjumping contests and camel racing appealed, but the guilt of completing her workload was a stronger pull.

The stables were eerily quiet, with no sound but the rustle of birds in the bushes and the occasional snort or whinny from a member of the riding school cast. The late afternoon sun cast beautiful shadows over the ground and Abigail felt peace wash over her. "But I can't trust you to behave, can I?"

In response, Muppet lifted her head and attempted to nibble on Abigail's ear. "You can't eat my body parts," laughed Abigail, smoothing her hand down Muppets taut neck. She eyed up Muppet's back. It would be so easy to slip a saddle on, now that Molly had equipped her with the skills to tack up. What's the worst that could happen, having a little trot around the enclosed paddock? Plenty, a voice in her head piped up.

Moody could buck, rear, bolt, shy at imaginary objects, or just generally dump her unceremoniously on the hard ground with goodness knows how many broken bones. Or worse.

Her reverie was interrupted by the crunch of tyres on the gravel driveway. A customer enquiry, deduced Abigail, knowing it wasn't the sound of the engine from Sam's car. There would be no other reason for anyone to call in.

Kissing Muppet briefly on her nose, Abigail turned and made her way along the short track to the courtyard. Emerging from a cherry red sports car was a tiny slip of a girl. From her build, Abigail would have sworn she wasn't old enough to be behind the wheel of a car, but there was something about her manner that instantly conveyed her maturity. She was dressed in a tailored riding jacket, with the uniform black jodhpurs and sleek riding boots to identify her as someone from Sam's world. Her eyes were obscured by oversized brown sunglasses that reeked of being a designer brand, and her spiky platinum blonde hair reminded Abigail of a bleached hedgehog.

"Hi," Abigail smiled. "Can I help you?"

At the sound of Abigail's voice, the stranger turned to face her and broke into an enormous smile. She pushed the sunglasses up onto her head, and appraised her momentarily.

"You must be Abigail?" She thrust out her hand and they shook hands. "I guess I beat Sam home then," she added, glancing around the bare parking spots. "I knew I would, I bet he's still faffing around, or stuck in traffic on the A34. I told him to come through Salisbury but oh no, the Sat Nav knows best. He never listens to me."

Abigail realised that she was expected to know who this jockey was. She racked her brain to remember whether Sam had mentioned anyone coming over this evening but she was certain he hadn't. She would have relished the thought of someone new coming over. Visitors were few and far between.

"Er.." Abigail wasn't sure what the expectation was. "Would you like a quick tour while we wait for Sam?"

"I'll tell you who I want to see. That little Muppet Monster!"

"Oh, OK, she's over in the paddock," Abigail replied. "Come with me."

The pair made their way back up the track. "Sam didn't mention you were calling in," Abigail said casually in an attempt to discover who this stranger was.

"Oh, no, it wasn't planned," she laughed in reply. "I couldn't resist betting Sam I'd beat him in the showjumping showdown this afternoon, and the loser had to buy us all dinner tonight."

"And he lost?" ventured Abigail, thinking with dread of the cost of dinner for four. Even at the Twin Oaks pub, food and drink for four could rack up quite a bill.

"Nah - I had no chance on Dancing Star. She's got no speed, can barely cope with hurdles and is as clumsy as a drunk giraffe, but I don't mind losing. It's a good opportunity to have a catch up with Sam. And chat to Molly. And meet you, of course. And, just as importantly, say hello to my little Muppet."

They were getting closer to the five-bar gate of the paddock, where Muppet remained standing dutifully in the spot Abigail had left her, and the mare visibly reacted to the sight of the girl. She pricked her ears forward and began nodding her head in anticipation.

"Hello sweetheart." She began fussing Muppet, who lapped up the attention. "May I jump on, for old time's sake?" She glanced at Abigail, her eyes shining in delight.

"Be my guest." Abigail was bemused. This girl was obviously a jockey, and knew Muppet, so she was aware of the risks. "I'll go and grab her tack."

"No need." The girl was already clambering up the gate, and with the deftness of a gymnast, launched her dainty frame onto Muppet's bare back. Abigail expected the horse to flinch, shy, or even flatten her ears back in disgust, but she watched in fascination as Muppet remained stock still. The girl patted her pocket and tapped her heels into Muppet's flanks, prompting the start of a steady trot off in a clockwise circle around the paddock. Before long, she had Muppet performing perfect figures of eight at a contented canter. No reins, no saddle, the instruction was all through the subtle pressure of the heels and thighs. Abigail watched, transfixed.

After five minutes, the pair returned to the gate, breathless with exhilaration. "She hasn't changed," she observed, jumping off with ease. Moody nudged the girl's jacket pocket persistently. "All right sweetheart, you win." The girl drew something out of her pocket and Moody Muppet snatched it greedily and chomped happily.

"What was that?" Abigail asked.

"Oh, I hope you didn't mind me giving her that." She grinned. "Isn't it a fantastic secret weapon?"

Abigail frowned. "What secret weapon?"

Realisation dawned on the girl that Abigail was clueless. She pulled another black snake from her pocket and held it up. "Black liquorice. Muppet goes mad for it. Quite a lot of horses do."

As if to demonstrate the point, a chestnut muzzle launched itself at the treat dangling from her hand and it disappeared with a swift chomp.

"I had no idea."

"You just let Muppet know you've got some before you mount, a little tap of the pocket, and she'll be as good as gold. Well, usually, apart from a few occasions on the racetrack, eh, you little minx?"

"You know Muppet very well then..." Abigail left her statement hanging in an attempt to find out more about this girl.

"I was her work rider for two years when I worked for Johnny. I rode her out at the crack of dawn pretty much every morning to stretch her legs on the gallops. I'm not sure who got the most effective workout, though, she's a powerful runner when she puts her mind to it."

"Yes, I found that out," replied Abigail, remembering the New Year's Day firework episode vividly.

They were interrupted by the sound of an engine, which Abigail identified as Sam arriving home.

As they made their way back towards the house, Molly catapulted herself out of the passenger door. "Jackie!" she shrieked.

Of course, Abigail admonished herself. This was Jackie Simnel - only the most successful female jockey on the circuit at the moment. Sam and Molly talked about her all the time, along with her monopolising headlines in the *Racing Post*.

Molly rushed up to Jackie and smothered her in an enthusiastic bear hug.

"You loser!" Sam taunted as he emerged from the driver's door.

"I let you win," Jackie replied with a grin. "I forced Dancing Star into crashing through that triple, otherwise we could have had a perfect clear round."

"Rubbish. The superior jockey won."

"Whatever," Jackie conceded, "just point the way to the pub. I guess the drinks are on me too."

Gathering up an eager Bessie, the foursome made their way up the gravelled drive and into the Twin Oaks pub. Anna looked up with a cheery grin from behind the bar, pleased to see customers before six o'clock. It would be busy later, she reassured them, with all the Easter holidaymakers returning from day trips. "In the meantime, I've just had to put up with Sol's company," she joked.

As if on cue, the graceful form of Sol glided through the bar on the return trip from the gents.

"Hi guys," he greeted, flashing them all with his charm and a wave. "Nice to see you all." His eyes rested on Jackie momentarily. Fresh challenge. Then he glanced at Abigail with a slight quizzical look before retreating back to his table where a pint and a paperback awaited him.

Conversation amongst the group was dominated by tales and gossip from the racecourses; names, places and situations Abigail couldn't relate to, but she smiled and nodded along, grateful for a decent meal and some company. As Anna predicted, the pub filled up around them and before long, the place had a convivial buzz.

"Do you have far to drive back tonight?" Abigail asked Jackie, alarmed as she poured herself a generous second glass of wine.

"Oh, I'm not going anywhere tonight," she replied, to Abigail's relief. "Sam's offered me up your sofa, if that's OK with you?"

"Or you can share my bed if you don't fancy Bessie licking your face in the morning," Molly offered eagerly. On hearing her name, the collie stirred from her resting place under the table and got to her feet, stretched, her tailing thumping rhythmically against the chair leg as she did so. Sol's spaniel, Daisy, spotted her and bounded over to sniff her over, giving Sol the excuse to rise from his seat and join the group.

"We can't have Sam hogging three lovely ladies all to himself," he protested, sliding a chair between Abigail and Molly on the circular table. This strategically placed him opposite Jackie, but where he could press his leg flirtatiously into Abigail's when required.

"I'm Sol," he introduced, thrusting a hand towards Jackie. She regarded him playfully before shaking it and telling him her name.

"You're either a fashion model or a rider," he stated confidently.

"I don't think it takes a genius to draw that conclusion, Sol," Molly rebuked.

Jackie regarded him neutrally. "I ride, but I don't like to be labelled. You probably don't like to call yourself an Old Etonian, right?"

Sol's eyebrows flickered as he struggled to maintain the upper hand in the flirtation. "Harrow actually, and I don't mind it at all." There was an awkward pause in proceedings, as the pair's eyes hovered on each other, daring to make the next move. Abigail nudged Sol's leg to get his attention.

"So, where's your mum this time?" she asked him, referring to his custodianship of Daisy, who had settled down under the table with Bessie. Abigail could feel the warm lump of fur on her toes as the dog's rump spilt outside the confined space.

"I've lost track," Sol smiled. "I just tend to keep hold of her until my mum asks for her back."

"Excuse me," muttered Jackie, rising from the table. "I'm just popping to the ladies."

The group watched her disappear, taking dainty steps like a ballerina as she navigated the slalom of tables and chairs in the bar.

"Mmm," Sol piped up predictably. "Where did you find her?"

"She's a friend," Sam replied with a knowing smile.

"And I wouldn't waste your time, Sol," Molly added, "she doesn't bat for your side".

"Oh Molly!" Sam scolded. "It was fun watching him try!"

29

It seemed Jackie Simnel didn't relish the thought of Bessie licking her face in the morning and rejected the sofa. Instead, she shared Molly's bed that night. Judging by the stories that were recollected over the remains of dinner and drinks, Molly and Jackie were well acquainted on the racecourses, and their friendship firmly established.

The most advantageous part of her visit had been the liquorice revelation. The next morning Abigail walked Bessie over to the newsagents where she bought a bulging bag full of black liquorice. Enlisting the supervision of Molly, she groomed and tacked up Muppet, slipping the horse a piece before mounting.

It may not be a miracle cure, a voice nagged at her inside her head. What worked for Jackie may not work for you. It was with nervous trepidation that she cantered Muppet around the paddock, but the mare was obliging. Molly tentatively offered advice on her posture and technique, clearly wary about Abigail snapping at her again, but Abigail accepted the critique gratefully. Molly built the jump up to thigh height, where Abigail had been ejected unceremoniously last time, but Muppet put her ears forward in readiness for the challenge. They repeated the jump over and over, Abigail improving each time, and growing in confidence; both in her own ability and in Muppet behaving.

As Abigail slid off at the end of the session, Muppet was rewarded with several handfuls of liquorice. She chomped them down, barely chewing.

"That was great," gushed Molly, "You'll be fine when the camera crew come."

It didn't stop her nerves when that day arrived, and her stomach churned as she heard the tentative approach of a vehicle promptly at the arranged time.

"Hi," she greeted the driver emerging from a blue transit van. She imagined that the crew would be a crowd, but it consisted only of a cameraman and the reporter. Wasting no time, the cameraman swiftly assembled kit in the back of the van, while the reporter scanned the yard, making a mental plan. He was in his forties with a theatrical face that reminded Abigail of a pantomime dame devoid of make-up. She longed for Sam and Molly to be at her side, but they were adamant that they would wait in the cottage and not put her off. She could sense their eyes on her, probably huddled in the upstairs bedroom together, peeking out from behind the curtain.

"So, Abigail, my name's Jonathon," the reporter began. "I think what we'll do first is leave Adam to get some general shots of the stables and the yard while we work out where to film your pieces. Can you show me what's what?"

Abigail and Jonathon made their way to the stable block where she told him about the horses, and then to the yard where the corporate sessions were held. He asked open, sensible questions, and Abigail was relieved that there was no hidden agenda, no trick questions, and he was excited and interested in her responses.

Abigail had already set the paddock up with a couple of jumps at the height she was confident at, and Jonathon nodded in approval.

"I imagine the Moody Muppet gets frustrated at jumps that low," he commented, "after all her hurdling successes".

"Sam and Molly take her over larger jumps," she admitted, "but I'm such a beginner compared to them".

"Oh? When did you start riding then?"

Abigail cringed. "About a year ago. Until I met Sam, I'd never been on a horse."

"Is that right?" Jonathon looked her in astonishment and Abigail could almost hear the cogs clicking in his brain and creative juices flowing. "This is great - the Moody Muppet is teaching YOU to jump!"

If only he had witnessed the debacle a few weeks ago, Abigail mused, remembering the sideways cantering, the veering to the side, the stopping dead and tossing Abigail like a rag doll through the air. Some teacher.

"Right, Adam, if we can get some close-ups as Abigail tacks up the horse, and a wide angle as she rides out of the yard, then we'll go to the paddock and get shots of the jumps. Then we'll finish off with an interview outside the stable."

As if overhearing the conversation, Moody Muppet gave a loud neigh from where she was being confined in her stable. Abigail and Molly had groomed her within an inch of her life that morning, so she gleamed like a supermodel, and was ready for her catwalk appearance. With Adam the cameraman set up and ready, Abigail tried not to feel self-conscious as she entered Moody's stable and led her out, tacking her up as she had been taught. She gave Moody a tiny slither of liquorice and tapped her pocket as she mounted and rode out of shot towards the paddock.

Adam and Jonathan followed behind, and then began filming again as she cantered around the paddock, popping Muppet over the jump each circuit.

"Good girl," Abigail praised, as Moody gave an exemplary performance, although deep down Abigail knew it wasn't loyalty to her that was contributing to her behaviour, but the sweet treat in her pocket.

"That was great," enthused Jonathan as she steered Muppet over to them. "All we need to do now is grab an interview with you back at the stables."

Abigail dismounted and rewarded Muppet with a generous portion of liquorice. The mare snaffled it greedily, and Abigail led her back towards the yard with Jonathan and Adam in tow.

"What do you do with yourself when you're not riding the Moody Muppet?" Jonathan enquired.

"I design and make clothes," she replied proudly. "I'm just working up a design for some clients who are going to Newmarket for The Guineas," she added to give relevance to Jonathan's world.

"I'll have to pass your details on to my colleague, Alison. She's doing the main presentation on The Newmarket Festival and will no doubt be on the lookout for a smart frock to wear on TV." Abigail suppressed a smirk at his use of such an old-fashioned term. "It would get your designs in front of millions," he added.

Abigail promised to forward her details, buzzing at the success of the morning so far.

"So, tell me about what goes on at Ashington stables," Jonathan asked five minutes later. Muppet was safely stowed in her stable, having been rewarded with plenty of liquorice. She now looked out over the door inquisitively as Abigail stood awkwardly in the yard with Adam pointing the camera straight at her. Jonathan stood to one side, off camera, feeding the questions and encouraging Abigail to look at him and not the camera lens.

"The stables were the brainchild of my boyfriend, Sam Ashington, last year when he planned to retire from racing. We offer normal lessons, but have devised a package aimed at corporate organisations to come and do team building exercises based around equine activities."

Having anticipated such a question, Abigail had rehearsed the answer in her head over and over. Moody Muppet whinnied loudly in the background, as if on cue for Jonathan's next question.

"And that timely interruption comes from a superstar of the racetrack, the Moody Muppet. Tell us about her involvement."

Abigail glanced back at the mare fondly and smiled. "Sam thought it would be a good idea to buy Moody Muppet for my Christmas present last year, despite me being a novice rider. She gets involved in the sessions now, with the winning teams being offered a ride on her as their prize... if they wish."

"Well, you looked good together in the paddock. She seems to have taught you some skills," Jonathan gushed. You charmer, thought Abigail.

"She probably realises she'll get a treat if she behaves herself, but yes, I've been able to get some experience riding. I must add that I don't teach the corporate sessions. That's down to Sam when he's here, and his brilliant assistant, Molly Packer."

"It sounds as though you wouldn't have time to be involved; I understand you run your own business?"

Ooh, an opportunity to plug the fashion business, thought Abigail. This was an unexpected outcome. "That's right. I run "April Smith Designs", which makes women's clothing. I'm currently working on collections of dresses suitable for wearing to the races, so I can't ever escape the world of racing!"

"Perfect way to end," Jonathan gave a little clap, and glanced over at Adam to check all was well with the technicalities. From behind the camera he gave a thumbs up and Jonathan transformed from presenter mode back to human.

"That was great, Abigail. I don't know when this will be broadcast- it's a piece that can go out any time - but it could tie in with our Newmarket Festival coverage in May. Rumour has it that Sam could be riding in the Queen's colours. Is that right?"

"Yeah, possibly," Abigail replied with as little commitment as possible. "It's still quite a way off yet."

Jonathan nodded sagely. "Too right, we haven't even wrapped up the jumps season yet." He thrust out a hand. "Well, good luck with everything, and thanks for today."

Abigail shook his outstretched hand, wished him well, and watched as he and Adam clambered into the van and left a trail of dust as they headed back off down the lane. She couldn't wait to go and report to Sam and Molly on how well Muppet had behaved, and how she was able to put in a plug for the corporate sessions and her dressmaking. With a beaming smile she hurried over to the cottage and pushed open the kitchen door. The scene inside made her jaw drop.

"What on earth are you two doing?"

30

"So, what *were* they doing?" Kate looked levelly at her friend over her glass of wine. It was a chilly Sunday evening early in April and the pair were catching up in the Ashington's kitchen. It was the night of the annual Grand National party, generously hosted by Sam's dad, Robin, each year as an opportunity to network with jockeys, agents, stable staff and anyone else that wanted to drop by. Whilst many of the revellers braved the savage breeze and cool temperatures outside on the sloping lawns, Kate and Abi had commandeered two bar stools at the island in the empty kitchen, and sat having a heart to heart. It was so therapeutic for Abigail to be able to speak to somebody about her turbulent thoughts.

"They were writhing around on the lounge rug, giggling, like children," Abigail protested, gulping the wine faster than she intended. "I thought they'd be looking out for me, giving me moral support behind the kitchen window, but no, they were play fighting over some video on Molly's mobile that she was threatening to post on TikTok or something juvenile like that."

"And this makes you think they're having an affair?"

Abigail paused, waiting for one of the guests to pass by the kitchen door before continuing. "Well, it's not normal behaviour, is it?"

Kate shrugged. "So, did they leap apart when you came through the door?" she enquired.

"Well, no," Abigail admitted. "Molly squealed at me to come and take her phone before Sam could grab it." As she relived the image in her mind, she realised that she was probably just being ridiculous. She had walked across the lounge in a slight baffled daze and reached down to Molly's outstretched hand, whilst Sam protested that Abi was a spoil sport. They hadn't seemed ashamed of their behaviour, nor caught in the act. "But it wasn't just that one occasion. I've seen them messing around in the yard, Sam carries Molly over muddy puddles if she hasn't got her proper boots on…that sort of thing. And she accompanies him to the races all the time, leaving me alone at the house. That's probably a good thing," she reflected.

"If you want my opinion…" Kate paused. Abigail did. "I think if there was anything sinister going on, they wouldn't be so blatant about it. It seems to me they're just good friends, and get on well. She's young and eager to please." Abigail rose from the stool and fetched the bottle of wine from the Ashington's enormous fridge, topping their two glasses up. "She's there now, isn't she?" Kate pointed out. "She's been left behind in Hampshire, holding the fort, while you and Sam come away and enjoy yourselves?"

Abigail nodded reluctantly. It made sense that they wouldn't flaunt their relationship in her face if there was anything going on. Which led her to feel that she was being unreasonable. Jealous even.

"Let's change the topic," Abigail suggested, and filled Kate in on the other development that had been borne out of the *Raceday One* filming. Jonathan's colleague, Alison, had been in touch to commission a "new frock" for the Guineas festival, which added pressure to her existing commissions from Harriet.

"I've got bloody promises coming out of my ears, but no friggin' income at the moment!"

"Umm, you said *two* swear words!"

Both Abigail and Kate jumped, and looked towards the doorway where twelve-year-old Penny lingered on the threshold of the kitchen. She grinned a toothy smile at them. Abigail was pleased to see she was wearing the ra-ra skirt she had made her for Christmas.

Kate fetched a can of Coke from the fridge for Penny, and indicated that she should join them, which meant curbing their language and topics considerably. Penny took the last remaining stool on the opposite side of the island, proud to be included in the adult's talk. They listened patiently as she regaled them with tales of school, the *Lucky Potion* concert, and life on the farm.

"And how's your fashion business going?" she asked Abigail. "Are you making lots more skirts like this?"

"I've been working on a summer collection, which Harriet is going to help me to launch soon. And I've got to make a posh dress that a TV presenter is going to wear on TV next month."

"And the Queen might ask you to make some dresses for her when Sam rides her horse. I heard Sam's dad telling that fat man with a funny waistcoat about Sam getting the job. That's brilliant. Do you think you'll get invited to Buckingham Palace?"

Both Kate and Abigail laughed. Such young naivety was refreshing. "Maybe, although I think the Queen has her own dress designers."

"Yeah but, they're dressing her like an old lady. She should get a bit more trendy and have a skirt like this!" Penny sprang off the stool and did a twirl in the kitchen, sending the flaps of the skirt twirling high.

"So, you're not making any clothes for Teen Zero then?"

She clambered back on the stool and took a swig of her Coke.

"I've not made any other children's clothes," Abigail confirmed, leaning forward conspiratorially at Penny. "You have a unique, one-of-a-kind skirt."

"Oh". Penny looked disappointed.

Twelve-year-olds were confusing things. Abigail didn't have any siblings, so never felt completely at ease around children. Nadine, who was one of six children, had always advised treating them as though they were adults, just without saying "bloody" and "friggin" in front of them.

"Isn't that a good thing, to have a unique skirt? None of your friends at school will be able to copy you."

"Yeah, I like that, but I'm sad for you. I thought that Teen Zero would contact you and ask you to make stuff for them."

If only it was that easy, Abigail thought silently. It was exactly a year ago since she set up her own business, and the income she'd received from the hours and hours of hard work didn't make much business sense to her. It was barely minimum wage work by the time she factored in the planning of each season's designs, the marketing, working on the website, keeping on top of the admin and finances, chasing payments, sourcing and buying fabric, the actual sewing, screwing pieces up and starting again, liaising with clients, and shooing Bessie from the top floor room. Would she ever get a contract that would turn things around for her? It seemed she was nearly always on the brink of something life changing, but never quite getting there.

Kate had fallen quiet. The name "Teen Zero" resonated in her head somewhere, like a deja-vu moment. She could see the logo of the kid's clothing company in her mind's eye, but wasn't sure why.

"Well I'm making stuff for Harriet Packer and her mum," Abigail reasoned. "If I do a really good job, they will hopefully want some more of my designs."

As if on cue, Harriet strut into the kitchen, flanked by two friends that Abigail recalled vaguely as bridesmaids. Despite it being an hour after sundown, Harriet's signature sunglasses remained on her head.

"Ah, just the person!" Harriet pointed a shiny cerise fingernail at Abigail. "A birdie tells me you're making Alison Raven's dress for the Newmarket Festival broadcast." Her tone bordered on accusation, and Abigail knew this was political territory. Harriet opened the fridge, scanned its contents and closed the door disapprovingly. "Hmm, no champagne. I really should scold Robin for this."

"I'm drafting a couple of designs for her, yes. Why?"

"I want Mummy and I looking better than her, of course." Kate suppressed a snigger; Abigail kicked her lightly under the island by way of warning.

Penny piped up, "Harriet, you always look like a princess! I wish I had lovely long blonde hair like yours. Mine's all mousey and flat and rubbish."

"Thank you, Penny, sweetheart, but it's really quite important to stand out at these events. Gok Wan will be milling around doing his fashion segments for Channel 4 and I was overlooked last year. I don't suppose there's any chance we can see what you're preparing for Alison when you come to do the fitting with Mummy and me?"

"I'll see what I can do," Abigail promised vaguely, and satisfied, Harriet waltzed out of the kitchen, presumably in search of something more appealing than Prosecco.

"Oh my God!" gasped Kate suddenly. Abigail jumped, sloshing wine over the rim of her glass. "Teen Zero!" Wide eyed, she covered her mouth in horror as the memory came back to her.

"What?" Penny and Abigail chorused in unison.

"I've just remembered. At MODA. Oh shit, I'm so sorry...."

Abigail was completely confused. "What is it?" she repeated.

Kate flushed and went on to explain that at the end of the day, when Abigail had gone to the toilet, a man had come sniffing around her stall, asking strange questions about kids' clothing. "He was looking through your collection, grumbling under his breath that it was all designed for adults. I thought he was a bit strange, so I tried to get rid of him, and he gave me a business card to pass onto you, suggesting that you call him if you were interested."

"And who was it?"

Kate scrambled off her stool and swept up her oversized tote bag from its abandoned position under the island. "I shoved the card in my handbag. I meant to give it to you but, you know, it slipped my mind... here!" She pulled out a square of card that had become dog-eared and grubby from several weeks in the depths of the bag. "Mr Callendine," she read. "Head Buyer, Teen Zero."

Abigail snatched the card from Kate's fingers and read the card for herself. "Bloody hell," she whispered in amazement. "I guess I'd better call him first thing on Monday."

"D'uh!" responded Penny, rolling her eyes. "There's only so much help I can give you."

And with that, she jumped down from her stool, gave another twirl, and skipped out of the kitchen, leaving Abigail and Kate staring after her in bewilderment.

.

31

There would have been a time when Sam and Abigail walked the mile between Ashington Yard and Sloth, but everything seemed to happen at a faster pace these days. In a hurry to pay a visit to Mrs Angel, then head back to the New Forest before sunset, Sam insisted they drove so that they could make a quick getaway afterwards.

"You know what she's like," Sam reasoned as he slammed the Jaguar down the country lane. "She'll make us stay for tea and cake, plough us with questions and stories, then insist we stay for more tea. If we then have to walk back to Dad's to get the car, we'll never get back to the stables before dark."

Abigail conceded that this was true, but felt a ripple of excitement as they drew up in the lane outside and walked up the path to her front door. She hadn't seen Mrs Angel for a while, and was keen to fill her in on recent developments. The lawn was in a state of abandonment again and the bush that bordered the neighbouring property was sprawling too high and too wide over the lawn. Abigail made a mental note to put some time aside to come and get the outside space ship shape again, just as soon as she could.

She rapped on the door, expecting a familiar call from inside to either 'come on in" or that Mrs Angel was on her way. Silence. Seconds passed, the breeze blowing through the garden, creating a rhythmic thwack as an unidentifiable weed tapped against the bay window.

"Do you think she's dozed off?' Sam suggested.

"Could have," conceded Abigail, rapping again. This time a little harder, with more urgency. Mrs Angel was almost in her nineties. She could be forgiven a nap in the afternoon, or a little deafness to the front door.

Nothing.

"She could be out?" Sam shrugged.

"I doubt it." Abigail moved over to the bay window and shielded her eyes as she peered through the glass into the gloom. With relief, she saw the familiar shape of Mrs Angel slumped in her favourite armchair, the newspaper laid neatly in her lap. Her head had fallen sideways to rest on the support of the winged armchair, her glasses slightly wonky as her head had tilted. "She's asleep in her chair," she said in a needless whisper to Sam.

"Maybe we should leave her for now." Sam longed to get back on the motorway and home to the stables. He felt like he'd had his fill of small talk for one weekend, and the prospect of nattering to an OAP over tea and cake with yet more mindless chatter wasn't his idea of a perfect Monday.

Abigail ignored him and rapped on the glass, but Mrs Angel didn't stir. "She can't hear me; let's go and see if the back door is open. She tends to leave it unlocked."

On a mission, she started off around the side of the property, fighting through the overgrown conifers that bordered the boundary of the plot. With an exasperated shrug, Sam followed like a puppy. As Abigail predicted, the back door was unlocked, and Abigail strode into Mrs Angel's kitchen, calling out in greeting as she did so. There was no inviting aroma of freshly baked cake, which Abigail found odd, and the cottage suddenly seemed eerie. Everything was in its place, just as Abigail remembered from her last visit, but there was something wrong. Something she couldn't quite put her finger on.

"It's only us!" Abigail announced loudly as she arrived on the threshold of the lounge. "Mrs Angel, wakey wakey!"

The body didn't stir in the chair and Abigail's heart started to pound as adrenaline pumped through her body. Her conscious brain hadn't dared to articulate the fear yet, but the body's systems knew.

Abigail approached the chair and reached out to Mrs Angel's hand that lay limply on the newspaper. With a startled scream, Abigail jumped back into Sam.

"She's stone cold," she whispered, tears suddenly welling.

"Are you sure?" Sam knelt by the side of the chair and gently touched Mrs Angel's cheek with the back of his hand.

"See?" Despite the shock, Abigail was offended that he hadn't believed her.

"Shit."

149

The pair simply gazed at Mrs Angel's motionless body, unable to form any sentences.

"I've never seen a dead body before," Abigail sniffed eventually. "She looks very peaceful. That's something."

Sam stood up and put a protective arm around Abigail. She leaned her head wearily into his neck, thinking how nice this small moment of intimacy was, despite the circumstances. "What do you think we should do?" she asked finally.

Sam released his arm and fished his phone from his pocket.

"What are you doing?"

He looked at her levelly. "Calling Dad."

Abigail sank helplessly into the other armchair as Sam paced the lounge waiting for his Dad to pick up. She wondered how long Mrs Angel had been there, cold, lifeless, waiting for someone to find her. She reached for the paper on Mrs Angel's lap and was relieved to read the date: yesterday. She hadn't got as far as opening it, so this was probably the post lunch sit down with a cup of tea that now remained on the coffee table, as icy as Mrs Angel's skin. She was probably gearing up to watch the gardening programme that afternoon, but hadn't got as far as putting the telly on. She'd probably been there about 24 hours. If only they'd visited yesterday before the party, maybe Mrs Angel would have complained to them about a pain, an ailment. They could have called a doctor to be on the safe side. But knowing Mrs Angel, she wouldn't have confessed to any pains. She just got on with it. Or maybe whatever struck her down came suddenly, taking her swiftly and hopefully painlessly out of her life. They couldn't have changed her fate, Abigail consoled herself silently.

"He's on his way," confirmed Sam, shaking Abigail from her thoughts. "He says not to touch anything nor call anybody. Just stay put."

"He'll know what to do," Abigail replied. No matter how old she got, a parent figure would always be the parent figure. Especially Sam's dad, Robin, who was cool as a cucumber, commanding respect whether at the racetrack or in his own garden hosting a grand party. Or gazing down at the corpse of Mrs Angel in her front room, as he was ten minutes later.

"Well, I guess she didn't suffer," he said gently, pulling both Abigail and Sam into a triangular bear hug. His chest was warm and the woollen sweater he wore smelled of hay. "We should call the doctor first and get the death officially certified. I guess she's registered with Doctor Adams; most people in Sloth are. Then we should try and find the family's details."

Abigail remembered the hassle of getting her granddaughter to come for dinner in London, and felt her hackles rise. That would have been a golden opportunity for one last encounter with this wonderful lady.

"And we should have some tea." He looked pointedly at Abigail, who nodded and disappeared to the kitchen, glad to have a task to occupy

150

her. She heard Sam's footsteps scamper off as Robin dispatched him on a mission too.

The next hour was surreal as the doctor came. He made small talk with Robin in the kitchen about the weekend's racing results, before accepting a cup of tea from Abigail.

"She hasn't been into the surgery to see anyone for several months," the doctor explained, "Nor was she on medication, which is astonishing for a lady of her age. This means that it's technically an unexpected death, so I will need to call the police."

Abigail felt her heart quicken. As the first people to find her, would she and Sam be suspects? "It's just routine procedure," Doctor Adams confirmed, with a reassuring smile. "I can also call the next of kin," Doctor Adams offered. "Their details should all be on our files."

The trio watched silently as he sat at the table and fired up his laptop, made a few calls, completed paperwork, then began to moan to Robin about the recent planning permission that had been granted for 200 houses on the road out of Sloth. It all seemed bizarre to be making banal chit chat with the stiff corpse of Mrs Angel still propped in the chair in the room next door.

Two police officers joined them within the hour, their thick stab vests puffing out their chests and making them look top heavy, like turkeys strutting around before Christmas. Despite having nothing to feel guilty about, Abigail blushed as she answered their routine questions about the order of events since arriving at the cottage that afternoon. The younger policeman, only a few years older than Abigail, jotted notes in his slim notebook whilst the older man plodded around the downstairs, glancing at Mrs Angel's nick-nacks.

Once they had no further evidence to offer, Sam looked at his watch and asked if they were OK to leave. They still had plenty of daylight left in the April afternoon but Sam wasn't very patient when it came to unproductive time.

"Of course," the policeman replied.

"No problem," added Doctor Adams, with a supportive smile. "We'll take it from here. Fanny's in good hands."

It was the first time anyone had revealed her Christian name, and Abigail would have giggled childishly in different circumstances. No wonder she refused to be called by her first name on *Where in the World*. Imagine wearing a badge on your chest that said "Fanny".

Robin rose from his seat at the table to hug Abigail and squeeze Sam's shoulder.

"Oh," added Abigail to the room. "If I wanted to come back and tidy up the garden when I'm back in the village, would there be any objection?" The group looked blankly at her, as though she had gone mad.

151

"I just don't like the thought of the cottage being neglected now that Mrs Angel won't be able to look after it."

"I can't see why not," shrugged the policeman. "But you might want to check with the family."

Abigail nodded, and the pair made their way out of the kitchen door. Like hell would she check with the family.

32

The cup of coffee on the bedside table had gone cold by the time Abigail woke the following morning. It had been late when they finally arrived back from Sloth the previous evening, and Molly was like an excitable puppy at their homecoming. Starved of conversation for two days, she appeared to be glued to their sofa as the clock's hands nudged past midnight, regaling them with every detail of the past couple of days. When Sam broke the sad news of Mrs Angel's passing to her, they expected Molly to respectfully retreat back to bed with her solemn thoughts, but it only seemed to make Molly cling more to their company, wanting to reminisce over memories of Gloucestershire life.

Abigail lay in bed now, still and listening to see whether she could calculate the time without looking at her watch. The coffee was stone cold, there was no sound from downstairs, not even Bessie snuffling around. Nine thirty, thought Abigail. Drawing her wrist from out of the covers she gave a contented smile to see her watch state that it was 9:34. With a grimace, she drank the cold coffee that Sam had made her two hours previously and rose to look out of the window.

In the yard below, Sam's car was gone. Newmarket today, if she recalled correctly. The boy never stopped working, although the alternative for him today was a journey to Redcar, which was a six-hour drive away. He had been known to make the long trip if the rewards were great enough, so she counted her blessings that at least he had just spent a whole two days with her. The days off had been sacrificed reluctantly on Sam's part, of course. He'd had to decline rides at Windsor. Maybe Sam had wanted to stop by Windsor Castle and see if the Queen was in the market for a new frock, she thought to herself with a smile.

She watched as Molly came into view, walking down the track with Bessie trotting along at her side. Molly carried a bulging carrier bag, which prodded Abigail's curiosity.

"It's some goodies from the farm shop," Molly explained twenty minutes later once Abigail had washed, dressed and descended to the kitchen. "Sam gave me some money this morning and said we should all have a treat. I can give you a hand cooking it if you want."

Abigail peered at the stack that Molly had transferred from the carrier bag to the table. There were some chunky white chocolate cookies, a large loaf of farmhouse bread, some jars of chutney, a bottle of damson wine and a selection of vegetables. "I've put the meat in the fridge. I got some lamb shanks and steaks."

"And Sam just gave you some money?" clarified Abigail, with suspicion. "Just like that?"

"Yeah, forty quid. I've put the change on top of the TV."

It was odd behaviour, but Abigail wasn't going to complain. In the six months since moving in together, he'd never once offered up money for food. It was an unspoken arrangement that Sam covered the household bills whilst Abigail sorted out the food shopping. Maybe he was finally starting to realise how precarious her financial position was. She really needed to get her act together and bring in some proper money through her business. Her eyes fell onto the Teen Zero business card that lay on the table. No time like the present.

As the phone rang, part of Abigail hoped that nobody would answer, or that Mr Callendine wasn't available and she would have to leave a message. She wasn't exactly sure what to say to him, and dreaded the next few minutes.

"Mr Callendine," came the abrupt answer from the other end of the line. For a split second, Abigail considered hanging up, but forced herself to take a breath and sound confident.

"Yes, good morning, Mr Callendine. My name's Abigail Daycock and I run "April Smith Designs". I believe you may have been wanting to meet with me at MODA in February. You spoke to my colleague as I was away from the stall."

There was a momentary pause, so Abigail took the opportunity to apologise for not getting back to him sooner and explained the mix up with her "colleague" forgetting to pass on his card.

The pause at the end of the line indicated that Mr Callendine still couldn't place Abigail, nor the situation.

"MODA, you say?" He had a sneer to his voice and Abigail pictured a Disney villain.

"Yes, I mean it's strange that you want to talk to me as I don't do children's clothing. I specialise in ladies' fashion for special occasions, like weddings, the races and such. I have adapted the odd piece for a 12-year-old friend as a present."

"Ah," a lightbulb had gone on in Mr Callendine's memory. "It's all coming back to me. Hang on a moment."

Through the empty air waves Abigail could hear papers rustling, and the occasional frustrated tut from the Teen Zero buyer.

"Yes, here we are," he said. "We received a letter in the office just after Christmas and it filtered down to me. I will read you what it says, word for word...," he paused for dramatic effect. "To the person at Teen Zero who decides what to sell." He paused again, and Abigail got the impression if they were face to face, he would look straight into her eye and raise an eyebrow. "There's a clothes designer called April Smith and I think you should get some of her designs in Teen Zero because she's really good. She made me a dress last year with red devils on it and lots of my friends asked me where I got it and wanted it for themselves. At Christmas she made me a skirt like I've never seen before. My mum says it's called a "ra-ra" skirt and it's really unusual and comfy. I only get five pounds pocket money a week (sometimes a bit extra if I do some smelly jobs around the farm to help out) but I don't buy clothes at Teen Zero with it because I think they are all a bit boring at the moment. But if you had April Smith's stuff in your shops, I would save up my pocket money for a month so that I could buy some. Her website is blah blah, and I think you should check her out."

"Penny." Abigail's heart went out to the girl for her sweet gesture. She pictured her happy face doing a twirl in the Ashington's kitchen less than two days ago, the ra-ra skirt swishing out with her movement.

"So, I have looked at your website, and I checked you out, but as you say, you aren't catering for the Teen Zero market at the moment."

"No, I've got quite a lot of commissions coming in for the upcoming racing season," Abigail started to protest, but Mr Callendine continued.

"That's not to say there's not a demand for your 'occasion wear' to enter the teen market. The rise of the school prom, for example, as well as parties, concerts and so forth. I think our range is, as Penny says, a little boring, so perhaps you could come up with a selection of designs for next year's spring / summer collection that you think would appeal to our customers, and potential new customers like Penny. I can't promise anything more than to take a look over your concepts, but how does that sound?"

It sounded fantastic to Abigail. Not only did she not have to contemplate trying to squeeze in extra work at the moment, but this could be a way of expending her horizons into a bigger audience. She would have time to explore ideas with Penny and work out the logistics of expanding production should Mr Callendine be impressed with her designs.

"That sounds perfect," she replied, attempting unsuccessfully to keep the grin from her voice.

They arranged a date for Abigail to travel up to London to show off her preliminary designs, and she hung up, invigorated and filled with renewed hope. With Sam at Newmarket and Molly mucking out, she settled for giving Bessie a hug and a kiss before retreating to her tiny room to carry on working on the dresses for Harriet and her mother.

33

Looking back a year, Abigail remembered how appalled she had been witnessing Kate and her then husband Callum arranging their week with separate diaries splayed open on the table, their paths meeting fleetingly as Callum travelled up the length and breadth of the country to take various rides. As the flat racing season intensified, Abigail feared the same was starting to happen to her and Sam. There was no sign of him retiring from racing to concentrate on the business as he had promised, but she daren't bring it up, as he had a way of making her feel guilty about not making the corporate sessions successful. The *Raceday One* piece still hadn't been aired, and paranoia nagged at Abigail that perhaps she had messed that up as well and it would never be broadcast.

"So, I can't borrow the car this weekend to go to Gloucestershire?" she asked Sam, as they sat around the table after their evening meal that night. She'd slow cooked the lamb shanks in red wine, and made a stack of creamy mashed potatoes and green vegetables. Despite Molly's offer of helping to cook, she'd remained sat at the table reading out snippets of gossip from Heat magazine whilst Abigail bustled around the kitchen. It was the first feast for a long time, although Sam nibbled at the food on his plate, pushing the food around, before giving Bessie the remainder. She'd noticed how little he was eating since it had been confirmed he would get the ride on the Queen's horse in the prestigious 2000 Guineas race next month. Although it maddened her, she bit her lip, knowing that his strict calorie control was a touchy subject.

"It's better if I drop you off on Friday morning," he negotiated, consulting his diary, "as I'm on my way to a schooling session near Newport, then I can pick you up on Saturday on my way back from Wolverhampton. It'll be quite late as it's their evening meeting so we could stay overnight with Mum and Dad."

Abigail shrugged helplessly. It was the only option available to her. She would stay with Kate on Friday night, as that was more appealing than staying at the Ashingtons without Sam. Kate had also offered to drop her at Harriet's for the dress fitting and photoshoot on Saturday. If only she could afford her own wheels, her life would be much easier, but she knew that was an impossible expense for the time being.

"Which means it's just me and you here Friday night," Molly pointed out, stretching out her slippered foot and prodding his thigh. "I can whip your ass on *Champion Jockey*."

The implication that Abigail's presence in the house stifled their fun stung her. She was also annoyed they were excited by the prospect of playing childish games on the console. Once again, Kate was the voice of reason.

"At least if they're playing *Champion Jockey*, they're not getting up to the other things you're paranoid about." The friends sat in Kate's garden that Friday, enjoying coffee whilst basking in a rare glimpse of sunshine. Spring had decided to make an appearance after months of grey sky, drizzle and nippy northerly winds. It was still early, as Sam had needed to leave well before breakfast in order to get to Newport by ten o'clock. That meant Abigail was unceremoniously dumped on Kate's doorstep at nine o'clock with a bulging suitcase of dresses and a packet of biscuits that she'd hastily purchased from the petrol station as Sam filled up the tank.

Toddler Aidan eyed up the biscuits from a distance as the girls munched their way through half the packet in the sunshine.

"I love having Fridays off," sighed Kate. "I don't know how I found the time to work five days a week." She had cut down her hours to have more time with Aidan, but this particular Friday was to be an exception, as Aidan was off to his granny's house, freeing up Kate to help Abigail attack Mrs Angel's overgrown garden.

"You sound like a pensioner," Abigail scolded, trying to work out when she last had the luxury of a day away from the confinement of her sewing room. "But it is lovely to think we have a couple of days to do whatever we like. Just not sewing or riding."

"I can't think of anything more satisfying than making Mrs Angel's garden look neat again. It's a perfect tribute to her. Right young man," she addressed Aidan. "We should get all your bits and bobs together for Granny."

Abigail hovered at the kitchen island, watching as Kate moved effortlessly around the lounge, sweeping up toddler paraphernalia and stuffing it into a large canvas bag bearing an elephant motif. The house looked a lot neater without Callum living in it, Abigail observed. No vases of dying flowers dripping brown petals onto the mantelpiece, the pages of the *Racing Post* no longer covered up sofa cushions, nor were there abandoned pieces of clothing - whether clean or dirty - forgotten on the backs of the dining chairs. The carpet looked vacuumed, the kitchen surfaces were clear and there was even a faint smell of polish in the air. Kate herself had gradually shed the surplus baby bulge thanks to boyfriend Dan's personal training sessions, and she had a motivated glow to her cheeks.

Once the pushchair had been loaded, they were ready to set off a few streets to Kate's mum's house to drop Aidan, then carry on up Sloth's sleepy main road to Mrs Angel's cottage.

"Let's hope she has plenty of tools in the shed, otherwise we'll have to go and see what we can pilfer from neighbours," Kate said, pushing open the wooden gate and negotiating the overgrown conifer to get to the back garden, as Abigail had done only five days earlier. The paint on the gate was faded, weather worn and peeling off in fat shards, and Abigail wondered whether they should give it a sanding down and another layer of moss green paint.

"A-ha!" Exclaimed Kate, wrenching back the stiff door to the shed. It had endured many years in the dank, shady corner of the garden, with fewer and fewer people opening the door over the years. Like the gate, its wooden exterior was neglected and getting beyond saving. With a twinge of sadness, Abigail realised the next owners of the house would no doubt take the shed down and throw it away, replacing it with something new. There would soon be no evidence that Mrs Angel ever lived in the cottage. "There's all sorts in here."

Abigail peered into the gloom. The lawn mower that she had used last year was still there with its cable dumped on top of it like a lazy snake. On the dusty shelf, amongst the cobwebs, was a box of rusty tools. Empty plastic plant pots lined the back of the shed, stacked up and leaning to one side. A column of paint cans dominated the corner, surrounded by aerosol cans, plant feeder, slug pellets and an ice cream tub full of nails.

"Shall I start mowing the lawn at the front whilst you attack the hedge and conifer?" Kate suggested, handing Abigail a pair of secateurs from the box of tools. Not knowing what to put the clippings in, Abigail located the dustbin, recoiling as she peered inside, where the stench of four weeks rotting kitchen waste rose up to her nostrils.

"I'll put the bin out when we leave. It's a bit overdue."

Kate was holding the cord for the lawn mower, realising that she would need a plug socket. "We're going to have to disturb the neighbours after all," she sighed, waggling the plug at Abi.

"Or..." Abigail skipped over the back door and tilted the plant pot to reveal a key underneath. Mrs Angel had told her the key was there "for emergencies". OK, this wasn't quite an emergency, but it was for a good cause.

"She wouldn't have minded, would she?" Kate concurred. "I'll plug it into a lounge socket and put the cord through the window."

In the spring sunshine the girls got to work, Abigail merrily hacking away at the greenery that she knew would grow back with gusto. Kate trimmed the lawns and started pulling up the weeds that had taken hold in the borders, which was the majority of the life growing there. Abigail suspected Mrs Angel would have been a proud gardener in years gone by, but her lack of mobility in older age had led to neglect of the gardens.

Neither girl heard the car pull up in the lane, nor the footsteps approaching the garden gate.

"Just what the hell is going on here?" A woman's voice boomed behind them.

Abigail spun around to face the lady, in her fifties, sharing Mrs Angel's unmistakable rotund genes.

"Carol!" Kate said hesitantly. "I hope you don't mind. We thought it would be nice to get your mum's garden looking nice again, and well, less neglected."

"Oh yes, it's Kate, isn't it?" Carol moved through the gate and hovered, eyeing up the scene in front of her. She looked Abigail up and down briefly, trying to decide whether she recognised her. The body language was frosty and defensive.

"I was so sorry to hear about your mum," Kate said softly. "I guess you've got a lot of things to organise."

"I've come down from Edinburgh this morning and will be staying the weekend. There's some paperwork to sort out and stuff to clear out." She waved her hand vaguely in the direction of the house. Abigail realised that they had technically broken in, and had the feeling that wasn't going to go down well.

"This is Abigail, by the way," Kate continued. "She was a good friend to your mum when she lived in the village last year. They even went on telly together."

"Mum did mention something about it."

They waited for her to elaborate but she just shifted her weight to the other leg awkwardly.

"There's all the parish jumble sale boxes in the back bedroom," Kate changed the subject. "I don't know what you want to do about them, but I can see if my mum can store them somewhere if you need them gone from the house."

Carol gave a cursory nod, and started to head up the path past Abigail towards the back door.

"Is there any news about a funeral?" asked Abigail. "I'd like to come over for it."

Carol paused, and was about to answer when she was distracted by the sight of the back door open.

"Has the door been unlocked all this time?" she demanded. "Who was last in here?"

"No, I have a spare key," lied Kate. "Just for emergencies and things. We needed to go in to plug the mower in, but we haven't touched anything."

Carol looked suspiciously between the door, Kate and Abigail, then strutted up to the key that was still protruding from the lock and yanked it out. "Well, I'll take this back if you don't mind," she said haughtily, "and if you can clear out those boxes by the end of today it'll be less crap that I have to deal with."

With that, she vanished inside the cottage and Abigail and Kate regarded each other not knowing whether to laugh or be offended.

"If she was more grateful, I'd be inclined to continue," Kate commented, removing her gardening glove. "But as she's not, I suggest we call it a day."

Abigail glanced around at their handiwork. They'd made it look half decent at least, but agreed with Kate that it was time to stop. "We'll get those boxes moved around to Mum's and then go and celebrate with lunch and Prosecco at the pub. We'll raise a glass to Mrs Angel."

As they padded up the stairs to Mrs Angel's spare bedroom, Abigail recalled doing this a year earlier, helping Kate to stash the boxes after the jumble sale where they first met. Such a lot happened in that year: she met Sam, they bought the stables, had everyone around for Christmas Day... the recollection of Mrs Angel enjoying family time in their warm cosy lounge filled Abigail with bittersweet memories. Then a thought struck her.

"Kate," she lowered her voice, aware that Carol was downstairs in this deathly quiet house. "There should be a suitcase of cash under the bed."

Kate giggled, thinking Abigail was joking. "What, from all her bank robberies?"

"No." Abigail pushed Kate deeper into the spare room and pushed the door shut. In a hushed tone, she explained how at Christmas, Mrs Angel had started talking about Robin being the executor of her will, and she specifically mentioned a suitcase of cash under the bed that she wanted Sam and Abigail to have.

Kate looked wary. "What if we're caught taking it out of the house?"

"We can bury it at the bottom of one of the jumble boxes."

Abigail got down on her knees and lifted the pink frilly valence sheet to peer into the gloom under the base of the bed. "There's nothing here." Needlessly, she stretched out an arm and felt around in case her eyes deceived her.

"Do you think she meant it was under her bed?"

"Maybe."

The thought of padding across the landing to Mrs Angel's bedroom seemed risky. Kate read Abigail's hesitation correctly. "Tell you what, I'll take one box down and distract Carol with some small talk whilst you nip into Mrs Angel's room."

"OK."

Abigail waited for Kate to get to the bottom of the stairs before trotting on tip toes across the landing and into Mrs Angel's room. It was brighter than the spare room, with the south facing window letting the April sunshine flood across the bedroom. It was also very pink. Loud roses adorned the wallpaper, the bedspread was cerise and the worn carpet was a strawberry and cream pattern. There wasn't time to stop and take it all in. Abigail crept to the bed, bent to lift the valence, but apart from dust and years of being untouched, the space was empty. How odd.

With relief that she wasn't having to smuggle a suitcase of cash from underneath Carol's nose, Abigail hurried back to rescue a box from the spare room and followed Kate's footsteps down the stairs and out through the front door.

34

Harriet Whittington-Packer crouched on the gravel with her camera held confidently in her left hand whilst her right hand pulled the lens into focus. Unlike many photographers that barked instructions to the models, Harriet worked silently, sliding like a crab around the horse and rider in front of her, whilst clicking away. Anastasia, the taut blonde atop Firefly the hunter, seemed at home posing for the camera, pouting, leaning down Firefly's groomed neck, twisting one way then the other, and finally sprawling back so that she covered Firefly's rump with her long fluffy locks tumbling down his hind quarters.

Abigail looked on in awe. This photoshoot was beyond her wildest dreams, and she bubbled with excitement.

"Ok, yah, thanks Anastasia, I think I've got everything. I'll take some on your smartphone so that you can Insta. I'm sure Tarquin will like it."

True to her word, Harriet hadn't forgotten her offer to Abigail in London, and Abigail had worked tirelessly to pull together the summer collection in the nick of time. It had taken every spare minute and most of the remaining contents of her bank account, but she had ten designs that she was happy with, and was able to get them made up into the correct sizes for Harriet's posh and breathtakingly beautiful bridesmaids. The absent party was Molly. Despite being a bridesmaid at Harriet's wedding, it was clear that Harriet didn't include her into her everyday social life, which was fortunate on this occasion as she was holding the fort in Hampshire.

"Are these pictures OK?" Harriet asked, indicating to Abigail that she should come and view the shots on the tiny digital screen. "I think we're lucky with the light this evening, but we need to be done within the hour I reckon." Abigail had been watching from the side lines, transfixed at the ease with which these girls showed off her dresses, and their ability to sprawl over the horses as though they were a couch.

Abigail peered at the small display as Harriet flicked through the shots. "Wow," she replied truthfully. "They're good enough for the pages of Horse and Hound."

"Yah, what a good idea. Mother's a good friend of the editor so I'm sure we can persuade her to run a little feature on the photoshoot."

One by one, Natasha, Imogen, Helena and Francesca strutted their poses in Abigail's glamorous outfits designed for a day at the races. With Daddy's fleet of hunting horses deployed as supporting cast, and the grandiose country manor, lawns, immaculate driveway and spotless stable yard all providing the scenery, Abigail felt like a spare part as the human and equine models took control of her future success. Alongside the pictures captured on Harriet's long lenses, snaps were also committed to smartphones and were out on social media in an instant, being shared by thousands of followers, before Abigail had chance to say thank you.

No sooner were the models stripping out of the dresses, than people were clicking on the links to Abigail's website and starting to send her messages to enquire how much the dresses cost and how they could order one.

"I can't thank you enough," Abigail gushed as they all gathered around the bar in the drawing room of Harriet's parents' country house. It was the most uncomfortable looking room Abigail had ever encountered, with a large chandelier dominating the pale space. There were armchairs and a sofa, but the co-ordinated cushions were so perfectly placed, it didn't look as though they had been sat on in their lifetime. There was a long, black granite bar between a marble bust on a plinth, and the glass cabinet holding hunting rifles. Harriet fetched a full ice bucket along with seven flutes and placed them on the bar, before disappearing again.

"Can we keep these?" Imogen asked Abigail, holding up her flowing scarlet dress and matching fascinator. "We're off to Newmarket next month so we're bound to be spotted and we can tell everyone about where these dresses came from. I was snapped by Hello magazine last year."

"Er, yes, of course."

Abigail winced slightly at the amount of money that she had spent on the material for the ten dresses, just to give them away to virtual strangers. On the flip side, if the girls' efforts brought in plenty of extra sales, it had to be worth it.

"I knew these would come in handy. They were left over from the wedding." Harriet returned with a couple of bottles of champagne under her arm.

"Abigail says we can keep these, so that's my Guineas outfit sorted," Imogen told Harriet.

"Well, Abigail has made Mummy and I the most amazing dresses for Newmarket," Harriet shot back. "Gok Wan is going to be all over us!"

The fitting had gone well earlier that day and both Harriet and her bony mother had gushed over the dresses, which thankfully fit the pair like a dream. Better still, they had paid her in cash, and taken her business card to distribute to friends. No doubt, they'd be friends in high places. With relief, when Abigail showed them the design for Alison Raven, the *Raceday One* presenter who would be heading up live coverage of the Newmarket Festival, they screwed their noses up. "Our outfits are much nicer. Thank you, Abigail," Harriet's mother confirmed.

As Harriet poured the champagne, chat turned to their social lives, which seemed to revolve around fancy balls, garden parties, skiing in the Alps and larking around on yachts on the Mediterranean. Every now and then, one of the hens would try to include Abigail by asking whether she was a good shooter, or where she went hunting, but Abigail's answers disappointed, and the chat moved inwards again. As the third bottle of champagne drained, Abigail hoped the hens weren't planning to go shooting that afternoon. Not only were they reaching the giggly side of tipsy, the spring sun was sinking rapidly towards the horizon, leaving precious little light for hitting targets.

"How did it go?" To Abigail's relief, she looked up to see Sam sauntering into the lounge behind Harriet's mother. Her saviour. She hadn't expected him until later, with the evening race meeting due to go on until 9pm, but a non-runner in the last race meant he could escape earlier. He'd clearly made a swift exit, with a streak of mud still crusted to his left cheek.

"It was great!" Harriet confirmed. "The horses were perfectly behaved and the girls were as stunning as ever. Want some bubbles?"

"Oh wow, I've got over a thousand likes already," Anastasia commented, looking up from her phone.

"I'm driving, but thanks."

"I guess I should go and check my emails for orders," Abigail took the opportunity to extract herself from the party. "And launch the photos on the website."

After another round of thanking Harriet and her shooting party, Abigail followed Sam out to his jaguar, which he'd abandoned on the gravel by the fountain; the centrepiece of the driveway.

"My God, this place is just...." she struggled to find a word to describe its obscene opulence. "You know, it feels like the houses of the upper classes in those Hollywood movies that are set in England. The country residence of Lord Snooty."

"Well, her Dad is Lord Whittington," Sam smiled. "And it sounds like we'll be living in a similar palace when your collection takes off."

He was only joking, but when Abigail checked her email back at the Ashington yard, her inbox was bursting.

"Oh, good lord," She exclaimed, glancing up from her laptop. "If all these enquiries turn into orders, how the hell am I going to churn this lot out from our tiny spare bedroom?"

He sidled up beside her and glanced at the emails.

"There's loads here asking for prices, bespoke designs, asking when the collection will be launched. It'll take me all night just to respond to this lot. Talk about pressure, Sam!"

"Tell me about it," he replied. "I've got to win for the Queen. Now that's pressure!"

35

Abigail spent a restless night, half sleeping, half dreaming of orders, emails, fabric, and invoices before Sam woke her early for their journey back from Gloucestershire to Hampshire. He was to drop her off before heading on to Windsor. Flat racing season was ramping up and Sam was in demand, his phone rarely stopped ringing with calls from his agent, trainers, owners, the media, and other jockeys on the circuit.

Abigail tried to block out the noise of his whirlwind lifestyle to concentrate on her business, but she still craved a relationship with him, otherwise what was the point of her living at the stables? If they were to be two separate ships that passed fleetingly in the night, then she may as well live back at her parents where she would at least have more space to extend her fashion empire.

This is ridiculous, she thought, surveying the spare room. Her sewing machine dominated the desk, whilst piles of fabric littered the floor. She had invested in a cork board where she hung notes, receipts, and important documents, but there were still loose papers stacked on the windowsill and floor. The printer sat on a stool, which had become a makeshift table, and wobbled precariously every time she sent something to print. Her laptop balanced on whatever surface she could find.

It was a daily battle to keep Bessie from the room, where she would wag her tail and send cotton reels and post it notes skidding over the carpet. It felt too claustrophobic to have the door shut while she worked in the room, and Abigail needed to keep an ear out for the landline downstairs, which rang at the least convenient moments with enquiries for riding lessons and corporate sessions. Occasionally there would be a firm booking for a corporate session; Molly held around one every fortnight. At this frequency they barely made any profit, so Sam's winnings on the racecourse were still a necessity for the stable's survival. *Raceday One* hadn't broadcast the piece with Abigail and Moody yet, so the publicity for the corporate sessions was reliant on social media and word of mouth.

"Do you want a cup of tea?" Molly called up the stairs a few days later. Abigail was immediately suspicious. In the six months that they had been operating together, the number of occasions that Molly had offered to make a drink could be counted on one hand.

Abigail agreed and a few minutes later, Molly appeared in the doorway of the spare bedroom, perplexed about where to place the mug. "I don't want to spill any tea on your fabric or anything."

Abigail rescued the drink from Molly's hands and smiled her thanks. "You OK?" she asked, as Molly continued to hover on the landing. It was also unusual for Molly not to take the opportunity to talk for thirty minutes about random topics that Abigail had no interest in.

"I have a favour to ask, actually," Molly replied sheepishly. "You know I'm going to the Newmarket Festival?"

Abigail knew no such thing and her mouth fell open, but before any words could escape, Molly continued in the way that Abigail was more familiar with: "Well, I'm going to be in the dressy enclosure, you know, rather than hanging about the stables as I usually do. So, I haven't got anything nice to wear. I don't actually possess a single dress: can you believe it? I wondered if you had a nice dress that I could borrow, or actually, two would be better as there are two days to the festival and I don't want to be spotted in the same outfit twice. I'm not sure if your dresses will actually fit me, as you're a bit taller and definitely slimmer than me, but maybe if you have something baggy or stretchy that would be suitable..."

"I didn't know Sam had invited you to Newmarket," Abigail managed to interrupt her flow. She was certain there was a flicker of a blush appearing across Molly's cheeks.

"He's giving me a lift up, yes."

"Oh." Abigail could clearly remember the conversation only a few weeks ago, where he had suggested that Abigail join him to see his victory in the Queen's colours. Admittedly she had dismissed the idea in a huffy rebuke, but it wasn't acceptable for him to then turn the invitation to Molly. Even though she had said she'd give a right kidney to go. It didn't seem right that Molly should accompany her boyfriend to a showy occasion on her birthday.

"I need to look gorgeous," Molly continued. "Everyone's used to seeing me like this," she indicated her scruffy jodhpurs and stained sweatshirt. Her big toe poked out of a hole in her threadbare sock. "I want to make people realise that I can be hot... maybe," she added with a little self-conscious laugh. "I need a certain someone to notice me."

The bloody cheek of it, thought Abigail, her sense of outrage boiling in the pit of her stomach. That girl had no boundaries. Abigail was certain there was nothing amongst her outfits that could make Molly look attractive to Sam.

"We can go and see what's in my wardrobe," Abigail put her cup of tea on the floor and stepped around Bessie who had wandered upstairs to join them on the landing. Molly followed Abigail into the bedroom, where she threw open the door to the second-hand wooden wardrobe that they'd picked up in a charity shop last year. For the first time in her life, she was having to share the space with someone else's clothes. Sam didn't have a massive assortment of garments, and most of his regular scruffy day clothes lived scattered on the carpet rather than on a coat hanger.

"I've got most of my dressy clothes back home in London," Abigail explained apologetically. She flicked through a few coat hangers, appraising the garments critically.

"That's nice." Molly put her hand out and clutched at the emerald green silk fabric of the dress Sam had bought her last year as a surprise birthday present. There was no way that was being loaned to anyone, especially clumsy Molly who would spill goodness knows what on it.

"What about this?" Abigail suggested to distract her, pulling out a jumpsuit. It had been bought from a vintage store in Shoreditch as a fancy-dress item for a seventies party in London, back in a different lifetime. It wouldn't be the slightest bit flattering for Molly. It was a shade of milk chocolate and made from cheap, scratchy nylon. Its puffy sleeves and flared trousers suited the party, where the aim was to look as ridiculous as possible, but for a Newmarket crowd? Abigail smirked as Molly squirmed.

"Or I have a maxi dress?" Replacing the jumpsuit, Abigail pulled out a floral, baggy dress. Its elasticated bust would accommodate Molly's ample chest, but holding it against Molly, she could see that the hem would drag on the ground.

"I'm such a mug," thought Abigail half an hour later as she set up the sewing machine's thread to take the hem up on the dress. It was the only thing suitable, and wouldn't make Molly look the slightest bit ravishing, but that was little consolation.

It had got Abigail thinking about all the lovely things she had in her bedroom back in her parents' house in Richmond. The floor-to-ceiling wardrobes in her warm pink room burst with dresses from boutiques, smart suits, kitten heeled shoes to die for, lovingly preserved in their shoeboxes, tubs containing clutch bags and fascinators, drawers with accessories, shawls, scarves and wraps. She felt a pang of homesickness, and momentarily missed the spontaneous nights out with Nadine.

None of her possessions would be any use here, she thought, glancing out of the window over the yard to the stable block.

Admittedly the cherry blossom on the tree was picturesque, and the sound of great tits celebrating the spring with the repetitive tweet of "tee-cher, tee-cher, tee-cher" was preferable to the drone of rush hour traffic crawling along the A305 towards Twickenham.

"I might go home for the weekend next week," she told Sam once he'd returned from a long day at Nottingham. There had been an accident on the M1, turning a three-hour journey into a five-hour nightmare. He was tired and grouchy, and it was all he could do to sit upright on the sofa to munch on a slice of toast. Molly had retired to bed, and Abigail was grateful for some time with Sam to herself, even if he was tetchy. She sat on the tatty armchair as Sam had his long skinny limbs stretched across the sofa and she hadn't the heart to ask him to move them.

"On our birthdays?"

"Yes. I understand Molly's going to Newmarket with you for the weekend, so there's little point me being here alone." It was a barbed comment that caused Sam to stop munching and raise an eyebrow at her.

"You had the chance to come."

"And I explained why I didn't want to. I'm sure Mum and Dad will take me out for a nice birthday meal instead."

Sam considered this for a moment and resumed his assault on the crusts. "I meant to say, I've arranged for a guy from the stables over the other side of Godshill to come and sort the horses out that weekend. He's a mate of Anna and Paul at the pub and comes highly recommended. You'll have to take Bessie with you, though."

At the sound of her name, Bessie lifted her sleepy head from where she was curled in her basket.

"I can't take Bessie!" Abigail protested, imagining the struggle with her luggage and an excitable dog on the tube across London. "She's Molly's fucking dog: she's not my problem!"

"Well, she can't stay here all weekend on her own," Sam sighed. "Can't you go home another weekend?"

"If I do, I might just stay there and not come back." Abigail hated herself for being so petty but couldn't help herself. Why was she always the one having to compromise all the time?

"Oh, grow up," sighed Sam wearily. "Everything's not always about you."

Abigail felt tears sting in the corners of her eyes and remained silent. Sam finished his toast and placed the crumb dusted plate on the carpet.

"By the way, Dad rang today. He's got the date for Mrs Angel's funeral. It's the Friday before Newmarket. In Sloth, not Edinburgh, thankfully. It's a burial in a plot next to her husband."

"At least that will be one day that we can spend together." There was an accusatory edge to her tone.

"Ah." Sam had the decency to blush in shame. "I can't go. I've promised some rides that day that I can't get out of."

"Not even for a funeral!?" Abigail was flabbergasted. "Seriously, Sam?"

"I would if I could," he pleaded in response, but Abigail had her doubts. Four legs always trumped two. Always.

36

"You can shed tears that she is gone, or you can smile because she has lived. You can close your eyes and pray that she will come back, or you can open your eyes and see all that she has left." As Mrs Angel's nephew confidently spoke, Abigail glanced about the church. It was full. She could see the back of Carol's head several rows in front of her, next to a tall slender man with half-moon specs, which must be husband Graham, the surgeon that stole Mrs Angel's only daughter away to Edinburgh. Next to him, the blonde girl staring at her feet must be Isabella. She found the effort to come for the funeral, Abigail thought bitterly.

The service was at St Mary's in Sloth, a parish church dating back to the 12th century. The building had no dedicated parking, just a gravel path off the quiet country lane, so cars littered the village, parked haphazardly wherever the mourners could find space. The church itself was cold and bare, despite the plentiful crowd that had turned up. The sound echoed off the stone walls and high rafters. "You can cry and close your mind, be empty and turn your back, or you can do what she would want: smile, open your eyes, love and go on."

Mrs Angel would be remembered fondly, Abigail was sure of that much. Everyone celebrating her life within these chilly four walls would have had a different experience of her, whether as a mother, aunt, friend, colleague, acquaintance, grandmother. In the short time that Abigail had spent with her, she remembered her sunny outlook, her enthusiasm for small things, whether a slice of cake or the thrill of a half hour game show. What would she think of Abigail's current misery? What would her advice be?

There was the creak of the door and Abigail turned her head, along with others, to see Robin creeping into the church. He glanced furtively around, seeking out his wife, but slipped into the back row rather than draw more attention to himself. Robin was able to take a break from the racing calendar, but Sam couldn't, Abigail reflected sadly. Her eyes skimmed around the church. There was Kate and her mum, complete with Aidan wriggling restlessly on her lap. Next to her was Dan looking smart in a suit. Penny's family from the farm were across the aisle, minus Penny who had been ordered to school, despite her protests. Countless other families represented extended family: friends from lunch clubs, villagers that knew Mrs Angel only from a wave each morning.

The service was over and pall bearers led the way out into the churchyard where a freshly dug grave awaited the coffin. Abigail hung back and let family take the front row around the hole. Outside, the warm spring continued, and fluffy clouds dappled the blue sky. Everything was solemn. The black clothes, the quiet whispers, the silent nods that people gave to acknowledge each other.

"All right?" Kate whispered, appearing at her side. Abigail nodded as her stomach growled in protest. Both girls giggled and enjoyed the momentary release of tension. "Just hungry."

The church clock chimed midday, and the sound appeared to signal the end of the proceedings around the grave, as people peeled away and began to shuffle into small groups. Conversations started up and became more animated. There was collective relief that the formal part was over.

The Carpenter's Arms bulged with people an hour later as the mourners drifted through the village to the pub. There were towers of sandwiches laid out on trestle tables in the back room, and a free bar. It wasn't clear who had put up the funds to offer free booze to everyone, but Abigail bet it wasn't Mrs Angel's family.

"I've got a good mind to go and confront Isabella," Kate said, shooting a glare across the room to where the granddaughter stood self-consciously with her mother and stepfather. "Silly cow."

"Oh, leave it," advised Abigail. "It won't achieve anything now." She threw Isabella a dirty look of her own for good measure, before turning her back to the family. "We were Mrs Angel's substitute family. And she knew it, too."

"It's a shame Sam couldn't make it," Kate's boyfriend Dan chimed in, returning from the gents and sensing a break in conversation.

"Hmm," Abigail responded. "He's racing at Chepstow. Just couldn't get out of it, he promised so and so." Her scathing words were lost on Dan, but Kate recognised the sentiment, having put up with the same excuses from her jockey husband for too long.

"Let me guess," she joined in. "He's got a dead cert on such and such, and if I let so and so down, he'll never ask me to ride again."

"You've got it," confirmed Abigail, downing her wine quickly and wondering whether it was too soon to get another. "I won't see him over the weekend as he's at Newmarket - with Molly - then Mondays are his long day..."

She stopped abruptly, realising that this occasion wasn't about her and her problems. She spied Sam's dad approaching, his lovely warm smile directed at them.

"Everyone OK?" he asked, beaming at the three of them. He put an arm around Abigail and drew her in to his chest, planting a loving kiss on the side of her forehead.

"Shame Sam couldn't be here."

He released Abigail.

"We were just saying that," Dan replied.

"I nearly didn't make it myself," Robin explained apologetically. "The work at the yard just never stops; I had to leave quite a few tasks to my staff down there, but fortunately they're a capable bunch." He checked his watch. "I can't stay long, though; I have to get up to Cheltenham this afternoon for a runner in the first race."

"Oh," Abigail's ears pricked up. "I have to catch the train back. Maybe I could get a lift to the station if it's not out of the way?"

"Not at all. I just need to pop back and pick up a few bits and check on some things, so..." he checked his watch again and performed a mental calculation. "I'll pick you up from here in 45 minutes?" Abigail could see the genetic similarity to Sam in those few seconds. Always on the go, never content to sit back with no plan.

She nodded her agreement.

"Perfect. Enjoy the free bar while you can."

Heeding Robin's invitation, Abigail managed to enjoy two more wines before bidding her Sloth friends goodbye and sliding into the passenger seat of Robin's Mercedes. A weariness fell over her.

She'd had an early start, walking the mile to Fordingbridge as Sam was too busy with the stable chores first thing to drive her. As she stood shivering in the misty dawn light on the side of the road for the bus to take her into Salisbury, she realised that there was no way of knowing whether the bus had already gone, was late, had broken down or was cancelled. She ran calculations in her head of alternative plans, working out what time she would have to find a taxi in order to connect with her train at Salisbury. To her relief, just two minutes later than the timetable declared, a bold, red and blue double decker stormed up the road and swished into the bus stop, flapping its doors open in welcome. Abigail boarded and bounded up the stairs to the top deck where she found the front seat empty.

The countryside passed outside, a blaze of emerald fields, encased in thick green hedgerows and clusters of trees, all bursting with life and energy following a period of warm weather and occasional showers since Easter. The bus barrelled along, slowing into villages every few miles, pausing at bus stops to let passengers on and off. Abigail still marvelled at how pretty this part of England was. Every time the farmland gave way to a settlement, the road became lined with thatched cottages and roadside pubs advertising weekend bar-b-ques and cream teas.

If she were serious about giving up on Sam and moving back to London, she would have to sacrifice all this nature and chocolate box beauty on her doorstep. "Then again," said the devil's advocate on her shoulder, "when do you ever get out of the house to enjoy it anyway?"

There was much time to think on the train journey from Salisbury to Bristol. Abigail had packed a paperback in her black handbag, but wasn't in the mood to read. The train was busy with commuters, many with their heads down, tapping away on their laptops, others taking the opportunity to rest with their eyes shut, and others reading. This was more like the London life she remembered. Carriages packed full of bodies, all ignoring each other.

At nine o'clock the train pulled into the airy glass structure of Bristol Temple Meads station and the passengers spewed out onto the platform. Looking at her watch, Abigail realised that the train had somehow become delayed on its journey and she had a frantic five-minute connection, jogging down the steps into the underground ant's nest, looking for the correct platform for the connecting train to Cheltenham.

She made it with seconds to spare, and sat in the first available seat, panting to get her breath back.

As Robin drove her back to reverse the journey, she found herself dreading it. She was likely to hit Temple Meads at the frenzied Friday five o'clock rush hour, and have to elbow her way on the train, desperately searching for a seat that wasn't reserved.

"Is Sam meeting you at the other end?" asked Robin, breaking into her thoughts.

"Hopefully," Abigail replied, "depending on what time he gets away from Chepstow and what the traffic is like".

Robin checked his watch, although Abigail suspected it was a reflex action and unrelated to either of their schedules.

"How are you finding his hectic itinerary?" It was as though he could read between her lines. "It's not an easy life for the spouses in the racing industry. Poor Liz has put up with a lot over the years."

Abigail sighed, fatigued. She would choose her words carefully, knowing the pride Robin had for his son's success, as well as not wishing to sound unsupportive.

"His winnings are keeping the stables afloat at the moment, so we mustn't grumble," she replied. "It would be nice to see more of him, but I understand his need to chase after the next win, I really do."

The devil on her shoulder sniggered and called her a liar.

"It's an addiction for jockeys," Robin nodded. "The thirst for more wins, bigger wins, more recognition. It becomes a vicious circle. The more they win, the more they want it."

"He did promise to retire from racing and concentrate on developing the stables." They had arrived at the station where Robin swung the car into a drop off bay and properly looked at Abigail. "Do you think it'll ever happen?"

"I wouldn't like to say," he replied quietly. "But if he's going to give it up for anyone, it would be for you."

Abigail smiled her thanks. Robin was a sweetheart but she wasn't sure she believed him.

37

It was no surprise to find that Sam's journey home from racing at Chepstow didn't align with her arrival at Salisbury. After a lengthy wait at Cheltenham, she caught the connections wrong at Bristol Temple Meads and finally arrived into Salisbury at seven o'clock. She dialled Sam's mobile, cold and exhausted, thinking that he may be approaching the area if her luck was in. Her tummy rumbled again, the sandwiches at lunchtime long forgotten.

"Ah - I'm still on the M4," he explained. "Just passing the junction for Bristol."

Bristol? Bugger, he was ages away then, she calculated with a sinking heart. "I bumped into Olly - you don't know him - and we went for a burger, so left Chepstow later than normal. It's good to let the traffic clear a bit."

And leave me stranded in Salisbury, she thought peevishly. Rather than stand around the draughty station for an hour, she preferred to keep moving, and walked across town to catch the bus back to Fordingbridge, before starting the mile walk down the lanes back to the stables. She was grateful that there was enough light left in the evening for her to feel safe. There was no way of walking this route when it was dark.

As she reached the Twin Oaks pub, there was a toot of a car horn behind her. Sam's Jaguar slowed and he waved, before accelerating off along the final hundred metres to their driveway.

"I thought it would take longer to stop and pick you up, than it would for you to walk the final stretch," Sam explained when Abigail protested a few minutes later. The kitchen was warm and soaking up the last of the rays as the sun sank over the horizon. Molly had made herself at home as usual in their lounge, the TV blared out a garden makeover show and she was as excited as a puppy to see them.

"How did it go?" she asked. She addressed the words to the kitchen and it wasn't clear who she aimed the question at.

"Tiffany's Charm was a disappointment," Sam replied, confirming Abigail's suspicion that they weren't interested in her day. She slung her handbag onto the least used chair around the kitchen table and pulled her hair loose from the band that had been holding it neatly back from her face all day. It felt good to release it all.

"...two furlongs out, Blake Seven shot up the outside, like he had a fifth gear and Tommy was like, ooh, you bastard, but Danny wasn't giving a shit..."

Abigail tuned back out of the racing chatter and raided the bread bin, where there was a single lonely slice remaining in the bottom of the bag. It would have to do. She popped it in the toaster and yawned, wondering if it was too early to retire to bed.

"So what time are you leaving in the morning?" She interrupted Sam's description of how Blake Seven's trainer nearly had a coronary cheering him into the winners' enclosure.

He paused, irritated at the intrusion.

"Early," he replied. He looked at Molly. "I thought if we leave here at seven, we can grab some coffee and a bite to eat on the way."

"Yeah, good with me," Molly confirmed.

"So, when shall we do presents?" Abigail asked. She'd bought Sam tickets to see his favourite band, The Almond Hearts, playing at Cardiff Castle in August. She hadn't bothered to see which race meetings it clashed with, and was determined to demand that they book a nice hotel and stay overnight. Any sign of hesitation on Sam's part and she was ready to throw in the towel. This would be the ultimate test, she figured.

"Sunday night's probably best?" It was more a question than a statement.

The toaster clunked and Abigail turned her attention to rescuing the warm bread. Without replying to Sam, she buttered the toast and hunted in the fridge for jam. There was still some of the posh farm shop preserve lurking on the top shelf, and Abigail slathered it on.

"OK," she replied neutrally. She kicked off her shoes and wandered over to the lounge, sinking deliberately into the chair that Molly favoured. "Mrs Angel's funeral went off well in case you were wondering," she called over to them. She didn't look at the pair as she bit into her toast, but could sense in the split-second silence the look that passed between them.

There was no coffee, cold or otherwise, on Abigail's bedside cabinet when she woke the next morning, and she was surprised that she had slept through their departure.

She sat up in bed and hugged her knees, analysing the subtext of Sam leaving without saying goodbye. Was he being considerate in not waking her, or was he so excited about getting to Newmarket with Molly that she didn't even cross his mind?

The latter seemed more likely.

"I'll make my own coffee then," she told Bessie, padding down the stairs. "I'm sure you'd make me a birthday cuppa if you could," she added, ruffling the collie's head as she passed. Bessie stood expectantly and slapped a wet tongue across Abigail's wrist.

On the kitchen table was a pyramid pile of wrapped presents. A note balanced on the top in Sam's scrawl saying, "To open Sunday night, no peeking".

As the kettle set about heating the water, Abigail regarded the pile. At the bottom was a rectangular box, about the size of the chunky VCR that Abigail's parents had when she was a child. She tapped it and sensed that underneath the paper wasn't a cardboard box, but something made of a sturdier material. The corners were more rounded than a cardboard box would be. Bessie whined and Abigail laughed. "I'm not peeking," she protested, "just prodding".

On top of the base present was a pile of cards. Abigail sifted through, identifying the sender from the handwriting. Most were addressed to them both, and Abigail realised that they would now be like twins, sharing the birthday together, receiving joint cards and sometimes joint presents. There was an A4 brown envelope at the bottom of the cards, with "Ab" on the front in Sam's writing. What on earth was that? She gave the envelope a flap. There wasn't anything as stiff as card in there, and the paper inside didn't run to dozens of pages, although there were definitely a few sheets by the weight of it. Her years temping in an office gave her an advantage to such detective work.

Next to the cards was another rectangular present, untidily wrapped up as though done in a hurry or by a child. She glanced at the tag, upon which was scrawled, "To Sam and Abi, Enjoy, Love Molly". Abigail picked up the parcel to determine its weight. It felt like a lunch box with something in it.

She turned her attention back to the boiling kettle. There was only a drop of milk remaining, and she remembered taking the last slice of bread last night. "Give me five minutes," she told Bessie, starting back up the stairs with her coffee, "and we'll go over to the shop".

They walked the long way to the farm shop to allow Bessie the opportunity to chase her favourite tennis ball over the heathland. Despite being May, the air had not warmed up yet, and a chill blew across from the west. Abigail zipped up her fleece against the wind and thought of Molly shivering in her maxi dress. Serve her right, she though with a grin.

She tossed the ball for Bessie once again and watched as she scampered through the bracken in pursuit. A smaller brown blur bolted up from behind them and followed Bessie, tail wagging happily. Bessie got to the ball first, retrieved it and began to trot back towards Abigail, the spaniel jumping excitedly at her side.

"Hello Daisy!" Abigail greeted Sol's dog and ruffled her ears as the pair arrived at her feet. Bessie dropped the slobber-soaked ball and waited for the game to start all over again.

"Ah, you've found your friend!" Sol addressed his dog as he broke into a half-hearted jog to catch them up. "Good morning," he smiled at Abigail. "Long time no see. How are things on Planet Abigail?"

Aware that she still owed Sol the money he gave her for MODA, she started with the good news about Teen Zero, and the launch of the new collection with Harriet. "I'll be able to pay you back soon. I'm just limited to what I can do in the tiny spare room."

"No problem," he waved it off, and she was grateful he was so trusting. "Are you heading towards Frogham?"

"Yes, I need to buy something tasty for my birthday breakfast." The pair began to saunter onwards, the two dogs sniffing along the pathway as they went.

"Ah, happy birthday! I hope Sam's got something nice planned for you today." He glanced sideways and met Abigail's eyes.

"He's away at Newmarket. He's riding one of the Queen's horses so he couldn't exactly miss it."

"Wow, the Queen! I presume he'll get knighted if he wins and beheaded if he doesn't." He chuckled at his own joke. "You didn't want to go and watch it?"

"To be fair to Sam, he did invite me, but it wasn't what I had in mind for our birthdays, so I said no. I regret it now, though."

"Oh, I'm not so sure, at least you can have something indulgent for your birthday breakfast. And you get to throw slobbery balls for Bessie." He nodded towards the disgusting mess in Abigail's hand. She made a mental note to get one of those plastic ball launchers. "Plus, you can spend quality time with Molly."

Abigail felt herself blushing. "Molly's gone with him."

"Ah." Sol sighed and looked intently at Abigail. His expression spoke more than any words could. She'd seen it in his face before, when she was heading to MODA and leaving Sam and Molly together. He'd made her feel like she was taking a risk to trust them together. He made her feel as though he was somehow disappointed in her for just being accepting of their relationship. He provoked those same feelings again now.

There was an awkward silence between them as they carried on to the fork in the path where Abigail needed to head left towards the farm shop. Sol's course meant he was turning right to head back towards home.

"Well, I hope you have a nice breakfast," he said in farewell, smiling sympathetically at her predicament. "Come on Daisy."

With a fresh farmhouse loaf bought and stowed into her backpack, along with some mature cheddar that she loved, Abigail walked back home, kicking Bessie's ball so that she could thrust her hands deep in her pockets. Her mind was in turmoil as she weighed up the pros and cons of leaving Sam. Maybe she should just move out for a bit, give them both a break to think about the future of their relationship.

As dark thoughts chipped away at her psyche, she felt the vibrate of her phone ringing. Expecting to see her mum's name on the display, her heart jolted when she saw it was Sam ringing. He never rang when he was racing. He said it distracted him, so he always turned his phone off and left it in the glovebox of the car. It was as though he had sensed her anguish.

"Hi, what's up?" she asked. It was so unusual for him to call; something must be wrong.

"I was just calling to wish you a happy birthday. Since you were so sleepy this morning."

"Oh, thanks, you too." In the background she couldn't hear anything. No car engine, no chatter or laughter from crowds of people, not even a distant racecourse tannoy blaring. "Where are you?"

"In the bedroom; I've just checked into the hotel before going to the course." In her mind, Abigail had a sickening image of Molly sat quietly in the room, leaning into the mirror and applying bright red lipstick in an attempt to attract Sam.

"Listen Sam, we... er... when you get home, we need to have a talk." She exhaled with relief. There, she'd said it. There was silence for a moment, and Abigail wondered whether they'd been cut off.

"Yeah, Ok. Well, I'd better be off. I need to prepare."

"Right. Well, good luck."

"Thanks." There was a click and he was gone. Abigail stared momentarily at the blank screen before shoving her hands back in her pockets and walking onwards.

38

The cottage felt cold and empty, and not even the bacon buttie that Abigail cooked herself for her birthday breakfast could warm her up. She resorted to lighting a fire and, as the flames set in and the warmth slowly penetrated the lounge, Abigail flopped on the sofa and flicked on the TV. She encouraged Bessie to join her, and snuggled into her soft fur for a cuddle. It felt indulgent to put her feet up in the middle of the day. She could even close her eyes and have a snooze if she felt like it.

She was just enjoying the relaxation when a sharp rap on the glass of the kitchen door jolted her back to reality.

Groggily, she disentangled herself from Bessie and waddled towards the kitchen. Through the frosted glass she could make out the shape of somebody tall and slender.

"Me again!" joked Sol as she opened the door to his smiling face. He thrust a bouquet of red roses at her and waggled a bottle of fizz in his other hand. "A little something for your birthday."

He'd changed into smarter jeans since this morning and had swapped his Barbour jacket for a sweater that was supposed to look casual, but Abigail could tell it was expensive cashmere. He'd styled his hair.

"Come in," Abigail remembered her manners and stood aside to let him over the threshold. "Thank you. You didn't have to."

"There's cake too." From a carrier bag swinging off his elbow he produced a supermarket bought, boxed cake, placing it on the table as Abigail looked for a jug to put the roses in. She knew there wasn't a vase in the house.

"Are you on your way somewhere, or have you got time to have a piece of cake?" she asked.

"For you, I have all the time in the world." His lines were sickeningly smarmy, but he delivered them with a flirtatious hint of irony that made them more acceptable. "Unless I'm interrupting you, don't let me intrude..."

"No, I'm not doing anything."

She filled the jug with water and hastily arranged the roses before setting out to find a couple of clean plates and a sharp knife to cut the cake.

"Shall I put the champagne in the fridge?" he asked. "Unless you want to open it now? It's chilled already."

She looked up and met his baby blue eyes. "Yes, you know, fuck it. It's my birthday and if I want to drink bubbles and eat cake in the middle of the day, I shall!"

"That's the spirit," Sol laughed. "Where are your flutes?"

"Oh, we're not posh enough for champagne flutes in this house," Abigail grinned, mocking his public-school clipped accent. "We'll have to make do with wine glasses."

She watched him surreptitiously from the other side of the kitchen as he removed the cage from the top of the bottle and began to ease the cork out. There was something sexy about watching a man take control of this. The bottle gave a grateful pop as the cork was released, and he filled the two waiting wine glasses, handing one to Abigail.

"May you have a very happy birthday. Cheers," he toasted.

"Cheers." They sipped and looked at each other.

"So what time is the race?"

"The big one is at half past three but Sam's got other rides, and they'll be doing a big build up on the telly." She checked the kitchen clock. "We can go and eat our cake in the lounge and have a watch?"

As they took their seats on the sofa, munching cake and sipping champagne, Abigail realised that watching Saturday afternoon racing would have been her idea of hell a year ago. She wondered whether Sol thought the same now.

The *Raceday One* presenters sat at a long wooden table on the studio, copies of the *Racing Post* strewn out in front of them. The team comprised an ex-jockey, who looked to be in his sixties, but may just have had a hard life and was actually in his early fifties. The reporter that had come to the stables, Jonathon, was also on presenting duty, and their colleague Alison Raven, sat between them, the rose between two thorns. She was in her early thirties with flawless skin and perfect makeup. Her glossy black hair sat in a fat braid around her crown, whilst ringlets fell beyond her slender shoulders. She had a generous smile as she dominated the chat around the afternoon's proceedings.

Abigail's heart sank as she realised Alison wasn't wearing the dress she had designed and made for her. She knew it had fitted, as Alison texted her thanks, confirming receipt. She hadn't said she liked it, though. Bollocks.

"Now we all know Sam Ashington has a great chance on Captain Tom in the feature race later this afternoon, but you've been to meet one of the four-legged stars that currently lives with him in Hampshire..." Alison started to say to Jonathon. Abigail sat bolt upright, and nudged Sol.

"Look, this is the piece he did here!" She put down her glass and pointed to the screen.

"That's right," confirmed Jonathon. "Whilst Sam's racing around the country, back home, one of his former mounts is actually teaching his girlfriend to ride!"

Both Sol and Abigail leant forward to watch as the feature started. The camera scanned around the yard, making it look clean and inviting. Abigail blushed as she appeared on screen, describing how Sam had bought the racehorse for her Christmas present.

"You look good in all the gear," grinned Sol. The film had cut to show Abigail and Moody cantering around the paddock and popping neatly over the thigh high pole. The jump looked pathetically low on screen, but Abigail was consoled by the fact that she looked confident and her seat was good. Over the image, Abigail described the business. "I must add that I don't teach the corporate sessions. That's down to Sam when he's here, and his brilliant assistant, Molly Packer."

"Assistant?" Sol looked at her, his teasing blue eyes sparkled. "That's one word for it."

"She's a Godsend," Abigail replied sharply. "She doesn't require paying either."

Sol gave her another lingering look that was loaded with unspoken thoughts. Before the TV piece had ended the landline began to ring.

An enquiry. As soon as Abigail noted all the details and hung up, it rang again. This repeated four times before Abigail decided to let the answerphone take the remainder of the calls. She knew it was a risky strategy, as some people didn't like to leave messages and would just hang up.

"You can't be expected to play secretary on your birthday," Sol agreed. "Your champagne will get warm. Besides, Molly should be here doing that, not going off for a good time with Sam."

"You're right, fuck 'em. Molly can pick all that up on Monday morning."

She returned to the sofa, the alcohol already having an impact on her body. Maybe it was best she didn't talk to customers at the moment; it didn't look good to be tipsy at this time of day.

They sat and enjoyed the first few races, chatting amicably about village gossip. Sam had a chance in the second race, but his mount appeared to run out of juice two furlongs from the winning post and was consigned to a losing position.

By the time the feature race was about to start, Sol was pouring the last few drops from the bottle, and Abigail felt unsteady. How much of the giddiness was down to the expectations of the race ahead, and how much was the alcohol pumping through her bloodstream was anyone's guess. They watched as the jockeys mounted and the horses cantered down to the start. One by one, the handlers fed the thoroughbreds into their metal cages. Some horses resisted petulantly, and it took the brute force of several men to heave the bulk forwards. Other horses - like Sam's mount, Captain Tom - strode passively in and appeared to nod their acknowledgement to the handler. Once the horses were all confined to their starting stalls, the handlers scampered away, job done. Abigail found she was holding her breath. She felt nervous for Sam, and wondered how he was feeling, waiting for the clang as the doors shot open and Captain Tom would thrust forward like a bullet. The commentator had no such nerves. Thirty years of narrating these two-minute dashes meant that he was relaxed, but excited. "They're forward, they're ready, and they're off," he said as the wall of racehorses shot out onto the openness of the track.

Sol squealed in excitement; Abigail continued to hold her breath. Unable to make sense of the flurry of colours, they listened intently to the commentary. "As they begin the journey for the 2000 Guineas race, Captain Tom is one of the first to show as they split into two groups. Captain Tom under the skilful hands of Sam Ashington leading the pack on the left, with Power Up, Amesbury and Flying Solo also up there…"

"He's leading!" cried Sol, putting his glass down on the coffee table as his hands naturally wanted to bang the air, urging the horses on. Abigail couldn't speak. What if this was Sam's life changing break, winning Newmarket's most prestigious race on behalf of the Queen? The enormity of it suddenly hit her.

Meanwhile, the commentator still sounded factual and relaxed. "On the right, Tripwire leads to Galway Bay and then comes Simba. Jackie Simnell is urging on Tripwire as she tries to make history today as the first female jockey to take the 2000 Guineas crown."

Abigail managed to take a gulp of her fizz. Sam was holding his lead, the gold braiding on his purple silks making him stand out from the crowd. "Windermere Lodge in the orange and red is right back towards the rear of the pack and Budapest is the back marker."

The pack passed the halfway point, and Abigail knew that anything could happen as the race got towards its business end. The horses knew it, lengthening their stride, the jockeys knew it as they instinctively sensed the field around them and planned their tactics in split second decisions, and the crowd knew it as the volume of the cheering steadily increased as the wall of thundering hooves approached them.

The commentator knew it too, speeding up his observations, urgency creeping into his tone. "As they head down past the bushes now, it's Captain Tom leading Tripwire. Amesbury and Galway Bay begin their challenges..." The two separate packs had gradually crept back into one mass in the centre of the course, a handful of horses extending their leads out in front, leaving others trailing in their wake. "And Tripwire powers on, Jackie Simnell on board coming towards the stands side, Captain Tom is after him and Amesbury is running a huge race!"

Sam was using every ounce of power he could muster to urge Captain Tom faster, but Tripwire kept a stride ahead, seemingly lengthening his neck as the finish line came within touching distance. "Tripwire still in front with Captain Tom trying to reel him in, but it's Tripwire and Jackie Simnell first across the line, making history, with Captain Tom second, and Amesbury third."

Both Sol and Abigail let out an exhausted sigh. "Send him to the tower and orf with his head!" Sol joked, poorly imitating Her Majesty. To her embarrassment, Abigail felt the sting of tears in the corner of her eyes, an uncontrollable and inexplicable sense of defeat engulfed her.

"Oh sweetheart," Sol said, noticing as a shiny tear snaked its way down her flushed cheek. "Are these happy tears? Second's good, isn't it?"

"Yes, it's very good," she agreed, but she couldn't articulate the emotion that came with the realisation that Sam would never retire from racing. Why would he want to spend his days running corporate sessions and riding lessons when he could experience the roar of the crowd up the Rowley Mile? She could never compete with the thrill Sam must get from taking part in a race like that. And if life wasn't going to change for Sam, then it wasn't fair on her. She needed to let him go.

39

Sam's jubilation was waning, as exhaustion crept through his muscles. A journey of 160 miles back to Fordingbridge wasn't what he really wanted to do now, especially as the hotel room was right there waiting for him. Several of his weighing room colleagues had made disapproving comments about leaving his girlfriend overnight on her birthday and he started to feel guilty. Maybe he had been selfish. Her voice on the phone that morning sounded oddly strained. She wanted to talk about something. Various scenarios flashed through his brain. Maybe she wants a baby? Maybe she's already pregnant, he thought in horror. She'd certainly been moodier recently. Or she could be ill? Whilst he'd tried to push the nagging thoughts out of his head and focus on the racing, once he'd completed his rides for the day, he knew he had to go home and talk to her.

Once clear of the Newmarket traffic, the roads were blissfully empty of Saturday evening traffic and he had a good run home.

"Hi Ab!" he called, entering into the empty kitchen. The TV was off and the downstairs quiet. Bessie rose to her feet and trotted over in welcome, so she wasn't out on a dog walk. He glanced around the scene, spotting two wine glasses and a champagne bottle on the coffee table. So, she'd had a friend over. He couldn't think who, but Kate or her mum may have come over to surprise her. Perhaps that meant that they had gone to the pub for birthday meal and drinks. She'd left the door unlocked though; he'd have to nag her again about the need for security in the countryside.

"Stay here, Bessie," he told the collie. Retreating from the kitchen, he locked the door and made his way across the yard in the direction the pub. He was almost at the gatepost when a silhouette over by the stable block made him double take. She was stood with her back to him. Moody stood patiently tied outside her stable. It was good that she had more confidence around the mare now, and when he retired, he looked forward

186

to spending more time riding with her and helping to develop her skills further. She appeared to be talking gently to Moody, stroking her smooth, taut neck.

He hurried towards her, on tip toe for the last twenty metres hoping to make her jump.

"Evening," he whispered into her ear. It worked, and she yelped in surprise.

"You're home," she stated needlessly, turning to face him.

He was horrified to see that her face was blotchy, mascara smudged, eyes red and still swimming in tears.

"Whatever's the matter?" He asked. He instinctively reached out for her, but she took a step back and he dropped his arm back to his side.

She tried to compose herself, bottom lip wobbling. "I've been trying to work out how to tell you that I'm leaving."

His face fell and he sat down heavily on a straw bale behind him. "Whoa. That felt like a punch in the stomach." Of all the scenarios that flashed through his mind today, that wasn't one of them. The image of the two glasses flashed into Sam's head, and it suddenly made sense. All those days that he'd left her alone in this remote hamlet, of course she was going to find someone else. Shit, how could he have been so neglectful?

He looked up at her. Her blue eyes held pools of tears poised to spill down her cheeks. She looked back at him miserably.

"Who is he?" he whispered.

"Who?"

"The man you're leaving me for."

Abigail spluttered, too taken aback to be insulted. "There's no-one else."

"Oh, I saw the champagne bottle and thought...". Sam had no idea what he thought. He just needed to rescue the situation. He stood up again, and momentarily felt dizzy. It didn't help that he hadn't eaten since having a banana and a coffee at the services twelve hours ago.

He reached out again and touched the side of her arm. Although she flinched, she didn't move her arm away. "So, what have I done wrong?" he asked gently.

"It's not just you, Sam," she protested, "I'm just thoroughly miserable." She gesticulated her arm towards the cottage, dislodging his grasp. "It's Molly, it's this place, it's being confined in that tiny room day in day out, it's not having any transport to escape the village, it's being lonely, it's the insecurity of money, it's never seeing you, it's feeling like we're not a couple."

She'd worn herself out and put her arms around Muppet's neck. "I feel as though Muppet loves me more than you do."

"Oh God, Abigail," Sam protested in frustration. "Of course I love you. I think you're bloody awesome. I just don't always tell you. I presumed you knew."

The sun had sunk quickly, and there was barely any light remaining across the yard. Sam shivered. Silence fell between them.

"I remember this time last year," Sam said softly. "We nearly didn't get together due to a misunderstanding, do you remember?" Abigail released her arms from Muppet's neck and turned to face him again. He ached to pull her to him, but he needed to work harder first. "All it took was a talk to sort it all out," he continued. "I'm sure we can work though this and put things right. Please?"

Abigail wiped her eyes with her sleeve and nodded. "Let's put Muppet away and then go inside," she conceded with a sniff. "It's freezing out here."

The warmth of the kitchen hit them like a welcome tidal wave as they entered. Without speaking, Abigail slumped into one of the chairs around the kitchen table, her body language telling Sam that this was going to be more challenging than his ride five hours ago.

He took the seat directly opposite so that he could look her in the eye. "OK. Run it by me again. What's making you most upset?"

The seconds ticked by as she considered this. "You mentioned Molly..." he prompted.

"It feels like there's something going on between you two."

"Now that's just silly. We're good friends, that's all!" Sam protested.

"You play those console games together, roll around on the rug play fighting, talk about horses and racing constantly, then you invite her away to Newmarket overnight. What am I supposed to think?"

"You have to trust me; we will never be anything more than friends. Molly doesn't like me in that way."

"That's not how it looks. Even Sol thinks so."

Sam bristled, suddenly realising who would have brought the champagne around. Not to mention the bunch of red roses that mocked him from the windowsill. He should have brought her flowers back from Newmarket. Damn.

"What the hell does Sol know?"

"Well, why would he make it up?"

"Because he's a shit stirrer that wants to get in your knickers," Sam spat.

Abigail took a sharp intake of breath, but to Sam's relief, she didn't attempt to defend him. He had to be careful: he didn't want things to escalate into a row.

"If you don't believe me, I'll ask Molly to reassure you. Oh, and for the record, I didn't invite Molly to Newmarket overnight. She's there as Jackie Simnell's guest. I was just the chauffeur."

Sam was keen to move on; there had seemed a long list of accusations to work through. "Shall we talk about your next gripe?"

"I hardly ever see you. Until you retire from racing, that's not going to change, is it? But I don't want to be the reason you retire if it's going to make you resent me."

"I *do* want to retire," Sam insisted. "I'm bloody exhausted working long days like this. And I will retire, I promise. After Royal Ascot seems appropriate; that's only six weeks away."

Abigail looked at him doubtfully. "You said you would retire a year ago," she replied wearily. "Your dad doesn't think you'll ever retire."

"Funnily enough, I was going to announce it if I won today, live on the TV interview. But of course, I didn't win." Abigail longed to believe him. "I've got another chance tomorrow. If I win the 1000 Guineas, I'll break the news to Alison Raven live on air."

"And if you don't win?"

"I'll have to get the news out in a press release. You can write the damn thing for me."

That seemed to cheer Abigail up, and she managed a faint smile.

"And with me at home more, you can have the car to get out and about whenever you like. Can we tick that one off the list?"

"I guess so."

"Now, you complained about being stuck in the tiny spare room."

"It's claustrophobic and not the sort of place I can expand my business from."

Sam risked a coy smile and reached down the table to the presents. He extracted the smaller parcels from the top and slid the rectangular base towards Abigail. "Let's start with this one. It's technically a gift for both of us, but I already know what it is."

"Who's it from?" Abigail searched for a label.

"You'll know when you open it."

Abigail peeled back the wrapping to see a battered suitcase. It had the musty scent of something that had been stored in an attic, and suddenly she realised what it must be.

"Mrs Angel's money?" She gasped. The case was locked with two cracked leather straps, and with shaking fingers she unfastened them and prised up the lid. "Oh my God." Like something out of a heist movie, the case was packed full of bundles of £20 notes. Abigail picked a wad off the top. It was held together with an elastic band. "She really did rob a bank. There's a small fortune in here." There were so many questions.

189

"No, she just never trusted banks and stashed any spare cash under her bed. For years, and years, and years."

"But Sam," Abigail looked around with wide eyes, as though expecting a squad to come bursting through the door with guns poised, ready to arrest them. "How did you get it?"

Sam smiled, enjoying her reaction. "Dad told me to go and get it from under her bed and stick it in his car the day she died."

Abigail dropped the wad in her hand back into the case as though it were contaminated. "This feels all wrong. I know she said we could have it, but what if the family find out? We could be in so much trouble. We only have her word at Christmas to rely on."

"Don't panic," Sam put a reassuring hand on hers. "She wrote a note to Dad after Christmas confirming everything she said here. It's all in writing if we ever get challenged. Which is just as well, because half of this isn't legal tender anymore." Sam lifted a couple of bundles to reveal unfamiliar notes underneath, dating from days before they were born. "We'll have to take it to the Bank of England if the local bank won't accept it."

Abigail closed the lid and ran her hand over the worn-out leather. There was so much history in the case. It was just as beautiful without its contents. "Are we doing presents then?" Abigail thought how her tickets to the Almond Hearts concert was going to look pathetic next to Mrs Angel's case.

"No, we're making things better for you," Sam replied. He slid the A4 envelope towards her, feeling more confident that she was being persuaded to stay. He watched her face as she slit open the envelope and tugged the paper free from inside. She frowned at the headed note paper from the local council, skim reading it before opening out the larger sheet that had been folded into quarters. She wasn't sure what she was looking at so Sam leaned over to help.

"That's the planning permission, and these are the architect's designs. Your own studio cabin on site, look, just down from Moody's stable, over a hundred square metres of dedicated space for you and your business. A place to store fabric, plans, your sewing machine, those tailor's dummy things and whatever else is piled up in that room. You can design the space however you like."

He could see that her eyes had lit up as the black pencil lines on the plans became real in her head. She could visualise a bright space where she would get away from the clutter and the landline and spread out, dedicate time and energy to the business.

"Can we afford this?" She asked.

Sam shook his head in despair. "You've got a whole suitcase full of money there. Take what you need."

She was smiling at last.

"Any more gripes?" He smiled back. She blushed and shook her head. Rising from his seat, he walked around the table, spreading his arms to invite her into a hug. She stood and melted into his embrace, grateful to feel his strong arms around her.

"So, you'll give me a chance?" he murmured into her neck.

"I suppose I can put you on probation," Abigail agreed. She pulled back and looked him in the eyes. "But if you don't retire from racing in six weeks, I'll be on the next train to Waterloo."

Sam's stomach growled unromantically, reminding him that he'd eaten nothing all day.

"I guess it's a bit late to take you out for a birthday meal," Sam apologised, releasing her. "But we can order in a takeaway?"

"Sounds good." He wondered whether to push his luck.

"Then maybe an early night?"

"Or..." she looked playful once again. "You can teach me the basics of *Champion Jockey*." If you can't beat 'em, you've got to join them, she figured.

40

There was still a small detail that was bothering Abigail when she woke the following morning. She instructed Sam to enjoy a lie-in, bringing him coffee in bed and offering to take Bessie out before they left for Newmarket. He'd persuaded her to join him for the second day of the Guineas Festival, and as the weather was glorious and there was a chance that he'd announce his retirement, she agreed.

"Come on, Bessie," she called to the excited collie, who jumped from her basket and bounced around the lounge, thwacking surfaces with her tail. Abigail spotted yesterday's knickers abandoned at the side of the sofa, and with a grin, swiped them up off the floor and disposed of them in the washing machine. It had been a perfect evening last night. Having grasped the basics of the *Champion Jockey* game, they had enjoyed hungry and spontaneous make up sex on the cushions in the lounge. Abigail sighed contentedly at the memory, marvelling at what a difference twelve hours could make. She would have liked to lie-in with Sam, cuddle into his warmth and lazily trace the counters of his naked flesh with her fingers. There was no time for that. She was on a mission.

She counted out notes from Mrs Angel's suitcase and put them into an envelope before retrieving Bessie's lead, making her way up the drive and through the village towards Sol's cottage.

"Sorry it's so early," she apologised, as Sol opened the front door, tying his dressing gown cord around him. He looked surprised and flustered.

"Not a problem, I...er...is everything OK? Do you want to come in?"

"I came to bring you the money I owe you," she explained, handing over the envelope.

"Fuck me, did you rob a bank?" he replied, peeking into to see the contents. "A bank transfer would have worked just as well. Look, come in." He opened the door wider as Daisy came snuffling to greet her four-legged friend.

"Thank you." She stepped inside the hallway. "I hope I didn't get you out of bed."

"No, I was just making coffee, actually." He shut the door behind her and led the way through to the kitchen diner. "You're welcome to stay for one."

Abigail agreed to a quick coffee, calculating that she didn't know what chance she would get later. As Sol poured from the cafetière, Abigail filled him in on Sam's surprise visit home last night. She skipped most of the detail, but told him about the planning permission and the plans to build her a purpose designed studio, as well as his promise to announce his retirement.

"Sounds like good timing," Sol agreed, "with the way all the calls came in yesterday for the corporate sessions". He took a seat and motioned for her to sit opposite.

"Also, he's adamant about Molly being nothing more than a friend, and I'm going to have a chat with her today," Abigail continued, "but there's one thing that I can't figure out".

"What's that?"

"Why Molly asked Anna whether there were any jobs for me at the pub."

"When did she do that?"

Sol reached for the sugar bowl and stirred a couple of teaspoonfuls into his drink.

"Don't you remember? You told me about it! It was the day I'd had some falls when I was learning to jump on Moody, and came into the pub. You force fed me brandy and said you'd overheard Molly asking Anna if there was any bar work for me."

Sol's eyebrows knitted together in thought. "No, I don't remember that."

Abigail sighed in exasperation. "It wasn't that long ago, Sol. Have you got dementia?"

"I remember the occasion," he protested, "but not my exact words". A small smirk came to his lips. "Most of what I say is bullshit. It's not worth wasting brain cells storing it to memory."

"Well, I was quite upset by it," Abigail replied sternly. "You implied that Molly wanted me out of the house in the evenings so that she and Sam could have more time together." She gulped at her coffee, sensing that she was going to need to make a sharp exit before too long.

"Oh that!" Sol gave a light chuckle. "That was just me messing with you. Don't ever take me seriously, Abigail."

She couldn't believe what he'd just said. "So... hang on, let me get this straight. You just invent stuff to make people upset?" She slammed her coffee cup down to demonstrate her irritation. Bessie looked up from where she had slumped and thumped her tail on the floor a couple of times. It was like having a canine cheerleader on the sidelines.

"People only get upset if they take what I say the wrong way." Sol's face had clouded over. He could sense the tension in the air too.

"How much of it was true? Did Molly ask Anna if there were any jobs going?"

Sol shrugged. "Not that I recall."

Abigail stood up and looked him in the eye. "That's a very childish game for a man of your age. What on earth possesses you to think it's a good idea? You can destroy lives with those tactics."

"Oh, you need to learn to lighten up and take life less seriously," he retorted. He remained seated and showed no intention of moving.

Abigail nodded curtly, patted Bessie to her and strutted out into the hallway in what she hoped was an assertive fashion. "Bye Ab," he called after her, but she was already making her way out of his front door and into the lane.

She was relieved that he had made it all up. It backed up Sam's version of events that Molly had no interest in him, but equally she was disappointed in his behaviour. What strange kick did he get from upsetting her like that, and planting ideas in her head? She remembered Sam's accusation last night that Sol was a shit stirrer that simply wanted to get in her knickers. There was no defence of that now.

Back at the cottage she had enough spare time to open the birthday cards that had been untouched. Her parents had sent a floral card and a gift voucher for a clothes store. Abigail had guessed correctly that Molly had wrapped up a lunchbox, but inside were a stack of homemade chocolate chip cookies.

Kate had sent a card and a dainty necklace with a horseshoe on. The purple envelope on the bottom of the pile rose Abigail's spirits. Nadine! It was a homemade card: a black and white photo of Camden Lock that Abigail suspected Nadine had taken herself, stuck onto card. A sheaf of notepaper fell from the card, which Abigail unfolded.

Happy birthday Ab!
I've been meaning to get in touch sooner, but things are completely chaotic at the moment.

Abigail smiled to herself. When wasn't Nadine's life chaotic? She read on.

Erik and I split up after a month in Amsterdam. He was only ever interested in himself and his intellectual friends were a nightmare. I can put up with a lot of weed induced debating (as you know) but these guys were on a different level.

He wasn't surprised or particularly bothered when I told him I wanted to come back to London, so I'm now back and sleeping on Dougie's floor. The guys are glad to have me around again and I'm helping out with their gigs, but I must get my life together like you have. I should be using my fashion degree, but apart from applying for a job in Top Shop I'm not sure where to start. I don't think I'm cut out for teaching after all. I nannied for a posh kid in Amsterdam for a week and she was a nightmare, and I realised that teachers have to put up with dozens of these little brats every day.

Anyway, please come up to London soon and we'll have a good night out and long overdue catch up.

Sending love and hugs
Nadine xxx

41

It felt like a new relationship again as they made the drive together to Newmarket. Dressed in the green silk dress that Sam had bought her for last year's birthday, Abigail stole glances at Sam as he navigated his way around the M25. Occasionally he let his left hand slip off the gear stick and rest lazily on her thigh. For Sam, the pressure was off compared to the previous day; whilst the second day of the festival was still a prominent day in the racing calendar, his rides today were all for his regular trainers and he knew he already had the respect of the owners.

"I just need to pick up my bag that I left at the hotel last night, and check out," Sam explained, pulling into the left lane to park up at the budget hotel on the outskirts of Newmarket. "Do you want to wait in the car? I'll just be a few minutes."

"Actually, I could use the loo," Abigail had been confined to the car for ninety minutes and her bladder was starting to nag.

"There's some in reception. I'll meet you back at the car."

Abigail was pleased to see that he'd only booked himself into a cheap chain hotel. She'd heard from Kate that there were some very posh spa hotels in the vicinity, and such extravagance would have raised her suspicions.

She burst into the toilets focussed on one thing only, and crashed into the stall with relief. As she sat, she realised she was not alone, as female voices rose from what she supposed was the vanity area.

"It's been a couple of months and I just don't think it should be a secret anymore."

"I know, that's what Sam said." Abigail froze. That was definitely the unmistakable sound of Molly's voice. "He texted me last night saying I should talk to Abigail today."

"He's right. You've got to tell Abigail. It's not fair that she doesn't know."

Know what? Abigail flushed the toilet and the girls fell silent, not realising that someone else had entered the loos.

"Know what?" Abigail demanded, striding out of the stall. Molly jumped, and the colour drained from her face. Abigail recognised the other girl as Jackie Simnell.

"Great timing!" Jackie beamed. She touched Molly's arm supportively and nodded towards the door. "I'd best be going but I'll catch up with you later. Probably after I've whipped Sam's ass in the 1000 Guineas." She gave a genuine smile in Abigail's direction and floated out of the toilets. Molly watched her go, then turned her attention back to Abigail, who was washing her hands patiently, waiting for Molly to answer her question.

"I don't know how to say this..." Molly admitted. Abigail's heart was pounding. Had her suspicions been right all along? Christ, was Sol right all along?

"Well, the thing is...Jackie and I have started seeing each other."

Abigail shook the drips from her hands and took stock. Had she heard correctly? "You're a couple?"

"Shhh," Molly put her fingers to her lips, although there was no-one to hear. "It's not public yet, although Sam knows. Jackie wants me to start telling everyone, but I've not come out yet, and the thought terrifies me."

"Oh Molly," sighed Abigail with relief. She pulled her in for a hug. "It's no big deal. In fact, I'm chuffed to bits for you. You look really happy together."

Molly squeezed her thanks. "Yeah, but not everyone thinks like that, do they?" She pulled away and checked her mascara in the mirror. "Jackie lost a couple of friends in the past when she came out."

"Well, they weren't friends that were worth having then, were they?"

Molly smiled sadly and nodded. Abigail could sense that she had more on her mind.

"Is Jackie your first girlfriend?"

"Kind of. I had a massive crush on one of the instructors at racing college, but that was a bit one-sided. No, I correct myself. It was entirely one-sided. That's what got me expelled."

"They threw you out for being gay? I don't think they're allowed to do that under the equalities..."

"No," Molly interrupted. "I was finding it difficult to take 'no' for an answer and I got a bit obsessive over her. I'm not proud of my behaviour, but at least I avoided a restraining order. Narrowly," she added with a wistful laugh.

Abigail wondered what she had done exactly, but didn't push it. She felt honoured that Molly had opened up that much to her.

"Sam's outside with the car if you want a lift?" Abigail realised that he would probably start wondering where she had got to. They made their way out of the toilets together, Molly chattering about how glad she was that Abigail had come, and that it was going to be a gloriously sunny day.

Swarms of racegoers were heading on foot from the town towards the racecourse, dressed in their finery, some men already swigging lager from cans. Sam pulled into the car park designated for jockeys and they got out and made their way across the gravel towards the grandstands.

"Good morning, Sam!" A voice called from behind them. The trio turned in unison to see Alison Raven heading towards them, tottering awkwardly on towering heels. Abigail's heart raced as she recognised Alison's dress as her creation. It looked fantastic on her, the wrap of silk emphasising her tiny waist, whilst the bias cut hugged her curvy figure.

"Are you confident of victory today?" She shielded her eyes from the glaring sun and beamed at them.

"I always set out to win," Sam confirmed. "Oh, and when I do, can you give me an extra minute in the interview? I want to make an announcement on live TV."

She raised her impeccably manicured eyebrows. "Ooh, curious. It's not a wedding proposal, is it? Do you remember Freddy Enright did that last year, and that didn't end well for him?" Her eyes scanned over Molly and Abigail.

"No, nothing like that." Sam suddenly remembered his manners and introduced the pair.

"I'm Luke Packer's sister," Molly added, shaking Alison's hand.

"And Jackie Simnell's girlfriend, I understand," Alison remarked. Molly flushed and looked horrified.

"I didn't know it was common knowledge."

Alison gave a relaxed laugh. "Well, Jackie's telling everyone, so it's going to be everywhere by the end of the weekend. And Abigail," she stretched out her hand. "Fantastic fashion designer, and you're able to control the Moody Muppet. What a talented individual you are!"

"I'm glad you like the dress." Abigail felt oddly starstruck in her presence. "I saw you had a different outfit on yesterday and I panicked that something was wrong with the dress."

"No, not at all. I love it. I'd seen that the weather was going to be hotter today and this dress was more appropriate. Anyway, better dash," she apologised, spotting a colleague with a clipboard motioning to her. "Have a nice day, and good luck today, Sam."

Molly and Abigail found a spot trackside to sit in the sun whilst Sam headed off to the weighing room. The grandstand started coming to life as the hordes arrived, flooding the bars and wandering around like aimless ants, checking out the facilities. The girls chatted amicably about the future of Twin Oaks, and about how the relationship with Jackie had developed. Abigail suddenly felt much closer to Molly knowing that she was no longer a threat to her relationship with Sam. She wished she'd given Molly a second outfit as the same maxi dress was making an appearance for the second day running.

"Good morning ladies!" The greeting came from behind them. Both girls turned to see Harriet striding towards them, a champagne bucket clutched to one hip and empty flutes dangling from her free hand. Unlike Alison Raven, she wasn't looking resplendent in the dress she'd made for her, and Abigail prayed she'd worn it yesterday instead. She made a mental note to up-sell a second dress when the customer was going to a two-day festival.

"I got this for you, as a thank you," she remarked, setting down the metal bucket on the grass at their feet.

"For us?" Abigail confirmed.

"Ya, the outfit yesterday was such a winner. We got spotted and interviewed by Gok on telly and Mummy was glowing for the rest of the day. He said it showed off her lovely figure, so she was like the cat that got the cream. He pecked her on the cheek and everything."

"Are you joining us?" asked Molly, preparing to shuffle up the bench.

"Oh, no thanks Mols, Daddy's got an executive box today and they'll be serving up the starters soon. He's trying to impress some sheik from Dubai, so I have to play the charming daughter role. Enjoy your bubbles!"

"Amazing!" Abigail exclaimed as Harriet strode back towards the glamour of the executive box. She hadn't brought much money with her, so a glass of wine had been out of the question, let alone a bottle of Moët. There was no doubting that Molly was penniless too. It's my second bottle of fizz in less than 24 hours, thought Abigail. At least Harriet had no ulterior motive.

The first race got underway, but neither Sam nor Jackie were riding in it. Molly still knew plenty of morsels of gossip about most of the riders, and provided her own Heat magazine style commentary as the field stormed past the finishing post.

The day grew hotter and the champagne made both girls feel giggly, then sleepy. Using the champagne bucket to guard their place on the bench, they approached the rail for the 1000 Guineas race, both wanting to scream their support for Sam and Jackie.

"I wonder how nervous they feel, waiting in the starting stalls," mused Abigail, watching on the big screen as the last half dozen horses were dragged reluctantly into their starting positions whilst the first loaders waited patiently. If they didn't feel nervous, she was carrying the anxiety for them. So much rested on the next few minutes: pride, glory, prize money and Sam's ability to announce his retirement on live television.

"And they're off!" The commentary over the tannoy system jolted Abigail out of her reverie and she watched the row of horses jump free from the starting stalls. She struggled to pick out Sam's blood red silks at first as the horses bunched together, galloping as one big mass, but after a few nail biting seconds, Sam's mount, Flora, began to edge forward of the pack. She hoped it wasn't too soon. Many times, she witnessed horses committing too early then running out of steam and being relegated to the back as the stronger horses swept past.

"Go on Jackie!" squealed Molly, although her encouragement was futile as the pack were nowhere within ear shot. Jackie's thoroughbred, Butters Bred, was also pulling out in front, and Abigail had the sickening feeling that the race was going to play out as a carbon copy of yesterday. Jackie had threatened to "whip his ass" after all.

Abigail looked down the track and could just about make out the bobbing heads of the pack storming up the straight. From trackside, it was impossible to distinguish who had the advantage, and Abigail turned her attention back to the big screen to check Sam remained in the lead.

In no time at all the thundering mass could be heard, and a glance at the screen told Abigail that Flora had retained her stamina and Sam silently egged her on, the peak on his jockey cap almost grazing her flattened ears as he waved the whip forwards to encourage her faster.

Sam and Flora passed them in a blur, with Jackie in her gaudy purple and yellow chequered silks just a neck behind. The tidal wave of hooves followed. Just thirty metres to go, now twenty metres... Sam was holding on and an enormous cheer erupted from the grandstand as the commentator announced that Flora had taken the finish first, winning the 1000 Guineas race. Despite her best efforts, Jackie failed to push Butters Bred any faster and she's ended up in a respectable third.

"Come on!" Molly tapped Abigail's arm, "Let's go and watch them arrive in the winners' enclosure."

The girls trotted through the masses that swarmed towards the bookies for their winnings, and pushed their way through to the back of the grandstand to the parade ring. The crowds around the ring were a dozen deep, so Molly and Abigail had to settle for perching on the steps and watching for Sam's arrival on the big screen. Alison Raven walked as deftly as she could manage to keep up with the long strides of leggy Flora as the perky filly headed in from the track. She thrust the microphone on its extendable pole up to Sam's face.

"Congratulations Sam, a confident ride all the way," she stated.

"Yeah, yeah," nodded Sam, keeping his focus whilst connections came buzzing around like wasps to a Coke can. "She's a great horse. You can just let her have her head and she gives her all. I just sat and steered."

Abigail watched anxiously. She knew that these interviews only lasted the length of the walk into the parade ring. He would have to announce his retirement quickly.

"Now, you're just being modest. What's next for Flora then?"

"Well, I'd imagine she'll be heading for Royal Ascot, maybe the Coronation Stakes, but as for me, I'll like to announce that I'm heading for retirement."

Sam looked down at Alison to check she wasn't on autopilot and that she had definitely registered his words. Alison was professional and had listened to his answer, her eyebrows shooting up in surprise.

"You're planning to retire from racing at the end of the season?" she clarified. "But you're so young. You've got years of winners left in you."

"I'll be retiring after Royal Ascot," Sam corrected, "and it will be hard to give up the thrill of racing, but I'm also excited to be ploughing my efforts into teaching more people the art of equestrianism, and will be building up the business at Twin Oaks".

Perfectly timed, horse and rider arrived into the winners' enclosure to a rapturous roar from the gathered crowd. Alison realised it was time for her to withdraw from the nucleus, which was sucking in more connections, media and grooms waiting with buckets of water and the winner's drape.

She turned to give a wrap up to the viewers, but was too late. The cameraman had kept the lens on Sam, following with a close-up to capture his delight at the adoration that met him in the winners' enclosure. Abigail watched as he stood up in the stirrups and cheered with the crowd, his victory salute and a farewell to Newmarket.

He dismounted and pulled the saddle from Flora's steaming back. As he received congratulations and pats on the back from the horse's owners, he scanned the crowd as inconspicuously as he could, searching for Abigail. His eyes found hers and she blew him a kiss. He gave her a smile and a nod, extracted himself from the owners and headed off to weigh in and make his win official.

42

It had taken Abigail two years, but they were finally going on holiday together. Choosing a destination had been laborious, with both offering up suggestions that the other rejected. With his pale skin, Sam was reluctant to go anywhere too hot, and he wanted somewhere with activities and action, as the last thing he wanted to do was lie on a beach all day.

By contrast, Abigail loved the sun, and although she needed to protect her fair skin with high factor cream and sun shades, she could lie around a pool with a book for hours. Rejecting clubs and nightlife, she wanted to spend the evenings in romantic restaurants, eating good food, drinking wine and getting tipsy with Sam.

"What about a riding holiday?" Molly had chipped in.

"A busman's holiday you mean?" Abigail replied dismissively, but when she looked online, there were endless possibilities of equestrian breaks in beautiful locations with luxurious accommodation and gourmet food thrown in.

"This looks lovely." She showed Sam the webpage detailing glamorous chateaus along the Loire Valley, with horse riding trails through forests and alongside rivers. Some of the hotels had azure swimming pools overlooking vineyards, and Michelin starred restaurants. The temperatures in May were manageable for his ginger complexion, and they suddenly had something they agreed on. It was satisfyingly expensive. It felt as though this was the prize for the hard work that they had both put in since their last birthday.

Sam kept his word and rode his final race at Royal Ascot. It helped to go out on a high, clocking up half a dozen winners over the five days of the festival, including another successful pairing with Flora, bumping up his prize money. The Twin Oaks Equestrian Centre went from strength to strength as Sam focused on boosting its presence on social media, and even

Jackie Simnell popped in every few weeks to help Molly run a session and create a buzz, and more bookings.

Abigail witnessed Sam transform from the exhausted ghost that existed on 1000 calories a day, back to the relaxed friend she had met in Sloth. He remained at home most days, and they spent time together, walking Bessie, riding across the heathland, playing *Champion Jockey* or enjoying Sunday lunch at the pub. They had a new routine in their lives and it had brought them closer again. It was inevitable that they would bump into Sol around the village, and whilst Abigail couldn't forgive him, she remained civil as they exchanged pleasantries.

People often asked Sam if he missed racing. Of course he missed the adrenaline rush of a win, he would reply, but he was enjoying the satisfaction of running the equestrian centre, and watching people develop their riding skills. It was a corporate response that omitted the other things he didn't miss. He loved not having to drive for hours on end, and the endless traffic queues that lengthened his day. He happily lived without the social media abuse that came from punters that had lost bets when he failed to get a favourite across the line first. He was able to eat properly now, without worrying about putting on weight, and he didn't miss the headaches that came from dehydration, nor the sore throats from when he needed to make himself sick. He did miss his friends from the weighing room and the camaraderie of the shared experience on the racetrack. He made sure that he still met up with as many of them as he could when they were in the area, and there were several trainers within a thirty minute drive that were happy for Sam to come and ride out for them when he craved a forty mile an hour thrill on the gallops.

"Molly will be fine without you," Abigail insisted, spotting Sam checking his phone as they waited in the queue to check in. "She used to do it all when you were racing."

Whilst that was true, the sessions were now more frequent, and there were more enquiries to deal with, more admin, more tasks. To reflect the increase in Molly's workload and responsibilities, they had promoted her to assistant manager and insisted she took a small wage from them.

They checked in their bags and headed through departures. Sam tolerated Abigail as she browsed the perfumes in the duty-free shop, and in return she entertained his fascination for sunglasses. After trying on over thirty pairs, he settled for buying the first pair he'd seen.

"Breakfast?" he suggested. Not having to worry about making weight for races meant that he could now indulge, guilt free, and they sat in the diner drooling over the prospect of a fry up. There was no reason not to pair it with the obligatory holiday glass of alcohol.

"Look, look, four o'clock," Abigail hissed, as a family sauntered past the diner. Mum was overweight and over-tanned, whilst Dad was lumbered with all the baggage. But it was the daughter that Abigail was drawing his attention to. Somewhere in the region of her early teens, her skinny legs were wrapped in a ra-ra skirt, the crocheted layers flapping over rainbow striped stretchy Lycra. It was the third girl they'd seen in the airport so far sporting an April Smith design from Teen Zero.

"Ker-ching!" laughed Sam. It had become their shared joke every time they spotted someone wearing one of Abigail's designs.

This had been her dream, to spot people wearing her ideas, bringing them to life. Sometimes she cringed when she noticed someone wearing something that didn't suit them, or wearing it wrong. However, mostly she felt nothing but pride. She couldn't have done it without space that the cabin provided, and she was grateful every day for the input Mrs Angel had had to that scheme.

She now also had Nadine's support in her business. With no other paid work to keep her in London, Nadine accepted Abigail's offer to share the cabin and work on some designs of her own. With the spare bedroom freed up, Nadine took up residence, and if Sam felt outnumbered by having three females around the place, he never complained. It was another pair of hands to walk Bessie, to make meals, to run errands.

"It's a bit like the commune I lived on when my parents joined the climate change protests at Heathrow airport," Nadine observed. "Although at least there's a flushing loo and running water here."

Nadine loved the open countryside and relished the opportunity to take Bessie for a long morning walk, taking a few minutes out to sit in the bracken with a spliff, dreaming up her next creations. She created a subsection on Abigail's website dedicated to her collection, and was delighted when orders began to flow. Although she stepped in to help Abigail out when she got overloaded, there was an acceptance on both sides that this was never going to be a business partnership. Abigail knew Nadine found it difficult to settle, and didn't feel it was wise to integrate her into "April Smith Designs". Nadine would admit herself that such a move would make her feel trapped and claustrophobic, and she was happier doing her own thing in her section of the cabin in return for helping out, such as holding the fashion fort whilst they went on holiday.

The waiter deftly delivered a pint for Sam and a Buck's Fizz for Abigail, smiling fleetingly before heading off on his next mission.

Abigail took the stem of her glass and held it up to Sam.

"Here's to us," she toasted. "To a well-deserved break."

Sam lifted his pint and chinked her glass. "Cheers darling."

They sipped in unison, enjoying the decadence as much as the cooling sensation.

"I wonder what we'll be doing this time tomorrow," Abigail mused. It would be their birthdays tomorrow, but she tried not to dwell on the awful day she'd spent on her previous birthday.

"Well, we won't be at a racecourse for once," Sam smiled. "But we may well be on horseback."

A wave of nerves swept over him at the thought of tomorrow. He contemplated the diamond solitaire ring hidden away in his suitcase. His dad regularly challenged him, asking when he was going to ask Abigail to marry him. He'd brushed off the question by saying he would ask when the time was right. He had to wait for a point when he felt confident that she would say yes.

Her lovely eyes were still regarding his, her happy, relaxed face being the only thing he wanted to look at for the rest of his life.

If   that   time   wasn't   tomorrow,   then   when?

Printed in Great Britain
by Amazon